THE
CONQUEROR

Aditya Iyengar writes novels, screenplays and poetry. His previous books include the critically acclaimed *The Thirteenth Day*, *Palace of Assassins* and *A Broken Sun*. He splits his time between Delhi and Mumbai.

THE
CONQUEROR

Adhir Iyangar writes novels, screenplays and poetry. His previous books include the critically acclaimed The Thirteenth Day, Palace of Assassins and A Broken Sun. He splits his time between Delhi and Mumbai.

THE
CONQUEROR

THE THRILLING TALE OF THE
KING WHO MASTERED THE SEAS
RAJENDRA CHOLA I

ADITYA IYENGAR

First published in India in 2018 by Hachette India
(Registered name: Hachette Book Publishing India Pvt. Ltd)
An Hachette UK company
www.hachetteindia.com

SRD

ISBN 978-93-5195-148-3

Hachette Book Publishing India Pvt. Ltd
4th & 5th Floors, Corporate Centre,
Plot No. 94, Sector 44, Gurugram 122003, India

Typeset in Arno Pro 11/14.8 by
Manmohan Kumar, New Delhi

Printed and bound in India by
Manipal Technologies Limited, Manipal

NOTE TO THE READER

In his brilliant work of historical fiction *Cuckold*, Kiran Nagarkar mentions that he uses contemporary language and colloquial phrases to strive for immediacy and not some academic fidelity that would appear simulated at best. As an approach, I feel it makes history more relatable to readers, and is one I've tried to follow while writing this novel.

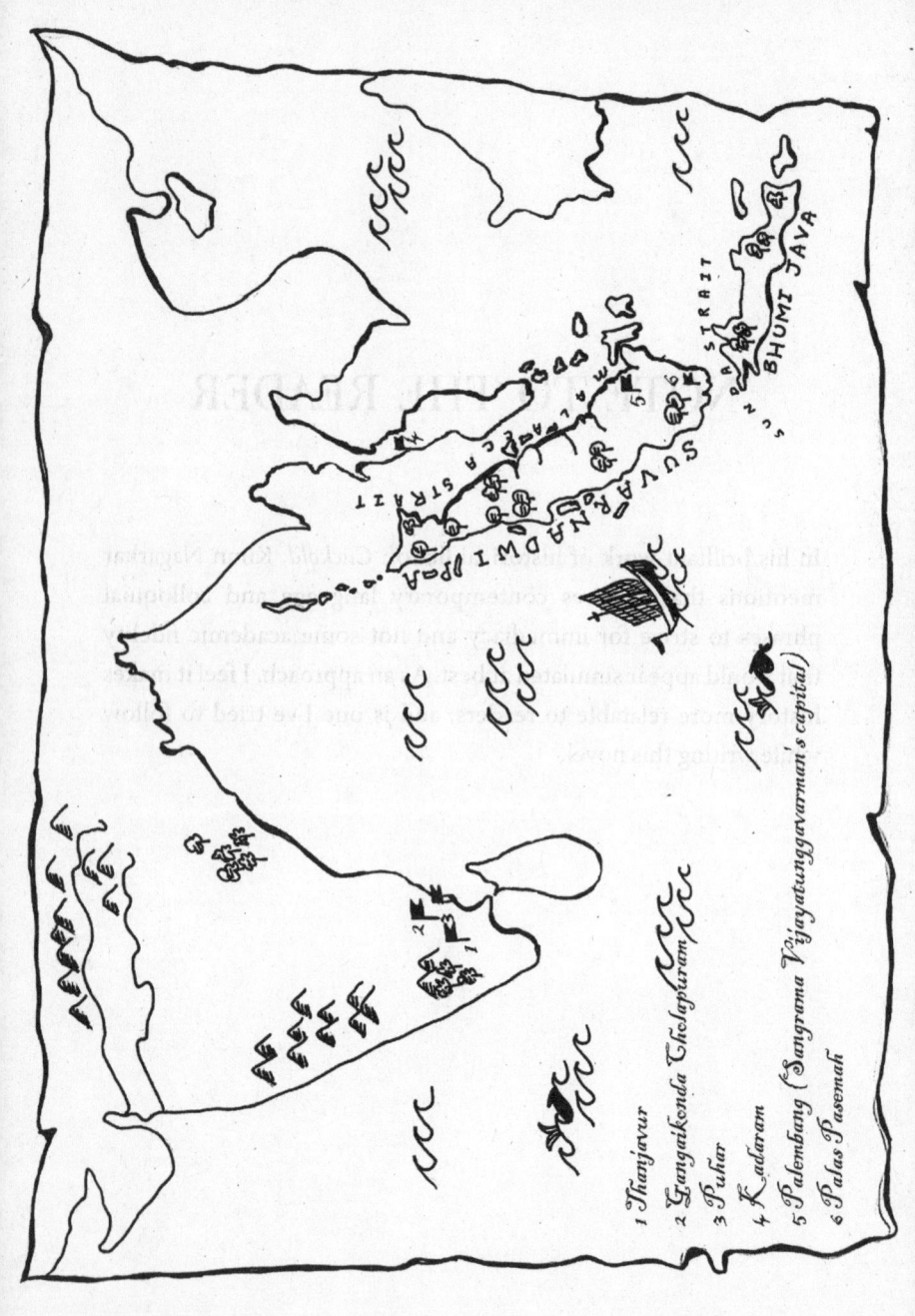

[Who] having dispatched many ships in the midst of the rolling sea and having caught Sangrāma-vijayōttunga-varman, the king of Kadāram, together with the elephants in his glorious army, [took] the large heap of treasures, which [that king] had rightfully accumulated; [captured] with noise the [arch called] Vidhyādharatorana at the 'war gate' of his extensive city, Śrī Vijaya with the 'jewelled wicket-gate' adorned with great splendour and the 'gate of large jewels'...

– Chola inscription at Brihadeeswara Temple, Thanjavur, 1031 AD

BOOK I

PROLOGUE

Namaskaram.

Welcome to my humble abode. It's not much to look at. The grey stone walls need paint and the floor hasn't been cleaned for days. But it will have to do. My fellow inhabitants that include a family of rats and, I think, a pigeon, do not mind the accommodation, but object to my presence for I take up too much space. It's only temporary, however. For if I heard the chatter of the guards outside correctly, tomorrow is the day my head will be placed on a stone platform and crushed by an elephant.

You're the scribe, aren't you?

The one who has been given the noble task of recording my final words. You're probably thinking, why should this man be given such dignity at the end? He has, after all, conspired to murder the emperor of my land, Rajendra Chola.

I'm sure there are many stories being told about me. And you've probably heard some version of the events that transpired yesterday through the rumours and gossip floating about the city like straw in the wind. It matters little, honestly. A king needs to tell his story. Even one deprived of his kingdom as I. This much I have learned from Rajendra. And while you may not be the most illustrious company, you will have to do. Perhaps you will believe my version of events over the others. Perhaps, if you have any skill with words, you will write my story and sell it for a handsome price and redeem my name in this land.

Perhaps by the end of it, you may even come to like me.

It all started when your king attacked my land unprovoked.

1

'Sire, we're under attack.'

I grunted. What kind of dream was this?

'Sire?'

I rolled over on my side, forming a mountain range on the mattress, and lay, hovering between sleep and semi-consciousness. A pair of cold hands clutched my arm and shook it hard.

'Sire!' more urgently this time.

'What?' I mumbled.

'War ships! Hundreds of them!'

'What?' I croaked, and prised open the stranglehold of sleep from my head.

'Cholas! They're here!'

I sat up in an instant. Let no one believe otherwise – I know what people are saying about me these days.

I cleared my throat of phlegm and spoke to Dhammavichai in an even tone.

'Is it confirmed?'

'Yes, Maharajah,' he sniffled.

I nodded at him curtly, stood up and walked briskly outside my bedchamber. The wooden floor of the palace was still cold. I soon gave up the brisk trot and walked in a more leisurely manner to the palace courtyard. To run or even jog would have been seen as the first sign of panic. My men needed to believe that I would take care of it, whatever 'it' was. The sun had not risen, but the sky was already dark purple. People were hurrying about like frightened mice on the palace grounds that stretched out before me under the soft glow of the torch lights.

Dhammavichai caught up with me.

'Where are the ministers?' I asked him as he trembled, more out of habit than anything else. He was a timid little man, but a useful slave.

'They're on their way, my lord.'

No sooner than I said it, a group of men appeared before us. Jayanagara, my minister of war, was among them. I ignored the others and addressed him directly.

'What's happened?'

'Cholas,' he said, pausing briefly to catch his breath. 'Their ships are coming down the river. Their army is marching towards the city walls. We've awoken five hundred elephants and every regiment at hand. Every man in the city is being given a sword to fight. General Samaratunga has already left for the river front. We're getting as many ships out of the harbour as possible to meet them on the river.'

I nodded. Samaratunga was a bull-headed man who listened to none but the crazy voice in his head, which made him a capable general. He was also not the sort who would leave a battle midway either due to fear, or by carrying out what other less competent generals called 'strategic retreats'. A useful quality in commanders. He would stay on his ships till he died, I was certain.

'I've also sent word to Srideva, and the other Daatus. Every kadatuan will know in a few hours.'

I shrugged. My vassals were not very reliable. When I had ascended the throne, I administered a *persumpahan*, or an oath of allegiance. It was a formal ceremony where all the Daatus of Srivijaya would have to bow to me, and take an oath of loyalty to my line. The oath was protected by a curse that if broken could have supernatural repercussions on the traitorous chiefs. Of course, it was all just for show. I doubted their loyalty from the moment I began warming the cushions of my throne. They were just waiting for an opportunity to rally together and overthrow me – like grass in a bonfire, just waiting for the smallest spark to go up in flames and burn everything around it. If I didn't drive the Cholas out from the city, no one would. It was all my father's fault. He had not been firm with the kadatuans, unlike my grandfather who had always kept them under his thumb.

What? Oh, a Daatu is a chieftain of a kadatuan which is a principality. The kingdom of Srivijaya is made up of several small kadatuans, but the kingdom itself is also called a kadatuan. As the Maharajah, I am the most important Daatu and the ruler of the other Daatus. Try, as far as possible, to not interrupt me; it ruins the flow of my story. Attempt filling in the details yourself. The listener is as much a bricklayer as the storyteller. Now, back to my tale.

'Maharajah, please leave the palace with the queen and the princess till we take care of matters,' said Jayanagara, a little stiffly, perhaps anticipating my response.

The sky was draining of its darkness quickly and was almost pink. I ignored Jayanagara's request.

'How far are they?'

'Maybe an hour away on the river, Maharajah. Their land forces are closer; they will reach our walls soon. Our scouts also report the presence of elephants, horses and catapults.'

The palace was at the centre of the city, a fair distance from the city walls. I was rather proud of the walls of my capital city. We had built them with the aid of Chinese engineers who had worked on repairing their own monstrosity that girded their nation from nomadic tribes – the wall they called the "Great Wall". Our walls were built of solid stone and rose at least twenty feet above the ground.

'How?' I asked, genuinely dumbfounded. There had been no word of any Chola ship sighted on our oceans, leave alone near my city.

Jayanagara looked down at the ground. 'We're at a loss, my lord. No word had been received. Our scouts have spotted at least one thirisadai and several smaller warships.'

Battle talk? Oh, yes. I forget, you wouldn't know. Thirisadai are what the Cholas call their largest ships. These can house many hundreds of your benighted race, I am told, and are used to carry troops and beasts around the sea.

Chola war ships were coming up the river and their soldiers around the city towards the city walls and my minister of war had no answer as to why. I would have him executed for this later. For now we needed every man able to carry a weapon.

We would meet them at the docks and the walls, I decided. Push them off the rim of our lands. I told Dhammavichai to get my armour and elephant ready and sent word to Samaratunga, through a messenger on horse, to hold the harbour. Jayanagara would assemble as many troops as possible and lead them there. I would take another group and mount the defence of the walls.

We waited in the palace courtyard and Jayanagara sent out orders to all the barracks to assemble at the docks. A gong was sounded and I knew that soon every able bodied man would be at the battlefront with whatever weapons they had at hand.

Dhammavichai soon came clattering behind me with two slaves who carried my armour.

An elephant was waiting outside the gate with its howdah upon it. She bent down and my slaves put a ladder against her so I could climb. Two steps up the ladder and one more into the wooden canopy with a seat that was the howdah. I had dressed the sides with curtains of mail that would protect me from stray arrows. An assortment of weapons were contained in the howdah. I strapped on the armour myself – a leather breastplate with my imperial seal upon it. There was no time for an attendant to do it.

Jayanagara inspected a helmet that his slave had brought him, and I told him to leave for the docks immediately. A regiment of the palace guards, with the exception of a few who would protect my Maharani and daughter, got into formation behind me.

Let no one believe I did not do enough to protect my family.

I picked out a bow and spoke to Dhammavichai who looked at me mournfully. I half-expected him to burst into tears. His greying hair was unkempt and he wore dirty white robes that I could tell had been worn in haste. An upper cloth that was slung around his chest left his left shoulder bare, and a baggy lower cloth, similar to your dhotis, that extended from his hips, sagged onto the ground. He wore no ornaments, no armlets, not even the necklace he normally wore while on royal duty. He looked more like a beggar than a royal steward to my house. On another day I would have laughed at the woeful figure that he cut.

'Watch over my queen and daughter,' I told him curtly. The elephant trumpeted and I told the mahout to take it forward. The beast was visibly restless. As she lumbered forward, the howdah shook from side to side. A group of soldiers and my royal guard followed, numbering no more than a hundred.

We made our way to the city walls, joined on the way by a ragtag assortment of horses and foot soldiers, whoever was at hand. As dawn lit the streets and the houses, I saw some guards going from house to house to wake up its residents, telling them to report to the armoury to get weapons and join us at the wall. The streets were slowly coming alive with noise – men shouting, hooves pounding, pots clattering.

We hurried our pace and reached the city walls at the point where the scouts had reported the Chola army had been sighted. My elephant trumpeted her displeasure again at being awoken so early and was immediately shushed by her mahout. The walls towered before us; I felt secure in their shadow. They had been crenellated too, meaning empty gaps had been built into the parapet at the top of the wall that allowed our archers to pour fury onto the attackers. The walls were unlike anything anyone had seen in this region. I had even designed a gateway arch on the inner gateway of the walls – a war gate to remind the men that passed through it of the glory of the land they fought for. It was called the *vidyadharatorana*, and it was a large arch of stone encrusted with all kinds of gems from across the many countries with which we traded or to which we extended our influence. A truly magnificent structure that inspired awe among all who beheld it.

But now was not the time to admire the *torana*. A flight of 168 stone steps led to the top of the wall and I wheezed my way upwards. The monsoon was going to arrive, and I had spent most of the dry season sitting at banquet tables. The weather in our parts does not swing as readily as in yours and is anchored by the rain. There are essentially two seasons: a dry season where it rains little, and a wet season, where it rains enough to fill the ocean.

I reached the parapet and acknowledged the salute of the captain in charge of the wall. I remember the light of the sun that morning, bright in my eyes. It made me put up a hand to block it, almost unconsciously, as I looked beyond the wall. The ground outside the fort was clear and unblemished by vegetation and, in the distance, I could make out men marching towards us followed by elephants and horses. They marched across the land in disciplined squares – almost leisurely, making clear their disdain for us.

A solitary man rode on a horse a little ahead of them. As he came closer, I saw that he was dressed in blackened leather armour with a coat of mail draped upon it. He was a heavily bearded man, with facial hair that grew down to chest, and long hair that had been tied into a top knot on his head.

'I will give the initial order,' I told the captain.

He grinned wolfishly then looked back at the men on the wall and shouted at them. 'Hear that, men! Your Maharajah is up here fighting for you.'

The men roared their approval.

I looked at the bearded man in black armour. He stopped just outside the range of my arrows and raised his fist. The soldiers behind him stopped their advance and formed a line of squares. My first instinct was relief. There didn't seem to be too many of them.

I could count four squares of foot soldiers with perhaps a thousand men in each of them. Each square wore a different regimental turban and, from a distance, they looked like a field of flowers. The men carried long spears, had swords fastened to their sides and large round shields that covered most of their bodies.

Behind the men were platoons of archers holding long wooden bows and quivers slung behind their back. They were followed by two rows of horses and two rows of elephants. The horses were of medium height, suitable for cavalry charges. Unlike Arab horses that were short and swift and the heavy Frankish horses from Europe that could pound through men as if they were grain, these possessed a combination of strength and speed, and had almost certainly been procured from the kingdoms north of Tamil territory, even as far ahead as lands on the silk routes. I made a mental note to find out where these horses came from once the battle was over.

The elephants stood placidly behind the horses and infantry. They were armoured in chain mail and had wooden howdahs perched on their backs. I presumed they carried four to six archers each. I was so distracted by the sight of the troops that I almost didn't notice the catapults being wheeled out from behind them.

The Cholas had attacked us before – nearly eight years ago – but it had been a naval raid. We hadn't been ready back then. Our ports had burned for days.

We were ready now.

I had an army of at least eight thousand men and a navy of three hundred ships of all sizes ready to do battle. I looked behind me and saw my troops in the familiar Srivijaya blue come out and form organized lines underneath the walls. More would join soon. The Chola army, if it could be called so, was more of a raiding party of two to three thousand men. A small force, but one that needed to be dealt with firmly and kept outside the walls.

Six catapults faced us. Though catapults come in different forms, these consisted principally of a large wooden arm with a sling at the end in which large stones were placed to be flung at a target. Each of them was manned by a crew of ten to twelve men.

Yes, there are specific military terms to describe each part, young scribe, but I fear you are not familiar with them. Which is why, when I explain things to you as if you were a child, it is for your own clarity.

For a moment, the trader in me wondered where they had got these from. The Chinese, maybe? I had not heard of Chola troops using siege weapons. To the best of my knowledge, they used elephants. And how much had they bought them for? The crews drew the arms of the catapults down and began loading their slings with heavy stones.

I was not afraid. My walls were firm; a few rocks wouldn't deface it. I waited patiently till they had loaded them. Then, the bearded man in the black armour led his horse to the catapults. He had a word with one of the men operating it and pointed towards the wall. The man nodded, and gave some instruction to the rest of the crew around the catapult. The bearded man raised his arm, and lowered it sharply. A great roar went up from the Chola troops as the catapult flung the stones in our direction.

The first two stones flew above us and crashed somewhere in the city; the third one broke against the parapet, spraying bits of rock over the soldiers. The catapult arms were lowered again. The stones rolled onto their mouths and were spat out vehemently towards our walls. This time three of the stones crashed into the centre of the walls without doing much damage.

They could fire their rocks all they wanted. Nothing was going to come of it. Along the parapet, my archers stood ready. Behind them were two lines of infantry men, with swords fastened to their sides and long spears in their hands, to repel anyone that dared cross the parapet. Below us more men were gathering in Srivijaya blue. They stood in small crescent-shaped formations outside the gate with their swords drawn. If the Cholas ever got inside, they would be slaughtered.

When I focused my attention back on the Chola troops in front of me, I noticed that something was the matter. A ripple passed through the squares of infantry. From each square now, groups of men emerged holding long wooden ladders.

I knew what was coming.

'Archers, ready!' I roared, and my archers flexed their long bamboo bows and fastened arrows onto them. The Chola soldiers burst out into their war cry. Like any good war cry, it was short, easily repeatable and was structured with alliteration.

Vetrivel! Veeravel! 'Victorious spear, valorous spear.'

We would see whose spear was victorious after the battle, I thought. The Chola troops whooped and screamed and charged while my bowmen waited patiently for the sea of troops to come within the reach of the arrows. Once they were close enough, a wave of arrows was released onto the troops, skewering many of them as they made their way towards us. A sea of dark red stained the flat ground, human ink on nature's parchment.

Still they came.

Their archers now began returning fire. Hundreds of arrows flew towards us, forcing us to duck. Six more stones were flung, and each of them crashed into our walls, blinding our archers with dust and rock.

It had been a distraction of only a few moments, but it was all the time the Chola foot soldiers needed to reach the base of our walls. They thrust the tall ladders against the parapet and began climbing. The soldiers on our walls tried to push the ladders off but were held back by the withering fire of their archers as their infantry scampered up our walls like monkeys.

I peered over the parapet to take stock of the situation. The cavalry had stayed back beyond our range but the elephants were now streaming forward. Behind the parapet, we heated coconut oil in large cauldrons that gave off a lovely fragrance. Once heated, the cauldrons were emptied on the men climbing the ladders. I saw the oil peel off the face of a Chola soldier who was climbing up the ladder and he fell onto the men who were coming up behind him. One of our sergeants lit a torch, and flung it onto the ladder; it burst into flames along with the soldiers trapped on it. The men below cleared away as the ladder and burning men fell among them.

But not all our attempts at thwarting the ladders had been successful. I saw one or two Cholas climbing over the wall but they were brutally hacked down by our men.

Suddenly, an arrow flew over the wall and embedded itself into the ground at my feet. I looked up to find its source and saw more of them flying towards us. The elephant archers, perched as they were at a height, were releasing arrows in my direction. We had no choice but to huddle together underneath the parapet of the wall helpless as the arrows flew over our heads. Some of the archers tried to stand up and return fire but were shot down almost instantly.

More Chola troops had begun clearing our walls, their red jackets mingling with our blue tunics. Two of them emerged directly in front of me. As soon as they touched the ground, they swivelled around with a mighty roar each and began hacking away blindly at anything in their path. I took a step back as a blow aimed by a soldier glanced past me. I clenched my sword as I waited for an opening and soon managed to slash my assailant across his neck. He tottered and fell a few feet away from where I stood. My bodyguards surrounded me and began fighting the Chola troops that were now steadily pouring over the parapet.

The captain of the wall came up to me.

'I'll handle it from here, my lord. We'll keep them from the city as long as we can.'

I nodded at him, and a group of the royal guard surrounded and escorted me down even as more red coats began to be seen on our parapet.

It had all happened so fast. I was sure of our victory and yet now we seemed to be barely holding the wall.

Arrows bit the ground around us and my men formed a cordon around me with their round shields raised. My troops were now fighting the Cholas for control of the parapet desperately. I was tempted, for an instant, to stay with my men and fight to the death there, but decided against it. I had to find a way to mount a defence of the city if they managed to overcome our walls.

My bodyguards managed to procure some horses and we left the walls and headed towards the palace. The streets were full of panicking people taking whatever possessions they could find at hand and running in no particular direction. Some of the fleeing citizens must have seen my armour with the Srivijaya royal crest and realized that the king was among them, and heading towards the palace. They set up a great clamour and blocked my path even as we tried to push our way back to the palace. One of my guards had a whip, however, and began using it mercilessly on the people, scattering them like pigeons, so that we were soon moving unencumbered through the dusty streets. The people moaned and followed us, assuming that the king would go where it was safest.

Now, why would they assume that? Hindu and Buddhist scriptures talk of the duty of a king as the protector of his people; that he must come in between his people and any harm. It logically follows that the king must be heading in the direction of danger, no? So why were my people convinced that I was looking to save my own skin and not theirs? Unless they did not believe I could protect them as a Maharajah anymore.

In that moment, I had ceased to be their Maharajah and become one of them.

This reflection came later, of course. At that moment, I kicked my horse in the side to get it to move faster, and we soon overtook the people and arrived at the palace gates where I dismounted. I was about to send word to the minister to arrange for troops near the palace when a man stumbled towards us.

'Maharajah...' he mumbled, and sank to one knee.

He was half charred, his face blackened by fire belch, the hair on his head burnt to a crisp and his clothes tattered. 'Maharajah, the docks are taken. The harbour is in flames. Minister Jayanagara and General Samaratunga perished in the fire. The army fights to survive.'

I could only nod in shock as my guards ushered me through the palace gates. What was I thinking, you ask? What could anyone think? My first thoughts had been the preservation of my kingdom. Now, though, I was reduced to worrying about my own hide. Like any other man.

The palace was surrounded by walls. Though not as robust as those of the city, at least they posed some kind of barrier.

The remaining royal guards set up a thin perimeter at the gates, waiting for the inevitable. I climbed up to the parapet of the wall to observe the advance of the Chola troops. The wall was barely eight feet tall. They would spring over it without a thought. Still, in that moment, I was grateful there was something between the marauding hordes and us. I thought hard. Who could I summon at such short notice? Srideva's kadatuan was a day's ride away at Palas Pasemah, and he was the closest to me. The others were more than two days away.

How could my entire army get obliterated between the dock and the walls?

Time seemed to freeze and, yet, it fled at an unimaginable speed. Before I knew it, the sun was high in the sky and the red Chola wave was upon us.

A few of them came hollering towards us, whooping their little cries of war and lusting for death – our death – as they crashed into the heavy wood of the gates. My men stationed on the short parapet of the palace walls drew their bows and fired into the swarm. Some died; the rest of them stepped back, waiting for reinforcements. We braced ourselves.

Dhammavichai stood cowering next to me, and I told him to keep the Maharani and my daughter inside the women's chambers until the fighting ended. An armed guard of ten men were dispatched to protect them and two of their attendants. The rest of the women folk of the palace were told to fend for themselves until such time that we drove off the Cholas.

Did I truly believe that we would drive them off? Yes. Yes, I did. Even at a point where my walls and docks were taken and I was Maharajah of only a few meagre footsteps worth of palace ground. If not by the force of our arms, then by the blinding glint of our gold – we would pay them to leave our lands as we had done before.

Another wave of Cholas soon descended upon the gates, screaming in that harsh gibberish that your people call Tamil. This time they came with a wooden battering ram protected by men bearing shields. The archers fired at them. One of them got struck in the neck and the battering ram fell down but another quickly took his place. Our archers continued to rain arrows upon them but they managed to bring it to the gates and then began pounding it.

From behind them, a platoon of archers began firing arrows at us. It became too dangerous for me to stand at the parapet so I climbed back down. My palace guard – what was left of it, some twenty-odd soldiers – circled around me. The charred man, who had informed me of the destruction of the docks, was among them, closing and opening his eyes as if he was in a trance. Then the wooden gate imploded with a cough of dust and both sides of the door tottered and fell to the ground like drunks in the mud.

We drew our swords and waited for the red coats to come. They poured in through the gateway arch and fell upon us like wild beasts. I lashed my sword out at one but he skipped past me and skewered a Srivijaya soldier in the same motion. However, my second stroke did not miss. It split a soldier's head and he fell to the ground with little grace.

This was my kingdom, and no one would take it away from me.

Strengthened by the thought, I swung my sword again and again until the swirling motion made me dizzy. I hacked and hewed and slashed and stabbed.

And then I realized that no one was striking me.

The rest of my troops were dead. I was quite alone. I stumbled over a body and looked down, horrified to see it was the charred man. The Chola troops had formed a loose circle around me. Were they saving me for the end? I gripped my sword tighter.

'Maharajah! Maharajah!'

I looked around. It was Dhammavichai running towards us with a sword that was far too big for him. He swung it wildly, shrieking at one of the Cholas who stepped aside. This, along with the weight of the sword overbalanced him and he fell over. A soldier promptly drove a spear through the small of his back. I looked at the soldier, and then at Dhammavichai, who writhed briefly with the spear protruding through his back and then became still.

A shield clattered against me from the side, and my hand released the sword. Before I knew it, I had been wrestled to the ground by a group of Chola soldiers. I tried to struggle but their arms knotted into mine and their feet pinned my calves into the dust. After a few moments I gave up struggling, and it was at that moment that I felt that I was going to die. The hands heaved me up and I found myself face-to-face with the bearded man in the black armour I had seen leading the Chola army. His smile gleamed from the forest of his unkempt beard and he muttered something I did not hear since everyone around me was shouting:

Vetrivel! Veeravel!

2

Had I known it would be the last time I saw my city, I would have kept my eyes open and not blinked. I would have willed my tears to dry before they reached the thresholds of my eyelids. I would have pleaded with my heart not to pound so hard as to drown out the noise of my city. I would have pricked my ears like a dog to listen to every plea, every cry being uttered that day. I would have inhaled every scent from the coconut palm to the jasmine flowers lying on the ground to the fresh grass that stood alive to the world under my feet.

I will not say the name of my city. It lives with me as a memory and little else. To call it by its name will only remind me of what I have lost.

So permit me this little deception, for the rest of my tale is as true as the prison we sit in.

Such a city it was! The Chinese sailors who sailed through it described it as a city where the roosters never stopped crowing. The city where the lights never went out. The city that had never known darkness.

Until that day.

A pair of cold hands bound my wrists together with rough cord. Another pair patted down my body to ensure I had no weapons on my person, or worse, a vial of poison. I could have – should have – told them not to violate my person, not to grope my thighs and cup my crotch as roughly as they did. Poison is not the way of kings. Certainly not of the Srivijaya monarch.

After my wrists were bound, my armour was removed piece by piece. Surprisingly the jewellery on my person was not touched. A minor relief. It meant that they intended to treat me as a king, until they decided to kill or maim me. I did not know of how Cholas treated captured kings, but I found myself wishing they were not like the Chinese who would tie up prisoners and kill them slowly over days by administering a thousand cuts to their body. It is a barbarous custom, I admit. We normally have men crushed by elephants. A quicker method for sure, and equally effective in scaring populations not to revolt.

But I digress. This story – my story – is not a straight and narrow path. Imagine it to be like a city with lots of little diversions. A visit to an orchard or garden here, a courtesan house there, a port at the very beginning and the end of the city, and many small pleasures hidden within its borders.

I was surrounded by a swarm of red coats. A large hand held the back of my head and bent it down, while two more pinned my shoulders firmly and did not allow me to struggle out of my restraints. I was marched briskly outside the palace gates. I could not see a thing, only the sandals of the Chola men around me as they crunched gravel, but the sounds I heard left little to imagination.

The streets of my city reverberated with death, and though I could not see it, I could certainly imagine it. Women crying, men screaming for their lives as swords cut into their naked flesh.

Children bereft, running around, looking for their parents – some harbour of safety, a harbour their Maharajah was meant to provide.

The hand on the back of my head relaxed after some distance, and I straightened my neck. A group of horses of different colours stood in front of us – the ones I had admired that morning.

One of the soldiers motioned me to mount one of them. Of course I refused. The soldier used the pommel of his sword to hit me in the stomach. As I doubled up, winded, two soldiers heaved me up and put me sideways on the back of the horse. One of them sat behind me for good measure.

The bearded man, who I assumed to be the general, barked out an order, and the rest of the soldiers got onto the other horses and formed a tight square around my horse. We began to move at a slow trot.

We were heading in the direction of the dock. The man sitting behind me put one hand firmly on the small of my back as we sat so I wouldn't push myself off the animal. After a little while, we stopped.

I peered through the legs of a horse to see what had resulted in the delay. Were my soldiers fighting back? Instead I saw a man lying dead on the ground. A woman sat naked next to him, trying to cover her body with her arms. A naked pair of legs stood in front of the woman. They were dark, hairy and heavily scarred and I could tell they belonged to a man. Another pair of legs, dhoti-clad, went up to the naked ones and the naked legs became stiff, standing at attention. They stood inert for a few moments in front of the dhoti-clad legs and then turned around and ran away.

The dhoti-clad legs bent down to reveal a torso, and then a face. It was the bearded man. He took a long piece of cloth and wrapped it around the naked woman, who did not seem to notice. He then stood up, and all I could see were his dhoti-clad legs again that walked briskly back to his horse. After he had mounted, we were off again.

I am ashamed to admit it but it was only now that I remembered my wife and daughter. You must understand, for those first few moments of my captivity, I only feared for my own life, and was reacting to my circumstances. Now, I tried to struggle off the back of the horse but the soldier behind me kept his hand pressed firmly into my back.

'Please!' I shouted in Tamil. 'My wife, the queen! My daughter!'

My cries went unheard under the trample of the horses and all I could do was writhe desperately on the back of the horse.

How could I know Tamil even back then? Well, I spoke four languages before being captured. Don't look so disbelieving now. I know Malay, Tamil, Chinese and Arabic – the outcome of being a Maharajah of an empire of traders.

At that moment, though, my empire was far from my mind. What was to be done to me? Was I to be executed in front of my subjects in the public square – a quick end, the flower of my life trampled underneath the foot of their army? Or was I to be dragged through the streets by horses – my flesh peeled off by the very rocks over which I presided as king? Was I to be squashed by elephants, like a watermelon between the thighs of a wrestler – all the anger in my head exploding out of it into the dust, then calming to a trickle as it oozed out? The Chinese, as I have said before, are ingenious for their knowledge of torture. They have an instinct for the things that can cause pain. Reportedly, they have a method of torture where they will not only pull out your fingernails, but also insert fine nails or sharp pieces of bamboo under your nail where the skin is the most sensitive to further prolong the pain. I wondered if the Chola rulers too approved of such depravities.

It turned out that my wildest imagination could not conjure up what would happen to me next.

We reached the dock or whatever was left of it – burnt wood and blood-soaked stone – without any resistance. There were bodies all over the dock and fire burned in little patches. The smell of burned flesh filled the air. Just that morning the scent would have been of camphor and jasmine and sandalwood – goods being packed up and sent up the river to the ocean that would take them to distant lands. The dock was silent too, apart from the occasional shriek that pierced the air. An eerie peace.

I was heaved off the horse, and two men escorted me firmly to the edge of the dock area where a small boat bobbed quietly on the water. I was pushed down the dock steps towards the river. For a brief moment, I thought I was about to be drowned, since my hands were still tied. Instead, we waited.

A small craft – no bigger than your *kattumarams* – rowed by two men bobbed up next to us. I was pushed gently – a sign to enter it.

Did I have a choice? So many, and yet none. I could have jumped off the boat and tried to float away to safety, hands bound behind me. Or I could have let the river have its way with me. I could have turned and faced down my captors and refused to budge. Instead, I quietly stepped on to the boat and took a seat.

I was soon followed by the bearded man who sat in front of me and spoke to me for the first time in Tamil.

'My lord, I understand that you know our language, so I will speak to you in our words.'

I did not respond.

'A Chola expeditionary force has invaded your kingdom upon the command of our emperor, the Emperor of Tamilakam and Chola Nadu, His Highness Parakesari Chakravarti Rajendra Chola. I am Brahmarayar, his senapati.'

So he was a general after all. I did not respond again, but I don't think he expected me to. Instead he continued.

'Your city is no longer under your control. You will be taken to our flagship to discuss further terms.'

'And if I refuse?' I asked, more to put on a brave face than anything else.

He smiled at me, teeth emerging through the forest, 'I think you will find it is more beneficial if you agree.'

I was a little taken aback. Perhaps they would give me generous terms of surrender? Give me back my kingdom in return for a few trunks of gems. Tamils are greedy that way.

Now there is no need to get agitated, scribe. I'm just telling you my story as I see fit. It is best you use my words as they spill out of my mouth. No one tells a river where to flow. This one will go where it damn well pleases.

Stop grumbling. You are under orders, and the sword that dangles above my neck hangs over yours too.

Where was I?

We sailed out to the flag ship, a large beast of timber painted red, with a wooden carving of the head of a tiger on its bow that also acted as a battering ram. So when the ship would hit an enemy, it would look like a tiger was biting its prey. You find it ingenious? It is most tacky, according to me. The Chinese ships have snakes and dragons; some of the ones from your land have boars or lions. The Arabs alone have no such pretences. None that I have seen at least. My own people, regrettably, also put all kinds of animals on the bow, much to my disgust. But a king has to look away occasionally.

The ship was larger than any I'd seen your people ply. It was even larger than the largest ones we operate in the Srivijaya empire. While most of the ships that made the voyage from your lands to mine were fishing boats or merchant ships, this one was different. It had, as we say, a stouter bottom, and towered over the ocean. A ladder was lowered from the deck and I was asked to climb up. It was a long climb, and I was greeted by a group of red coats as I arrived on top.

The general escorted me as we walked on the deck. From the moment I set foot on it, all eyes on the ship were on me. The deck was filled with swarthy figures who were speaking harshly to each other while giving me angry glances. The general and I then descended down a wooden staircase into the belly of the ship. We walked along a narrow, dimly lit passageway – ships don't have too many torches, you see. With all the wood around, there is always a risk of fire. Men walked past us hurriedly, stopping only to bow to the general. From somewhere around us came the trumpet of an elephant. The ship obviously had at least two levels including the upper deck and stored animals in addition to men and food supplies. I tried to gauge how many men a ship like this could carry but couldn't. It looked massive from the outside. No wonder the Cholas had been able to send an army across the sea.

After walking for a few minutes, I was led into a chamber guarded by a soldier, who nodded as we entered. The chamber was lit by dim firelight and was well appointed. A solitary window at the side of the chamber was covered by a curtain made of fine cotton to block the sun's rays. Two carpets adorned the floor, and a small desk lay next to them. A large bronze statue of a dancing girl, exquisitely carved, stood at an angle towards me. A mattress with round cushions of the brightest yellow occupied the centre of the room and was partially covered with a green sheet the colour of fresh grass. An empty bird cage hung in a corner.

Brahmarayar told the guard to look after my needs and, with a courteous bow, left the chamber before I could ask him what was going to be done to me. So I sat on the mattress feeling grim and helpless. My mind was so focused on the bitterness of my new situation that I didn't notice the ship setting sail.

It was only when the salty breeze of the sea tickled my nose that I realized I was being taken away from the mainland. What trickery was this? Were they planning to drown me in the middle of the ocean so my people would not learn about the death of their king?

As I stood up the guard blocked my path. I looked at him and then turned around and looked at the window; he took a step towards me, prepared to launch himself towards me if I entertained the notion of using the window as an escape route. As the idea occurred to me, I took a step towards the window. The stern expression on the guard's face melted into horror then progressed to piteous fear. Had I taken another step, he would have probably folded his hands and prostrated at my feet. I assumed he was under orders to keep me unharmed.

The door behind us opened before I could make another move and another man walked in. A young one this, and with the exaggerated facial hair of one trying to hide the deficiencies of youth. A dark moustache crept over his face like a jungle vine. From the way the guard bowed his head, it was obvious that the new man stood higher in the hierarchy. A senapati perhaps. But he looked far too young to be one. Maybe an apprentice? The son of a nobleman who would inherit the mantle one day?

'Please be seated,' he said in chaste Tamil and an even voice. I kept standing in defiance.

'There's no reason to be alarmed. We mean you no harm. You are a guest on my ship here.'

I glowered and looked closely at the man. He was dressed in a white dhoti and a pristine white coat, and wore gold plated armour with a tiger head embossed on it. He was certainly someone important. Perhaps a man of the ruling class. His hands would give me some indication. I looked at them, trying to judge the quality of jewellery on them. His fingers were laid flat against the front of his thighs. All of them were adorned with rings studded with precious stones but one stood out. A fat ring on the left middle finger was larger than the others. In the dim light, the ring looked like a seal of some sort. I realized that it was a signet ring that all kings kept on their person when they had to stamp off on royal decrees.

Was this Rajendra himself?

Wince all you want, young scribe, but Rajendra is a king, as I once was, and equals have the privilege of addressing each other by their first name. Rajendra he will be for the rest of the story.

If you don't interrupt me, or try to act fresh, I will finish the story quickly so that you can go on with your squalid life – drinking, whoring, gambling or whatever it is that scribes do.

The thing about news is that it travels very slowly overseas. I hadn't heard much of Rajendra in my time as Maharajah, the title that I had inherited from my father nearly eight years before the Cholas arrived. My knowledge of the outside world was restricted to what the merchant guilds would tell me. I had no way of knowing what your king looked like. In the usual ornate descriptions furnished by your traders, the emperor came across as a young and virile man with a fearsome moustache, like the whiskers of a lion, and the God of War guiding his arm. When they spoke of his conquests, they did not mention any other princes or generals. They simply stated that, 'Rajendra Chola did this, and Rajendra Chola did that,' ascribing the deed to a single man, rather than to the people of the kingdom.

It was reasonable then for me to surmise that the young man in front of me was a king. I had not heard his name before I came to power. He must have come to the throne around the same time I did, or perhaps some years before. So I looked him in the eye and, without preamble, told him that we needed to discuss terms. I was the Maharajah of the Srivijaya empire. Son of the Sailendra dynasty. Lord of Melaka and Sunda, and the lands across them. I would reward his kingdom with more wealth than it had ever seen if I was given back my land.

He looked back at me and nodded.

'My kingdom will discuss terms with you at a suitable time. For now, you are my guest. Please join us on the upper deck for some breakfast.'

He had referred to the kingdom as his. I was right, he was indeed the king.

The deck was teeming with activity, but everyone stopped what they were doing as soon as I entered. The sun poured its golden bounty upon our heads and I had to squint to make out my captors. They were dark, darker than the dwellers of Srivijaya, and small and wiry.

A man came bearing a silver plate that had coconuts and slices of salted ginger. He offered this first to his king then me. I refused.

'I would have the ginger,' said the king. 'You don't want to fall ill.'

I knew that, of course. Your king, after spending two weeks on the seas, thought he could explain its ways to me, who had lived at its shores since I was a child? Ginger and acidic fruits were being consumed by our sailors to boost their immunity at sea for centuries now, and here was your king trying to regale me with its benefits?

I waved it off as politely as possible, as I fought against the indignation I was feeling. 'My lord, there is no reason I should be taken captive. Give me back my kingdom, and we will negotiate a treaty. If it is the taxation that's bothering you, I can relook at the rates.'

He smiled at this.

'Yes, taxation is something that will surely be discussed. But the high seas are no place to discuss a treaty of any importance.'

I felt my spirits lift when he said that. Was he taking me back to my kingdom to negotiate a settlement?

'But I'm afraid, I can't take that decision. I am, after all, not the final authority.'

He said this with a swift glance backward and then upward towards the sun that was spitting fire at us.

I took that to mean that he would consult with his Gods. Some kings wanted divine approval in every little thing they did. They would bully astrologers or dissect birds and look at their entrails or even sacrifice humans. I was not having it. Being a kingdom of traders, we know how to force our way through arguments like battering rams.

'We have Hindu priests in the city. I see no reason why we can't conduct our talks during auspicious hours there.' I said, a little impatiently.

He looked confused for a moment.

'We will, of course, consult your "higher authority" before we do anything, Emperor Rajendra,' I explained, trying hard to hide the exasperation in my voice. I also wanted to indicate to him that the game was up. I knew who he was. Normally, a king introduces himself to another king at the very outset of a meeting. There had been no need for him to conceal his identity. He was simply trying to humiliate me as a conquered king. Well, I was having none of it.

He was silent for a moment and then burst into laughter. The laughter rippled across the generals who were standing next to us, and then cascaded across the sailors across the deck. The whole ship was laughing at me.

'Maharajah Sangrama Vijayatunggavarman,' he said, taking my full name for the first time, 'pardon me for not introducing myself at the outset. I am not the emperor.'

Her story is not told. And perhaps she never desired it to be. Like the dew in the morning, it should disappear just as any light falls on it, she would say if one desired to tell it. She would cite the ephemerality of stories and tell the storyteller of the futility of it all. What are stories but meteorites that create a brief blaze across our minds, and then extinguish themselves forever, she would say laughing. Let the story not be told. Let it rest under the ground of time. There is fresh manure being placed upon it every moment, burying it further in any case.

But stories have a life of their own. They obey neither the wills of kings nor the obstinacy of princesses.

Her story begins at a little distance from the palace in which she has spent her entire life. She is a young girl. Her father is the king – *was* the king, her stricken attendants tell her. They tell her that the Cholas have attacked in the morning and her father rode out to the city walls to protect the kingdom.

Princess! They beseech her. Take some horses and speed away from the palace that has already begun to burn.

So she runs. For the first time in her life, and maybe the last. She climbs on a pony the shade of red clay after the rains – disregarding the customary palanquin she is used to. A troop of sixteen guards accompany her, her mother and four lady attendants, chosen for their youth and energy, who will be able to serve both the princess and the queen while they are away. The princess protests at first, but is told that palaces often take the brunt of conquest, and a palace without a king becomes a graveyard for women young and old. The queen is not yet forty and the princess is nearing sixteen herself.

She runs with the stories of Cholas swirling about her ears – like a storm that unsettles her. They rape their prisoners and commit all sorts of atrocities. They get elephants to trample the heads of royal prisoners and ground them into the dust. They attach a man's limbs to four horses and then steer them in opposite directions, literally tearing the man apart. These aren't stories that have been passed on through the benevolent coos of her mother and grandmother, but ones told in the night in the whispers of house-maidens and the gossip of servants. Stories that reveal more about the dark side of man than the light she is accustomed to seeing as royalty.

An hour after they leave the palace, they look behind to see it burning. They are in a little field now. A forest lies ahead – an excellent hiding place till the Maharajah restores order.

The princess is tired. She hasn't ridden so far and fast in her entire life. The horse is frothing at the mouth and the princess would too, she feels, if there was any water in her to spill. But the escape party carried little by way of supplies. Speed was most essential to their survival.

She looks sadly for a moment at the palace.

'If we enter the forest now, we may be able to find shelter for the night. Tomorrow we will take our next decision. Hopefully the Maharajah will have brought everything under control by then.'

He tries to sound optimistic. Pavitran is an old soldier. One of many who was put to pasture in the recesses of the palace once he had survived enough battles, and had enough fight left only for old age, a battle he was losing slowly, impeded by regular exercise and a spare diet. The rest of his troop are young and are among the best and most ambitious in the empire. The palace is as much a hunting ground for young soldiers as it is a pasture for old ones.

She nods at him and decides not to look at the palace again. She doesn't want to remember it the way she has seen it, with black plumes of smoke jutting out menacingly like some devil's horns. They ride towards the forest.

The roads leading to the south of the city, away from the Chola invasion, are choked with Srivijaya families escaping the sword. The crowds part reverentially though when they see the royal retinue. The presence of two female riders among a bodyguard of lancers heading away from the royal palace tells its own tale. Most of the crowd is silent as they pass, but some can be heard grumbling.

'What do they have to grumble about', asks the queen. 'There have been no wars, no raids for the past eight years. By all accounts, your father has taken care of his people. Trade is up, and taxes haven't been increased for at least a few years. Surely, in our times of trouble, they should be more sympathetic.'

'They're peasants, my lady,' says Pavitran in a placatory whisper heard only by the three of them. 'By nature, they are whimsical. The moment the threat to their life is gone, they'll be back to singing praises of the Maharajah who has given them so much.'

The queen nods, but she isn't convinced.

They reach the forest by mid afternoon and ride through the evening. At night, the guards, tired as they are, set up watch, even as the princess and her mother sleep next to a fire.

The princess can't see anything. The firelight is dim; it illuminates only her mother and four handmaidens who huddle up next to it. The forest is quiet, almost solemn in its silence, bereaving the loss of the kingdom. Suddenly, a twig snaps, breaking the sombreness. The men immediately draw their swords and take a battle stance. An ululation is heard from behind followed by shuffling feet and the death swish of swords in the air.

The princess doesn't know this but the soldiers are trained to fight at night. A handmaiden screams and sets off the others. The queen scrambles across the fire to her daughter and presses her desperately to her bosom. The princess hears grunts, and then a man falls on the fire, extinguishing it. The princess can't make out if he is one of her retinue or not. She clings to her mother who clings back. She closes her eyes, hoping it will be over soon.

A few moments later, everything is silent.

A voice calls out. A familiar one. Pavitran.

'Your highness? Princess?'

'Pavitran!' says the queen, her voice shaky.

They find each other in the dark and Pavitran takes command of the situation. A fire is lit again, and losses counted.

'Bandits in the night. Rabble trying to make good the invasion.' The princess can sense he wishes to use stronger words.

'They thought we were travellers and would be easy prey,' he continues, wiping blood off his sword.

'Two of my men killed. Three of your women taken.' He does not look at the princess and queen.

'They're not just your men, Pavitran, and neither are the women ours. Both belong to the kingdom of Srivijaya, of which I am queen.'

Pavitran looks a little surprised at the outburst, but he lowers his eyes, a little sullenly. The princess wonders what he is thinking.

The youngest handmaiden has been left behind, a girl called Sumitra. She seems to be of the princess' own age. The queen leans across to her scoops her into her arms and she breaks down crying. The palace women are a family unto themselves. Tonight, her sisters have been taken away from her.

There is no point in staying in the forest any longer, the queen decides. They will travel further and try to move beyond the forest and into the neighbouring kadatuan of Palas Pasemah ruled by the Daatu Srideva. Perhaps he will help throw the Cholas out and restore the kingdom.

The group moves in silence through the night. The princess wonders what will happen to her three maidens. Will they be sold off in the flesh markets of the port cities? Or will the bandits have their way with them and keep them chained in their caves or wherever they came from? They will become hollow bowls of longing for men – to be filled up when the men please and thrown away when they are a little worse for wear. The thought chills the princess. She has never been at the receiving end of such cruelty before, though she has seen it enough in her father when he would put people to death in his kingdom. For the first time since the morning, she realizes that there is nothing that separates her handmaidens and her anymore. That she is as likely to be taken off in a raid, her body parts used to contain the lust of men, and then thrown away. She begins to weep, not just at her plight, but at that of her sisters as well.

Pavitran's horse nudges up against her and passes by, and though she can tell he sees her heaving and weeping, he does nothing to comfort her.

3

To understand my story, young scribe, you need to know the story of my people. It sounds sweeter in Malay, our language, but Tamil will have to do for now.

I am the *sangam*, the meeting point of two of my island's most esteemed royal houses. To make things clearer, you must first look at the map I'm drawing. Here. We are a number of small islands divided by the sea, but also united by our seafaring. The two largest islands are controlled by us, as well as the waterways between them. My ancestors found out early on that the royal houses that controlled the largest islands also controlled all the trade. The two largest islands are Bhumi Java and Suvarnadwipa.

Suvarnadwipa was traditionally controlled by the house of Srivijaya who owe their origin to my ancestor Dapunta Hyang Sri Jayanasa. A man with such ambition, he undertook a *siddhayatra* – an expedition of conquest, not unlike your *ashwamedha*, but without a horse – taking 20,000 troops across the island, conquering everything in his path. My ancestor's appetite for conquest was insatiable; he swallowed up the Tarumanagara and the Kalingga empires and controlled the entire trade of the island of Suvarnadwipa by controlling the Melaka and Sunda sea passages.

Bhumi Java, on the other hand, belonged to a family called the Sailendras. You may recognize that word. It is of Sanskrit origin meaning "Lord of the Mountains". How a dynasty that prides itself on the sovereignty of mountains became the rulers of an island and the sea, I have not the patience to tell. The origins of the dynasty can be traced back nearly four hundred years, though there were learned men in my court who said that our dynasty went back to when time itself was a twinkle in the almighty's eye. Somewhere along the line, the two dynasties met and married and subsequently controlled most of Suvarnadwipa.

Our islands are inhabited by strong-willed men and women. We are no good at taking orders but excellent at taking initiative. A king does not give out orders and his vassals don't obey him due to fear or the pain of death. Instead, each Daatu of a kadatuan pledges loyalty through a *persumpahan*, or an oath of loyalty, where the Daatus are told they will be cursed with unimaginable consequences if they betray the Maharajah of the Srivijaya empire. After that, the Daatu controls his kadatuan with minimum interference from me. Taxes are paid, treaties are kept on the foundation of trust rather than fear. We work together to ensure that the Srivijaya empire prospers. In doing so, we are a group of small kingdoms rather than a large unified one. This, of course, means that the balance of power can shift between kadatuans over the course of a generation. A Daatu who manages to gain more trust from the other Daatus than the Maharajah walks away with the kingdom. That my dynasty held thrall over the islands is a testament to the sway we had over the kadatuans and the people.

I can tell you about the generations of rulers before me, but for the sake of my story you probably only need to know of my grandfather.

My people have a proverb: 'When elephants fight, the ant between them is killed.' Srivijaya was the elephant of its time. But it was not the only one. Another power was threatening us from Bhumi Java called the Medang kingdom.

I see your eyes glazing over. Fine, I won't trouble you with too many more names.

The history of Medang is not relevant except that they grew out of relative obscurity and quickly conquered much of Bhumi Java before we knew of it in Suvarnadwipa. It came to a point, a little more than forty years ago, that they became the only power to rival our strength under their ruler Dharmawangsa, a thoroughly unscrupulous man who, inspired by our ancestor, old Jayanasa, decided to conquer everything in his path.

Dharmawangsa invaded our lands with his navy and nearly overran us, so much so that my ancestors needed to seek the protection of the emperor of the Song dynasty in China. With the help of the Chinese we began to slowly beat back the Medang. By the time my grandfather, Sri Maravijayottungavarman, ascended the throne, our kingdom was weak, but still alive.

My grandfather was a shrewd man. He dealt with the Medang kingdom that was growing stronger in his own inimitable style. How he did it is perhaps a story to be related by someone less strapped for time than a man on the brink of death. Just that, by the time the war with the Medang had finished, there was no kingdom left to speak of.

More significantly, my grandfather recognized the need for allies to build an empire.

The Song are powerful. Perhaps more powerful than we know. Our traders have not been able to go through their whole land, crisscrossed as it is by walls and encircled by a larger one – a great wall – that keeps away the barbarians from civilization; much like our city walls, only far longer and bigger than those in our islands. The only thing protecting our kingdom was the ocean, and who knew for how long? Ships are able to sail longer and faster than ever before.

So my grandfather did two things. He tightened his kingdom's defences and ensured every kadatuan in Bhumi Java and Suvarnadwipa was well equipped to stand an attack of any nature. He also made an ally of Rajendra's father, Rajaraja, as a counterbalance to the Song. In return, he gave both the kingdoms favourable trading rates. He also opened up trade between kingdoms in Bharata like Chola Nadu and the Palas as well as the Song and established our island kingdom as a central port where both Bharata and Chinese traders could dock and replenish their supplies.

Both the Cholas and the Song were happy with the arrangement; the Arabs, too, enjoyed the trade. Suvarnadwipa was truly an island of gold in those days.

Rajaraja was so happy with the arrangement and his friendship with my grandfather that he even built a *vihara* – a Buddhist monastery – called the Chudamani *vihara* in our name, funded by the revenue of an entire village.

My father, Sumatrabhumi, was weak, as I've told you before. He favoured the Chinese over the Cholas since they paid more. Trade was more vital for China than your people, you see. After learning one year that the levies imposed on trade were increasing, the Chola merchants created commotion in the coastal city of Kadaram out of spite. That year, Tamil pirates were spotted around our coast with increasing regularity. They raided the kadatuan of Kadaram with little success, though I later found that they spoke of it with greater distinction than it deserved. That was before my reign. By the time I ascended, they had grudgingly accepted my father's terms. When I learnt that the demand for Chinese products had increased in Tamil lands, I promptly raised the taxes and duties to profit from it more. Any good trader would.

And so the Cholas came.

She awakens to the smell of horse manure, and realizes she is slumped over the neck of her horse that has been walking slowly all night. Pavitran had tied all the horses together with a stretch of rope so that they wouldn't wander; he led the way. The horses walked at a gentle pace all night; when the princess finds her nostrils assaulted by the odour of their excrement, it is already mid-morning. The sun was high, and glared angrily through the leaves of the trees around them – angry, perhaps, at their abandonment of the kingdom. She rubs her eyes, and closes them again, hoping she will wake up and this will all be just an unpleasant dream.

No such luck. The horse neighs and shakes its head vigorously. The princess opens her eyes with a sigh, and peers into the distance. The horse at the front, Pavitran's mare, is at a tiny rivulet. The other horses reach there soon enough and begin drinking their fill. Pavitran says they will rest here, in a tone that does not brook discussion. If the queen is perturbed at his giving the command without asking her permission, she does not say anything. The group rests for a few hours under the shade of pine trees, their leaves pointing upwards towards the sun in supplication.

She has heard a story. The earth, when she was a maiden come of age, was set upon by millions of demons each wanting to possess her. They put their hands on the surface of her body and their hands were instantly severed by the sun, her protector, around whom she wanders to this day. The severed hands of the demons withered in the angry heat of the sun and became trees. The blood from their arms froze in the sunlight and became the leaves of the trees. The sun still watches over the earth and, at night, when its light has extinguished, the demons try to reunite with their arms, which is why trees grow at night and their progress is halted with the dawn.

It is a child's fairy tale, but it is, like many of these tend to be, a reminder of a great human truth – that avarice and greed can have fatal consequences.

She hopes the Cholas suffer.

Pavitran has fallen asleep with orders not to disturb him. Everyone sits and waits till he wakes up. The queen and the princess decide that they will play along. The queen announces loudly to no one in particular that she is taking the princess and the maiden upstream to bathe. The guards bow respectfully, and let them leave. Upstream, the princess washes her face and lets the rushing stream sweep across her body while the maiden keeps watch. She disappears into the stream of the river. The cold river water batters her face and body until they are numb. She takes a deep breath and dives into the water, holding her breath. The water shuts out the world for a few moments.

When she emerges she sees Sumitra standing and talking to one of the guards who informs them that Pavitran has awoken and they need to leave immediately. The princess looks around and sees her mother next to her. The queen tells the guard that they will finish bathing and come, and Pavitran will just have to wait until they're done.

The guard looks confused, but nods and leaves.

The queen calmly washes her hair, taking infinite care to separate each strand with her fingers. After she is finished, she tells Sumitra to bathe, and waits for her and the princess to finish. When their ablutions are complete, they walk back towards the horses. Will they still be there, wonders the princess. The same thoughts perhaps run through her mother's mind too. Only Sumitra walks behind them completely trusting her fate to them like a puppy.

There is no sign of the soldiers when they reach.

All three women look around. The queen begins to shout, but stops herself before the 'Pa' of Pavitran is uttered. She will not seek protection from her servant. She turns around to face the princess and Sumitra, and the trio look nervously at one another for a few moments. The queen wonders if she has sentenced her daughter to death by playing her little game of power.

The sound of wood cracking breaks the reverie. A soldier on a horse, with two more, emerges from the trees.

'General Pavitran has gone ahead with the rest of the troop. He asked me to bring you with me.'

'There are only two horses here and three of us,' the queen says.

'General Pavitran wanted to keep the horses fresh, your highness,' the soldier says nervously. He is young and fresh-faced but knows he is just a pawn in a game he cannot comprehend.

The queen is tempted to tell him to get off his horse and travel on foot so Sumitra can travel by horse. But what use would that be? A tired soldier is one less line of defence against what may come their way. She asks Sumitra to sit behind the soldier on his horse, and they make their way through the rivulet and onto the other side. They walk their horses through the forest in silence. The queen wonders if Pavitran will be bold enough to set a trap and get them killed. She thinks desperately for a way to find value in her presence. Her title has no meaning now.

They reach a clearing after a few hours where the soldiers and Pavitran are taking rest. Pavitran doesn't even stand up to greet the queen and her daughter. He speaks from a distance to them. 'We'll be out of the forest in an hour or so. Just before sunset. Then we can see what is to be done.'

He says it in a way that implies that he will not be responsible for them after that.

The queen speaks in a firm voice that carries. 'Srideva, the lord of the kadatuan beyond the forest – Palas Pasemah – is known to me. We will ask him for shelter and reinforcements to take our kingdom back.'

Pavitran has not considered this. The princess can tell by the surprise unfolding on his face. He looks slyly at the queen.

'They say the Chola army is larger than that of the Song. They have been hankering for Suvarnadwipa for many years.'

'Do you doubt the bravery and the ability of our forces?' The queen looks at the other soldiers.

Pavitran stammers, 'No, no, not at all, your highness. But it may take more than the lord of Palas Pasemah to overthrow them.'

'Not if we're quick enough, soldier. Stop dawdling. We need to get there immediately.'

The other guards are galvanized by this and start picking up their weapons and mounting their horses. Pavitran realizes he has little choice and slowly ascends his horse. Inside, the queen knows he is seething. By referring to him as a soldier, the queen has reduced his status in front of the rest of his men.

They reach the palace walls of Palas Pasemah before sunset. The city gates have been shut but are opened instantly when they learn that their queen has arrived in their midst. Before they know it, they are in the garden courtyard of the palace of Srideva.

4

'I am not the emperor. I am his son, Virajendra,' said the young man with the strange moustache.

'So, where is your emperor?' I asked, a trifle impatient.

'Chola Nadu. Gangaikonda Cholapuram to be exact. You will discuss terms with him there.'

'There? We have to go all the way to Chola Nadu?'

'Yes. But we are quite lucky. The winds favour us at this time. We should reach the mainland in a little more than a month, conservatively.'

'But what will happen to my people in the meantime? Who will look after them?'

'We'll take over administration temporarily, until we've made back the cost of our expedition. After that, we will leave the throne with anyone who wishes to take it.'

I bellowed and tried to lunge at him – an ill-advised move. His guards were upon me in an instant. They twisted my arms and pushed me forcefully to the ground, pinning me to the salty wooden deck. My face scraped against the uneven finish of the wood. I roared again and again and the men pushed me harder against the boards. When my lungs finally gave up and I was left panting, his voice spoke calmly from above.

'There is no reason to be disheartened, my lord. Who knows? Your negotiations may be over by then, and if they go favourably, you may return to rule yourself. We're already recovering the cost of expedition, from what I learn. A commissariat has been set up in the city, and we're making gains with your treasure. The Vijaya Torana from your city walls is quite a find. We had to use our elephants to tear it from your palace gates. It will join us on another ship soon.'

'It's called the *vidyadharatorana*,' I said through gritted teeth. 'What about my family? The queen and princess? Promise me you won't harm them, and I will guarantee favourable rates of trade for you. Please!'

He was quiet for a moment.

'I had given instructions to my generals to tell the men not to defile the women of the palace. As for your family, I believe they've escaped the palace precincts. My men had been given strict orders not to harm you or them. Perhaps your family believed otherwise. I assure you, if they are found, they will be returned to the palace without harm. Now stand up and face me peacefully.'

The guards hauled me up and released me, but they remained by my side.

Virajendra continued speaking in his matter-of-fact way.

'Our ships are already raiding the port of Barus as we speak. We will sail back within ten days. Of that you have my word.'

'Is this all really necessary?' I asked. 'Send me back to my land. We will discuss terms. I promise they will be favourable.'

'My lord, I cannot discuss terms with you. There is a process to this. I advise you to be patient.' He turned away from me and towards his general, who had been waiting for some time to show him some charts.

As they became busy discussing the destruction of my city, I was escorted back to the chamber. I sat on the mattress and weighed my options.

Why on earth did they want to discuss terms with me in Chola Nadu? Perhaps because I had no standing there and could not rally troops as I could here. Or perhaps, as young Virajendra himself said, he really was not equipped to discuss terms, though as a prince he should have been. A poor prince, indeed, I thought to myself with no little satisfaction. I was discussing matters with my Daatus when I was nearly half his age.

Who was left in the kingdom to fight for it? The Srivijaya have been ruled by queens in the past and our land has had the yoke of its destiny guided by feminine hands too. It is not like this in every empire. In many lands west of Srivijaya, women are not given access to the world of men. They are kept under lock and key, like the Srivijaya keep their gold, and are protected by armed eunuchs. I couldn't be sure if my own queen would fight for the kingdom. I felt a momentary stab of anger at her and the princess. Why couldn't they have stayed back and fought for the kingdom, which was as much theirs as it was mine? I realized my thoughts were fast becoming irrational and felt a great weariness and a reluctance to deal with the world. I closed my eyes and let my worries drift away like smoke after a dead fire.

I slept like a log for a few hours and when I woke up, I saw a large tray placed at the foot of my bed; it contained a bowl of sour rice gruel – what you call *kanjika* – along with small fried black gram cakes called *vatakas*. I learned later that these were the staple of your seamen. There was also a soup of parched rice, pomegranate, coconut and, of course, ginger. Two coconuts full of juice leaned against each other on the tray.

The guard from the morning continued to stand passively near the door of the chamber. I bit into the *vataka* and could feel the taste of ginger, pepper and aniseed ripple on my tongue. A blob of mango pickle was placed on the plate and I swiped a few fingers of rice gruel on it, smearing it across the plate. I ate a meagre quantity. My mind did not care for my belly at the moment, but recognized the need to keep it quiet.

The guard was looking at me. 'Here, have a coconut,' I said, and threw the coconut from the tray at his chest. He spun around and caught it with one hand and threw it back at me without wasting a motion.

'I've already had my fill, my lord.'

'So have mine. It's a command. You wouldn't want to offend a guest, would you?' I said lightly and tossed it back at him.

He looked unsure.

'Just have it. Otherwise I'll tell Lord Virajendra of the unspeakable cruelty being meted out to me by my bodyguard.'

I smiled at him, and he pouted.

'What's your name?'

He did not reply. Instead, he used a knife at his side to cut open the coconut and dig into its flesh.

'A man without a name. How do you ever get on? What does your wife call you when she gets angry? You do have a wife, don't you? A big strapping man like you.'

He carved a large piece of flesh from the coconut and put it in his mouth, chewing it thoughtfully.

'Refreshing, isn't it? If you don't give me a name, do you mind if I give you one?'

There was no reply.

'Splendid. Give me a little while. A name is a serious thing. A matter of earnest consideration. I took nearly a week to decide my own daughter's.'

A picture of my daughter, the princess, flitted through my head and distracted me for a moment.

He continued to look mutely at me.

'This is going to be a very long trip if only one of us is going to talk.'

When this did not elicit a response from him, I lay down and closed my eyes; eventually, after an hour, I went back to sleep.

The whole day, and the next one, was spent alone with the silent guard. I asked him whether anyone would come to get me. When I got no response, I once again threatened to jump out of the window. He said nothing but continued to regard me impassively.

Another idea struck me. I took a deep breath and began shouting for help in the loudest voice I could muster. The sound was hidden by the ocean rhythm and the sound of oars splashing the water. My voice did not escape the lower deck upon which my chamber was situated but it rattled the guard who looked around and put up his arm to shush me.

I shouted again and again; he looked around helplessly. Finally, the door behind him opened and two men barged in. One of them was Brahmarayar.

'What is the matter?' he asked, puzzled.

'This is fine hospitality you show the Maharajah of Srivijaya. You leave me alone with a mute guard and a few scraps of food and believe your duties as host are over?'

Brahmarayar looked disbelievingly at me. He opened his mouth and closed it and finally spoke after a few moments.

'Perhaps you are right, my lord. Won't you come with me? Let me show you our ship.'

We walked through a long narrow alleyway and came to the centre of the deck where a staircase stood, leading to the upper deck. I could hear the trumpets of elephants and the snorts of horses again as we passed by. Brahmarayar gestured for me to ascend the steps. He then barked out an order and an old sailor wearing a loincloth and a head scarf came up to him. He was dark as night and took out a device the size of my palm and gave it to Brahmarayar.

It was a compass. I had seen many of these before. We even used them at Srivijaya, though they were more ornamental than anything. I had not seen one like the one Brahmarayar held in his hand. It was a small square metal plate with several Tamil markings on it. Upon it was transfixed a wooden tiger that was carved in the middle of a charge. The tiger turned around and round and then came to rest with it face pointing towards the south – towards Suvarnadwipa.

'Like it? It's a special Chola compass, made by our mariners in our lands.'

'The Song have one with a turtle.'

'True,' He said with the hint of a smile. 'The Song call it the "South Governor" or *sīnán*. We've only begun to use it over the past hundred years. Some of our ships have fire throwers. Also Song creations. You'll find much of the Song in our vessels.'

'I guess the Song are a greater empire.'

The smile evaporated off his face and he looked away, but before he could say anything, Virajendra came up to us.

'Stretching your legs, eh? Good! A little exercise is quite necessary on these long voyages.'

'I wouldn't know,' I replied coldly. 'I've never had to visit any land beyond my own.'

Virajendra ignored me and continued to speak. 'I always find sea voyages very inconvenient. And yet, that's all father believes I'm capable of.'

The general looked aghast. 'Don't say that, my prince!'

'Well, it's true. Rajadhiraja is the regent. He was appointed as soon as father was crowned. Rajendradeva is the governor of our Northern and Eastern territories, which leaves the ocean for me. Chola Samudram! I've fought the barbarians of Eelam, crushed the tribes of Manakkavaram with its islands strewn like pepper grains on the sea, and now this.'

'Your father has great faith in your seafaring capabilities, my prince.'

He shrugged and looked out at the sea.

The prince adjusted the cloth that covered his torso but kept his left shoulder free. All the Chola noblemen and senior generals draped cloth around their body. The cloth was made of fine Tamil cotton with an elaborate trim. They wore short dhotis that extended up to the knee. The boatmen were naked except for loinclothes. Some of them wore head scarves to protect against the heat, a marked difference from the soldiers who wore jackets and short dhotis.

'I saw your army this morning. They are significantly better equipped than your navy. The Srivijaya equip both the army and the navy the same way.' I spoke loudly, hoping to find the ears of the troops and build resentment among them.

Virajendra laughed. 'Your eyes deceive you, my lord. Our navy is young. We're not seafaring people. The first invasions outside where the land ends in Chola Nadu were conducted by my grandfather. You have him to thank for trade as well.'

'Our sailors are paid in gold coins. Solid coins for their work. They have homes and land. They enjoy the best of Jambudwipa, the Arab lands and China. They take our camphor, gold, silver and wood and trade it with your civilization and make more money than even some kings have seen in their lifetimes,' I continued.

Virajendra squinted at me in the sun.

'You paint a beautiful mural, my lord. But don't try to deceive my men. They work for the greater glory of the Chola empire. They work for the privilege of calling themselves conquerors of lands their ancestors had not even heard about. They are not mere tradesmen like the Srivijaya, who have forgotten how to fight because their arms are weighed with gold ... and porcelain.'

He spat the word 'porcelain', almost disgusted at its delicateness.

The men around him laughed at me. I looked him in the eye briefly and walked away, down to the lower deck. Brahmarayar followed me and did not say anything. He left me outside my chamber, bowed slightly and went back to the upper deck. I spent the rest of the evening in a silent rage inside my chamber with the guard for mute company. Soon after, with nothing left to be done, I fell asleep again.

In the morning, I was awoken and summoned to the top deck. Was my little outburst going to be my death?

What? Yes, I know I'm alive here talking to you, but allow a man the flourishes of his story.

At that moment, I really thought I would be thrown off the ship in the middle of the ocean, perhaps with an iron weight manacled to my legs so that I sank deep inside its heart and became a feast for the fishes. My legs shook a little; I have no shame in admitting it. They always do when I go to war. Why should it be any different when I die? Let others think it is a form of fear. I believe it is a form of release. The fear gets shaken out of my body before I go into battle like the large snakes that you call *aanai conda* – elephant killers – that shed their skin and are reborn into a new mould.

I walked up slowly, determined to die like a king of the mountain as my ancestors had been. Virajendra greeted me with a smile.

'You're just in time, my lord.'

I looked ahead and saw a port.

It was Kadaram. I had seen the silhouettes of its buildings and the curves of its beaches invite me to its shores like a long lost lover far too many times not to recognize it.

'The kadatuan of Kadaram is ahead. They have heard of our invasion by the looks of it.'

I could see Srivijaya ships in the port – large ones with catapults mounted on them. Behind them were smaller ones with archers and marines that could weave through the water and cause havoc. I won't bore you with the technical details, scribe. You, who have probably never seen the ocean in your life. Know this, the large ships carried catapults to bombard the smaller ones or lay siege to the fort. They would mostly stay back, away from the range of arrows or stones pelted at them from the docks or city walls. The smaller ships contained marines and sailors who would try to board enemy ships and take control of them. In a naval battle, as in a land one, the one with the most ships left at the end wins.

The Chola ships were larger but fewer since smaller ships wee unable to sail across the ocean. The Srivijaya ships were smaller. I could make out that many of the river boats had also been assembled for the battle. We had never encountered a navy like yours before then. Our navy was built to protect our coasts and our rivers, so our naval ships, unlike some of our trading vessels, did not need to be big enough to sail across the ocean, but small and manoeuvrable. I saw Srivijaya marines assembled on the ships, their weapons shining in the daylight.

I am not normally sentimental. The throne offers little room for any emotion other than paranoia, but the sight of my navy often brings out romanticism of the worst kind in me. There they stood, their bodies taut and strong, fed by the rice of my land, their hands holding her steel in her defence. The ships rose proudly above the water, a floating chain of wood and iron that secured my lands.

Man for man we probably outnumbered the Cholas, though in my estimation, one of ours was worth three Tamils in the water. Our marines were equipped with the best equipment available in China including firethrowers that would shoot fire out at ships and burn their occupants. The only deficiency, as I saw it, was Tamil steel, which was valued by both the Arabs and the Chinese. Tamil metallurgy is perhaps one of the few things the world covets. The Arabs say that 'Hinduwani' steel is the best in the world. They even introduced it to the weapon smiths of Damascus – the capital of the world when it comes to weapons – who create the very blades of hell from it. The Persians even coined a phrase after it – 'to give an Indian answer', meaning to cut with an Indian blade. That and the cotton you make at Uraiyur – as thin as a cloud – is perhaps the only reason your civilization still survives.

But let's get back to my story. We have no flab, as they say, when it comes to time.

Our attack crafts were light and quick and headed towards the Chola vessels. The smaller attack crafts of the Cholas greeted them while the larger ships followed at their languid pace.

Catapults flung stones from the city walls, and they exploded into the water near the attack crafts that were just joining the battle. The flagship upon which we stood held back, and parallel to it ran three other large ships. Men were spilling out onto the upper deck dressed in red jackets and dhotis. The sails were stiffened and the pace of the oars slowed as we nearly came to a halt in the waters.

Virajendra looked on at the battle that was just beginning. Brahmarayar was nowhere to be seen.

'I'll tell you what,' he announced magnanimously, 'the greatest seafaring nation in the world is facing down the Chola empire. If your Srivijaya forces defeat us today, we will leave your lands, and I will relinquish all claims to your kingdom. A boat from my royal galley will take you to the port of Kadaram and leave you in your kingdom. We will return as supplicants next time without mention of your capture. This is my word as Prince of the Chola empire.'

My spirits lifted. On land, coupled with the element of surprise, the Chola army could defeat us. In the ocean, it was another matter altogether. The Srivijaya navy would cut them to pieces.

The Cholas had arranged themselves in three parts. The first was the attack group that was made up of only small- and medium-sized crafts. The second group contained a group of thirisadai ships that included the flagship. The third group included more small- and medium-sized craft – a retreat group of sorts.

I watched as the attack crafts began shooting a sea of arrows at each other. Grappling hooks flew across the water and pulled vessels closer to each other. Their men jumped aboard each vessel, their swords in hand or flat between their teeth. Some men fell between the ships to be lost forever in the infinite waters.

Virajendra was listening to an old man dressed in a pristine white dhoti, upper cloth and a jewelled turban who held a map and explained the formation of the ships. I thought for a moment if there was any way I could weaken their cause. A quick distraction? Something that diverts their attention from the battlefield? I could snatch the map and throw it away and hope they didn't have another. Perhaps I could push Virajendra off the ship. I took a step closer to him and immediately two guards came between us, blocking my passage. I grinned wryly at them and looked back at the battle that was unfolding.

I could jump into the ocean and swim to the shore. The swim would be fatal for these ground huggers who only felt secure when they had mud between their toes. Srivijaya, on the other hand, were taught to treat the ocean as a second home. We spent more than half our lives in it, our ships tumbling and playing across its surface, like an infant in his mother's arms. I weighed my chances and decided against it. The risk was too great. A stray catapult stone or a sheath of flame gone awry could easily be the end of me.

So I stood, and hoped the battle would be done soon. I was reasonably confident of our ability to hammer the Cholas, not least because they were outnumbered by our ships, nearly three to one, by what I could see. More importantly, the sea was our element. It was a battleground that decidedly favoured us.

The battle raged on and the Cholas struggled gamely against our ships that were faster and more brutal in their attacks. Soon, the Chola ships were breaking formation and the ones in the front were already heading back.

'Retreating? Already?' I asked softly of the guards who stood in front of me. They were too well-trained to respond. Once the battle was over, and Virajendra came as a supplicant, I would buy some of these troops as mercenaries for Srivijaya.

The Chola attack craft retreated to the line of thirisadai ships even as the Srivijaya ships surged towards them like eagles picking off snakes. The attack crafts fanned out and away from each other in their desperation to head back into open sea.

The thirisadai ships were virtually stranded as the Srivijaya ships bent their sails to propel their ships faster towards their prey. I would have done the same thing. Strike as they retreat, and strike so hard that they never think of coming back. My ships steered towards their ships that were fanning away rapidly, but not fast enough. Some Srivijaya ships broke off and headed towards the thirisadai – another move of which I approved. The largest ships carried the leaders. To destroy them would be to destroy the navy.

That's when the Cholas struck back. The retreat craft, the third bank of ships that had been arrayed as part of the Chola battle formation, now began sailing towards us and joined the attack craft that turned around. Two banks of ships formed one behind the other and began to attack my fleet from the outside, like a pincer. Imagine a grape. Two fingers squeeze it with enough force, it bursts open.

I saw the danger. I shouted at my ships to retreat. No one stopped me. They knew my voice wouldn't carry. The trap was set, and my ships had unknowingly entered it. A plume of fire shot out from one of the Chola ships and I realized that the retreat ships had fire-throwers.

You've not seen these, of course. The Chinese call them 'Pen Huo Qi' or 'fire-sprayer'. It is a box in which fire oil is pumped out with bellows through a long cylinder. As the oil is sprayed out of the cylinder, it is set on fire with a match, creating long shafts of hellfire that can fly several feet in the air.

The fire-throwers were wheeled out onto the deck, and they spat flames onto our ships. Why the Srivijaya vessels did not reply in kind – for we had fire-throwers of our own brought from the Chinese – I will never know. I suppose it was because they had been outmanoeuvred. Almost all the ships had been committed to this disastrous frontal assault.

The ships began huddling towards each other in the centre to escape the fire. Numb, I watched as my ships crashed and collided with each other. The Chola pincers pressed harder; the ships caught fire.

Fire on the ocean is like the plague. It affects everything in its vicinity. Soon my ships were a blazing mass of wreckage. A few of them that had disentangled headed back towards Kadaram and were given chase by the Chola ships. I tried to look over the fiery broken ships but the flames grew taller and completely blocked my view of Kadaram. Two thirisadai now detached from our company and followed behind the attack craft.

Virajendra came up to me. 'The land forces contained in the thirisadai will sack the city and Brahmarayar and his men will occupy it until we have made up the cost of our expedition. Our guilds will arrive after a few days and will be allowed to trade without any hindrance. In the meantime, you will return to Chola Nadu with us, and we will discuss terms for your return … after the rain has fallen. Perhaps when the winds pick up next year.'

I let my feet quake their fear away as he spoke and took in the last sight I would ever have of my land, my Suvarnadwipa, silhouetted amidst the wreckage of my navy, glowing golden amidst the fire in the sea.

Srideva is a man who senses an opportunity. The princess comes to this conclusion the moment she lays eyes on him. Trading is in the Srivijaya blood and children are taught to recognize risks and gambles early on, be it tossing against the ocean or making deals with merchants.

He has scanned them, three women not at their most resplendent, followed by a guardsman whose disdain for them cannot be hidden by his outward show of formal respect.

They are the queen and princess of Srivijaya's ruling kadatuan, that is certain. Srideva has seen them in royal ceremonies before in the great palace hall where all the Daatus of the kadatuans would assemble and talk about affairs of the state before food and wine would batter their senses and the women folk would leave.

Maharajah Sangrama Vijayatunggavarman was a good host. The rice would come piled high in plates scented with jasmine and expensive saffron from the east and fried till brown and heavy with the flavour of eggs or meat or coconut. Appams, steamed pancakes, jackfruit, bananas, beans, lotuses, potatoes in all varieties of preparations. And the meat! Succulent legs of pork and lamb and venison from the forest. Fish from the seas, salty against the lips, and delicate fresh water fish whose bones needed to be traversed carefully by the tongue.

Srideva controlled his thoughts before gluttony got the better of him. He was a man of strong habits, but also a man of discipline, his flat belly the outcome of daily work rather than a divine gift. He prided himself on his parsimoniousness, and his brutal efficiency in dealing with matters of economics.

He sits in *maharajalilasana*, the royal position, in which one leg is folded upright against the body, while the other lies flat against the cushion of his throne. His right arm balances lazily on the knee of his vertically folded leg. A posture that makes him appear relaxed, languorous, almost bored, as if the people in front of him aren't his queen and princess, but humble petitioners.

On any other day, he would have stood up and bowed obsequiously to the queen and would have gone out of his way to show that he was a vassal of her husband's. However, this is not any other day. His mind works rapidly even as his body displays indolence. Should he take on the Chola might and drive them away from the nation? Rumours flew around the city that the king had ridden off to the wall and had not been seen since; that the Cholas had dismantled the *vidyadharatorana* and had taken it, along with the city's wealth. Another report told him that the Cholas had taken over the port of Barus and the port of Lamuri and were heading towards Kadaram. All the four principal Srivijaya ports of trade were in their hands. What chance did he possibly have? Even if he approached the Chinese for help, or the Tambralinga kingdom or even what was left of the wretched Medangs, what could possibly be done?

Nevertheless, he greeted the princess and the queen with graciousness. That would at least put the impertinent guard who appeared to slouch in their presence back in order. 'My queen, your very presence fills my court with light.'

The queen nodded, accepting the customary compliment and provided one of her own. A clumsy attempt, but it was all she was capable of at the moment.

'Your court shines like the sun. It has no need for any more.'

The compliments and extravagant titles flew across the court, Srideva and the queen exchanging them languorously, almost caressing each other with their words. After she felt that she had shown adequate respect to the Daatu, she began to talk about more important matters.

'The Srivijaya kingdom has been overrun by Cholas. We have lost our kingdom and need your help to retrieve it.'

The ministers in the court began murmuring amongst themselves.

'The Chola have come from across the seas, no doubt angered by the taxes and duties we have imposed on their goods. They will leave too. The Maharajah is still probably fighting them as we speak, and once we have word that he is alive, we will join the struggle too. Until then, we cannot do anything,' Srideva said, his tone of finality brooking no discussion.

The queen cursed herself for being naive. Why had she expected his loyalty? Every kadatuan bore a potential maharajah. Why should Srideva be any different?

'Will you shelter us in your kingdom, Daatu?' she asked.

'For a little while, surely. But if word gets out that we are sheltering the queen and her daughter, and the Chola troops find out, it may become inconvenient.'

'Inconvenient?' said the queen bitterly. 'You swore a *persumpahan* to never betray your king, and yet we stand in our hour of need betrayed?'

Srideva stood up.

'I am the Daatu to my people too. You ask me to put their lives at risk to save the Maharajah who may already be dead? Find word of his existence and then come to me. You may stay here tonight and leave tomorrow in search of the Maharajah.'

'If the Maharajah hears that you sent his wife and daughter out of your kingdom, you know the consequences, I hope?' The queen's voice was flat, emotionless.

Srideva did not have an answer for a moment. He opened his mouth and closed it repeatedly like a fish out of water. Finally, he seemed to make a decision.

'At sunrise. Tomorrow. You will leave. All of you!' he declared, looking at the guard who had remained straight faced.

The princess was afraid that they would be relegated to the streets, or worse, the stables. Thankfully, the queen, Sumitra and the princess were led into one of the guest rooms of the palace and provided with clean robes for the night. The room was small and sparsely decorated and situated near the palace lawns. But it was clean and well lit and smelled of jasmine and wet grass. The princess and the queen did not speak to each other, and they fell asleep almost as soon as they lay on the mattress.

The next morning, a palace slave woke them up gently telling them it was time to leave. The horses had been prepared and three days' supplies had been hung in neat satchels along the sides of each horse. Pavitran and other soldiers had assembled too; the captain of the guards greeted them with a surly grunt.

The queen and her retinue were escorted through the city by a troop of soldiers. It was a pretty city, thought the princess as they passed by, full of gardens and large houses. A group of monks in saffron passed before them and the troop of horses stopped reverentially and let them pass. One of the monks raised his arm and blessed the group.

The retinue passed through the city to the city walls of burnt brick. They weren't as large as the wall at home, observed the princess, but they were there nevertheless, an outcome of her father's reign.

The soldiers left them outside the gates to the south on the other side of the city.

'There must be some mistake. We want to exit through the North gate that leads to our kadatuan, not this one.'

The guard escorting them spoke in a monotone, his face expressionless. 'Daatu told us to leave you here.'

'My kingdom is on the other side of the city, and we have been told not to enter your city. How do we get back to our lands?' asked the queen.

The guard shrugged and, turning his horse around, he went back into his city walls.

'What now, your highness?' asked Pavitran. There was an edge to his voice. 'Ahead of us lies the Medang kingdom and the edge of Suvarnadwipa. There is no way to go back. Where do you suggest we go?'

The queen did not answer him but led her horse towards the forest. The princess and Sumitra followed her.

'Answer my question, your highness!' Pavitran shouted.

The queen continued to ignore him.

'Answer me!'

The three women continued down the path towards the forest.

'So we'll take your leave then, your highness!' The queen did not look back. The princess heard the scuffle of their horses moving away in the opposite direction and hoped it was the last they had seen of him. Another forest, the second in three days. This one seemed less familiar than the one in their kingdom. Trees loomed over them, watching these strangers enter their home curiously.

The princess wanted to ask her mother what they would do now. Heading into the Medang kingdom, or what was left of it, could not be an option. It would mean certain death.

She hadn't been born when the *Mahapralaya* happened; she'd heard of it from her nanny, a woman as old as the hills, with cracked red skin and pendulous breasts that drifted nearly to her navel. The woman had passed on since then, but her story was among the first the princess had heard.

She had been fed on a steady diet of cautionary tales as a child. Ones where she would be eaten by *rakshasa* demons if she went out alone into the forest at night or ghosts may enter her tumbler of milk in the morning if it wasn't despatched immediately into her stomach as soon as it was taken off the fire. Ghosts were scared of fire.

The old woman would tell her these stories with the flair of an actor. She would flip her eyelids inside out and bare her teeth and growl to give the princess an idea of the hell that awaited her if she did not listen to her mother. She would conjure up fangs with her forefingers, protrude claws with a thrust of her nails, and howl into the moon like a wild dog to terrorize her young ward.

This story was different, however. It was told in a low voice and with an expressionless face, and an unspoken understanding that this was the princess' initiation into the world of adult stories.

Years ago, the Medang kingdom, under the rule of Maharajah Dharmawangsa, sought to overreach their ambition. The Medang held Bhumi Java but also desired Suvarnadwipa. They launched an attack with their navy, sailing across the sea, destroying everything in their wake. They overran Palas Pasemah, and reached the gates of the Srivijaya capital city.

The war lasted sixteen long years and many generations of Srivijayans died against the iron of the Medang. When it looked like the Srivijaya were about to lose their kingdom, the Srivijaya ruler, Sri Maravijayottungavarman, did something that would taint the name of the Srivijaya forever, but also save their empire.

King Wurawari of Lwaram was an ally of the Medang but had been getting increasingly disgruntled at his share of the spoils. Sri Maravijayottungavarman reached out to him with his spies, and a plan was discussed.

There was no stopping Dharmawangsa. His kingdom, Medang, was the most powerful in the two islands. He further sought to cement his status as the pre-eminent ruler of the island by marrying his daughter to one of Bhumi Java's oldest noble families.

The wedding was the biggest any of the two islands had known. All the noble houses of Bhumi Java had been invited and some even from Srivijaya's Suvarnadwipa. The streets were filled with people, and the cooks of the royal kitchen did not sleep for two days before and during the wedding. The royal palace was resplendent with gold and silver.

It happened in the evening when all the guests had left, having eaten and drunk their fill. Fireflies lit the palace grounds and the croaks of the frog was the only music in the air. The royal guards were drunk too.

King Wurawari of Lwaram, who had play-acted being drunk along with his men, opened the palace gates. A troop of Srivijaya soldiers came in stealthily and dealt with the guards of the palace walls quickly. They entered the palace, and Wurawari stationed his own men outside so that none could escape. The Srivijaya soldiers then went inside the royal hall of the palace and dealt with all its occupants.

The old woman would leave the story at this critical juncture, and move on to its message. The princess was too in awe of her caretaker to ask her what happened next, and so she sought answers from other women of that generation. One of them, an old washerwoman, nearly as old as her nanny, completed the story by flattening her palm and running its edge slowly across her throat. As her palm moved, she rolled her eyes back in their sockets and stuck her tongue out. This done, she cackled.

'Oh, young princess! We slit their throats, that's what! We locked 'em in and butchered the bloody lot. I once bedded one of the soldiers who was there during the raid that night, and he told me they were ankle deep in blood by the end of it. They got the family down into the hall and slaughtered 'em one by one. Even the bride. Dharmawangsa tried fighting but was cut down soon enough. An evil man that. Met an evil end.'

What happened after the death of Dharmawangsa was common knowledge.

The family was dead, except for the king's young nephew who was the groom and betrothed to be married to Dharmawangsa's daughter. It was rumoured that he escaped into the mountains never to be heard from again. Wurawari tried hard to take the place of Dharmawangsa but fell in one of the many wars that followed to control Bhumi Java. Finally, though, no clear victor emerged, and the land was parcelled out among the various warlords of the region. All the houses in Bhumi Java and Suvaradwipa began to call the death of Dharmawangsa, 'Mahapralaya' – the great destruction, since it represented a calamity of enormous proportions. The land was still known as Medang even though no real trace of the kingdom was alive. Wurawari's line had seen its end, and the Srivijaya were loathed in Bhumi Java.

The princess wondered why the queen was leading them towards it.

5

Shall I call you Ganapathy? You write so diligently. I suspect even
if I were to stop, you would continue, much like your elephant-
headed God who wrote the Mahabharata. You haven't told me
your name yet, sullen as you are and have been since your superiors
foisted this exercise upon you, to write the story of a defeated king
destined to die very soon. A story you believe will be forgotten, no
doubt, since it possesses not a valorous hero or a heroine with the
gait of an elephant and high breasts that open out like lotus flowers
to the dawn.

But we have only begun the story, my friend. There is indeed a
valorous hero, a heroine as well, and plenty of murder and intrigue
and all the other ingredients that make a story palatable.

And there is that most potent of seasonings: revenge.

But first there is a journey. The Chola expeditionary fleet
routed the Sriivijaya navy. Its thirisadai ships docked and the army
gushed forth and committed all kinds of atrocities on my beautiful
Kadaram. There was a time when mariners called Kadaram the
jewel of the ocean as its shore that glittered in the sunlight promised
them untold riches. Now, all that was left was smoke, and a memory.

I lay in bed in my quarters, and fever ravaged my body. I slept and woke up in the middle of the night, the sheets soaked in my sweat. I would scream, without reason or knowledge why, and I would weep. Virajendra's own physician attended to me, and apart from bleeding me dry and applying a foul smelling poultice to my forehead every evening, he did absolutely nothing for my condition.

'He suffers from melancholia,' was all he could muster when Virajendra asked him bitterly why his royal guest could not partake of royal hospitality. Truth be told, rather selfishly, I hoped I would die on the journey. My wife and daughter were dead. Even if the Chola invasion had spared them, my own kadatuans could not be relied upon. My queen wasn't the kind of person who would assert herself in these matters.

Your king had taken everything from me.

There's no need for you to get upset, Ganapathy. I'm a man who has come to terms with his loss. Every man has his winter. I have, in my life, had my fill of the world, both as king and as commoner, as executor and observer. And if I've received, I've given back as good as I've gotten, as Rajendra himself would agree.

We have not much time left so it's best I leave the reminiscing for my own spirit rather than scatter it like the petals of a flower across all and sundry. A few diversions are pleasant, but I must keep time in mind.

The ship of my being was passing through a storm. My head spun and tossed and I fell frequently unconscious. I would rise out of the depths of sadness, and would be pulled back into its murky infinity. I lay in bed for weeks, praying to my lord, the Buddha, to take me away from the world. I focused on him as my pole star, the one who would bring me to shore.

Then, one day, all of the sudden, the storm was over.

I woke up dazed, and stumbled to my feet like a newborn foal, nearly tripping over myself. My guard opened my chamber door and bellowed for a servant, two of whom slipped in and positioned themselves underneath my arms, determined not to let me fall back down onto the bed.

I was given soup and *kanjika* along with a cup of milk. Virajendra entered the chamber, relief etched across his face.

'I'm so glad you're well, my lord,' he said nervously, as if showing me disrespect would render me comatose again. 'We've docked at Poompuhar. It's one of our largest ports. In an hour or so, we will be ready to leave. What fortuitous timing! The Gods, it seems, want us to parlay.'

Convenient it was. After an hour, I was hauled up like a broken battleship by the servants and taken to the upper deck for some fresh air. I knew of Poompuhar – or Puhar as it was known by our merchants – as a port city in the mould of Kadaram. The eye of the needle through which the Chinese and Arabs threaded their trade in Bharata. A city that sailors said was known for its grog shops as well as its high art.

Where I come from, your land is known by many names. The northern part is referred to as Hind by the Arabs. The Chinese call your land Tianzhu, and I've heard people call your entire mainland Bharata or Bharatavarsha, or more commonly in my parts, Jambudwipa. The region that your empire occupies is called Tamilakam or Chola Nadu. There are as many names for the land you live upon as there are stars. And every kingdom proclaims its superiority over the others. The Chalukyas or the Palas or the Rashtrakutas are as foreign for you as we are from beyond the seas.

I will keep it simple and try not to confuse you with names of distant lands like Persia or Byzantium, names you may be familiar with but have little imagination of. Your country, the kingdom of the Cholas, shall be called Tamilakam or Chola Nadu while the rest of the main land I shall call Jambudwipa, since it is the name that best appeals to me.

I was put in a small wooden craft made of large logs of wood bound securely together, and bearing rudimentary seats and a solitary sail – a *kattumaram* – and taken to the dock. A gangplank was helpfully placed between the craft and the dock that the servants helped me ascend. Virajendra was waiting for me. A man stood behind him holding a red umbrella and another one waved vigorously a white fan made from the feathers of birds.

'Welcome to my land, Maharajah Sangrama Vijayatunggavarman. We will first go to my mansion here and help you recuperate and then visit my father and brothers in Thanjavur. Bhaskaran here will take care of you.'

He turned and walked away from me. A crowd of men and women gathered outside the dock and cheered as he walked past into a horse-drawn carriage. The prince waved back at them, basking in their adulation, and the horse-drawn carriage set off slowly through the crowd.

Bhaskaran was a tall reed of a man who stuttered a greeting and bowed low. He was fair and somewhat dolorous with a short, well-clipped moustache. He wore a silk dhoti that extended down to his ankles and a neatly folded upper garment that was placed with care across his left shoulder. A matching silk turban with a huge ruby in the centre crowned his head.

'Welcome, my lord. I will be your humble host for the next few days.' He snapped his fingers and two men bearing umbrellas and two more bearing fans appeared next to me. We walked slowly towards the gates that took us into the city. Bhaskaran was a young nobleman, one of the prince's companions, the grandson of the chief treasurer of Rajendra's father, he told me.

The was dock area that was a sight in itself. You've never been to Puhar, have you, Ganapathy? It is that rare city that lives up to its legend. A city of plenty where warehouses are overloaded with the produce of many lands. Mangoes, plantain, bamboo, sugarcane, pepper, tortoise shells, camphor, beeswax, all kinds of woods – tough ones, aromatic ones. Everything the world has conjured finds a temporary home in Puhar, it is said.

The city is an entity of two distinct parts. Maruvurpakkam that is near the sea to the east, and Pattinappakkam to the west. Both parts are separated by gardens and orchards that play host to daily markets. Maruvurpakkam, the Eastern City, is the vibrant part of Puhar. Since it is near the sea, most of its residents are salty old traders, merchants, fisher folk and even foreign Yavanas who are too finicky to go inside Tamilakam. Beyond the actual dock, where the ships harbour, are large warehouses with windows in the shape of the eyes of deer. A curious shape, no doubt, but I've never bothered to find out why. The Western City, or Pattinappakkam, is meant for residents who have deeper roots in the land than the ocean. Regular citizens ply their trade and live out their lives in their community's quarters here.

We walked out of the dock area where a horse-drawn carriage waited to take us into the Eastern City. Its body was golden and had the Chola tiger embossed on it and was drawn by two white horses. It was obviously a royal vehicle.

Like a well-bred young man, Bhaskaran did not enquire about my recent misfortunes, instead focusing on the city of Puhar itself. The last few days had seen rioting. The city guards who were Yavanas from far countries had been caught completely unawares and the city council had to ask the emperor to send in the army. The riots had been quelled and the city was back to normal now. What was the cause of the riots? There had been grain shortage for some time. But now, fortunately, grain had come from Uraiyur so the citizens were getting enough to eat.

We never needed city guards in my city, Ganapathy. Riots were unheard of.

I see you stifle a yawn. It's already late, and you haven't got what you came for. So much of the story is done, and scarcely a mention of your beloved emperor? Fear not, for he comes soon. But not a moment before I want him to. In my story, whether they be kings or slaves, they come at a time of my choosing. Much like the city of Puhar, your emperor, too, had two sides to him. One he revealed to the outside world, and one I believe he revealed only to me. Yes, we shall talk about him soon.

We rode in the carriage through the dusty streets of the Eastern City. Men and women of different colours, who obviously did not belong to Tamilakam, walked along the street as if it was their own city. There were more places to find food and drink than permanent lodging. The most prominent feature of the Eastern City was its lighthouse that stood on the edge of the land, a little distance away from the dock. It was a tall and wide stone pillar with a flat platform where a huge bonfire was burned to guide ships towards the harbour at night. We made our way past a row of gardens and crossed on over to the Western City of Puhar.

The first indication that we had crossed into another city were the *gopuram* of temples that rose like crowns into the sky. This was a city grown fat with riches that rapidly added layers every day to feed the greed of its people. The houses rose high, beyond three storeys, even as the city grew sideways. The houses had large circular terraces where families would congregate in the evening to escape the Tamil heat. The roads were wide and paved. Some of the more popular streets were even lined with torches that would be lit at night. We travelled for a long time, a good deal of it spent cajoling two bullocks that had decided to squat in the middle of a junction and block traffic. By the time we reached Bhaskaran's mansion, I was feeling unwell again.

The horse-drawn carriage dropped us outside the gate of his mansion. A boulevard lined with neem trees and manicured bushes led to his house. Bhaskaran went inside first, and returned promptly with two man-servants who supported me as I walked. I took off my sandals and left them at the threshold of the mansion, and we walked inside together, slowly.

The smell of hibiscus and rose hung in the air as we entered the courtyard of the mansion. Large stone pillars painted white and embellished with carvings of men holding swords stood towering over me. We walked past the pillars into a door and the inner courtyard of the house. A jasmine plant grew in the centre of the courtyard and filled the space with its rich scent.

Three women stood in front of me representing all the ages of man. An old, crooked one in a magnificent green saree with a gold border, a middle aged one with a streak of grey running through the centre of her head, and a young one, a teen or a little older, in the first flush of youth. I looked at them and smiled weakly, folding my palms together in greeting. I hadn't forgotten my manners. A prisoner I was, but still an ambassador of the Srivijayas in a foreign land. They would know that we conducted ourselves with the utmost dignity in every circumstance. They looked at me impassively and I was led into a room that contained a large bed and an ornate swing that hung from the ceiling.

The ground felt cold against the soles of my feet. I suppose that was really the moment it struck me that I was going to be living in another land. The palace floor in my city was tiled with stiff oak wood that would be cleaned every day and scrubbed with oil on occasion. The floor of this house was made of red clay that felt cold against my feet, as if it didn't want me to step on it. It was only later that I learned that many homes in your land had floor made from this clay to keep its inhabitants cool during the summer months. The clay could be very cold during the end of the rains and the winter but was inviting enough in the summer.

When the servants deposited me on the bed delicately, like some expensive gunny sack, I closed my eyes and feigned sleep so that Bhaskaran couldn't make conversation. I finally fell asleep curled into the centre of the bed and did not notice when the lamps of the room were put out.

The next morning I woke up to a mynah singing to the sun. Two servants stood respectfully at the foot of my bed, holding towels.

The sleep had been restful and brought clarity that I had lacked through the voyage. There was no point living timidly. I would not be afraid of the cold floors and strange smells of this distant land. I was the Srivijaya Maharajah. I would die a Maharajah. I would lead my life with the same abandon that I had before.

Let's see who dared to stop me.

I groaned loudly, startling them, then yawned loudly and stretched my arms to their full extent. Standing up, I took the proffered towel and a drink of warm water with honey and lime that I gargled in my mouth and spat into a spittoon. I let the servants lead me to the washing area and bathed myself, applying sandalwood to my skin for fragrance. A man with a razor shaved my face that had grown thick with hair and cut my hair short the way

I liked it. The clothes of your land – a dhoti and an upper cloth, an *angavastram* – were given to me and a silk turban that was already tied and which I had to only tighten after I fixed it upon my head. The bath had done me a world of good; I felt like a king again. I swaggered back towards my room in the mansion and found Bhaskaran waiting outside for me, his hands folded in front of his body. He smiled when he saw me.

'Maharajah, it's good to see you this morning.'

I nodded.

'Thank you for your hospitality. I did not feel well last night. I'm much better today, thank you.'

His smile stretched wider.

'I imagined as much. A sea voyage of that length does no good to the constitution. No wonder sailors die young.'

I was about to remind him that I belonged to a seafaring race and that our life spans were very long unless a battle or a family feud cut them short. I decided against it but nodded graciously.

'There is a vihara close by and a Buddhist temple if you would like to offer prayers. If you like, we could visit it first and then have breakfast. The emperor has always stressed that all religions need to co-exist in peace. He is unique that way. Different from so many others.'

I smiled and nodded. All religions thrived in Srivijaya too. I personally gave money from my treasury for the upkeep of temples and also encouraged the study of Sanskrit. All my ancestors did. As far back as six hundred years ago, the Srivijaya kingdom was a place where monks from all over the East would come and learn Malay and Sanskrit before proceeding to Jambudwipa. The Chinese monk Yi Jing spoke of 'Jinzhou' or the 'golden coast' – the Chinese name for Srivijaya in his travels – and recommended that everyone visit it. Thousands of monks came to my city every year. It was a place to prepare for cultural exchange, and to prepare for the sheer unfamiliarity of Jambudwipa. There was nothing special about your king in that regard, even though he appeared almost otherworldly to Bhaskaran.

I declined the offer of visiting the temple, though it would have done me good. I would do as my host did for the day, more as a gesture of politeness than anything.

We went to a dining hall where we sat on the floor that was less cold now in the morning heat. Huge palm leaves were placed in front of us. I watched as Bhaskaran splashed a little water around the leaves and said a brief prayer. A small army of men then entered and put small portions of rice, curd, pickle, vegetables and curry on our leaves.

We ate in silence, or rather, I ate in silence, ravenous as I was. Rice gruel is good for the sea, but I had not had a good meal in over two weeks and filled my stomach till it hurt. Bhaskaran hardly touched his food, and when I asked him why, he said that he had eaten shortly after dawn and would eat lunch when the sun was directly overhead next.

I learned that he was the head of the Town Architectural Committee and would leave as soon as breakfast was complete to discuss additions to a local temple. More travellers were coming from the north to Thanjavur and Gangaikonda Cholapuram, he said, and the Temple Trust needed to find a way to enhance the structure at Puhar.

Life seems to be one long pilgrimage for you people, Ganapathy. I have never known a race more obsessed with their Gods. There are so many of them here. A priest I met told me there were over 330 million of them, perhaps more than the stars in the sky!

Bhaskaran told me the people in your lands visited their local temples every day and went on elaborate yatras to different parts of the mainland, stopping from temple to temple before they arrive at their destination, much like the ships that go from port to port. Your temples are like our ports. They pump people that are the lifeblood of a kingdom into the veins of the city, though I only realized the extent of this later during my travels through Chola Nadu.

There are Hindus who worship Shiva and Vishnu in the lands of Srivijaya, too, though we consider the Buddha sacred above all else. And there are Hindus who worship the supreme one-ness, Brahman, much in the same fashion we worship the Buddha. As a Buddhist monarch I was always respectful of your Hindu traditions. I also paid grants to build temples in my land, as I've said before. Mention this when you tell my story. Anyone listening to it must know there was good in this man.

While we ate breakfast, Bhaskaran told me he had to leave but assured me that he would return soon. Till then his whole house was at my disposal. I was suspicious of this meeting. Who goes off leaving an enemy Maharajah unattended, even in their own kingdom? I found the Chola treatment of me surprising as well. No chains or manacles. No lashes or humiliation. It was as if I was a guest of the emperor and not kidnapped by his army in a cowardly surprise attack.

'I have arranged for four guards to look after your security,' he said, almost divining my thoughts.

Security? The guards were to ensure I did not run off. Though where would I run off to? I did not know the city, and there were probably no Srivijaya traders at the port who would take me back home.

'You may wander Puhar if you so wish. It is a beautiful city, quite like Kadaram.'

'Kadaram that is burnt to the ground now?'

He blushed a deep red and looked embarrassedly at the red floor, more concerned, no doubt, about offending his host and incurring his master's wrath than any feeling for the people of my land.

'The delights of Puhar are recorded in poetry,' said Bhaskaran weakly. 'You can visit the gardens and the theatres, or perhaps a musical sabha. Or you can go to one of your Buddhist temples. If you're feeling hungry, and would like to eat something in particular, perhaps my household can arrange it.'

I was feeling particularly vehement.

'Delights, you say? A musical sabha and a walk in the garden? What delights are these? Why do you not mention the pleasures of wine and the company of women?'

His hand started shaking as he blushed further, almost boring a hole into the ground with his eyes.

'...with small hips and heavy breasts the way you Tamils like them...'

I thought he would start crying. Bhaskaran seemed to be a bureaucrat through and through. An efficient workhorse with little idea of how to grease the wheels of friendship. A man who could do the work rather than get it done. What fool had they picked to be my companion?

Too his credit, however, he responded gamely enough. 'I'll, ah, um, arrange what I can, Maharajah.'

Throwing kingly decorum to the wind, I slapped my thigh with my left hand and clutched the flesh, making a lustful face and giving him a fair idea of what I was expecting. The colour drained from his face and he almost turned pale, which was quite a feat given he was almost as brown as I was.

I continued eating my breakfast and let him ponder over the problem of my entertainment. After I was done, a woman came with a small silver pot bearing water and poured it on my hands. I rubbed them clean, wiping away the debris of rice and vegetables into the leaf below.

Bhaskaran left in a hurry and I was left alone in his home with no company save my guards. The women of the house did not make an appearance – not only, I suspect, because of their reticence to join male company, but because Bhaskaran had probably told them it was best to stay away from me. I was tempted to think that they were treated like chattel. Srivijaya and our preceding dynasties had been ruled by queens. Our women could command men not through the space between their thighs but the space between their ears.

I spent the rest of the morning alternating between swinging on the teak swing and lying on a bed. I could not read Tamil, so it made no sense to ask for a manuscript of poetry. Though that would have been scant entertainment. I was always more fond of the outdoors and spending my time at the sea or on a horse.

In the middle of the day, a man announced himself at my door. He was a Brahmin, and wore a sacred thread that hung over his small pot belly. He said that he was a poet and had been sent by the prince of the Cholas to keep me company. I thanked him for visiting and told him that I had no benediction to give, no gift or reward for his poetry. He told me he was taken care of by the kingdom and a gift was not necessary.

He sat down, his feet folded in the lotus position, and began reciting his verse in Tamil in a clear and steady voice that could have sounded over the ocean but was tempered to suit my room.

The story he recited was about Krishna and Sudama.

Legend says that Krishna and Sudama were childhood friends in Mathura or Dwarka or wherever Krishna was from. Do not expect me to remember these details. Krishna was from the ruling family, and Sudama was somewhat impoverished. Krishna becomes a king and a warlord and general do-gooder – a celebrity if ever there was one. Years later, Sudama falls on hard times and decides to visit Krishna. He doesn't know if Krishna remembers him, but goes with some beaten rice as a present – Krishna's favourite dish from their youth. Krishna greets him with great love. He eats the rice and enjoys it and the company of Sudama who promptly forgets what he had to ask for. Sudama realizes this on his journey back and is despondent but when he returns home he finds a mansion in place of his impoverished hut and more wealth than he knows what to do with.

The storyteller used the word 'palace' to describe Sudama's home, and then corrected himself and said 'mansion' and smiled at me. I smiled back, and told him that I had enjoyed the tale thoroughly, and he must come again to tell me another.

'Yes,' he replied, 'one must never confuse a mansion for a palace.' He smiled mysteriously, bowed and left my room.

Was this some kind of veiled taunt? Was he rubbing the fact that I was no longer king in my face? Or was he trying to tell me that though I was a guest of the Chola emperors, this was not my home and I had to be watchful? To what purpose?

I beat the thought out of my head. I was paranoid. That was all. After the poet had left, I spent my time thinking about my wife and daughter and what had become of them. I would ask Bhaskaran to find out. As his guest, that was the least he could do for me.

Bhaskaran returned early in the evening and apologized profusely for the delay. Stone was in short supply in Puhar, and they had to arrange for it from the rocky highlands further up north in Chola Nadu, closer to Chalukyan territory. The Chalukyas, I understood, were like the Medang for us. Bitter rivals of equal power who wished to occupy the same land. Obtaining the stone from those quarries would require more money since the area was susceptible to Chalukyan raids. Now taxes would need to be increased. An announcement needed to be made, but on the back of a grain riot, it probably wasn't the most prudent hour.

He looked troubled, and I did not probe further. We ate dinner together, away from the female folk of his house, served by men. The food was roots and beans and all kinds of vegetables with no meat. I wondered if he was one of those Brahmins fastidious about eating only vegetables with no animal flesh in their diet, much like the Jains and even many Buddhists. I was tempted to ask him for some, just to see his face turn purple, but decided against it.

We finished the meal and Bhaskaran offered me some areca nut wrapped in betel leaf that you Tamils find so soothing to the digestive system. He walked me to my room, and as he bid me good night, he told me that we would be travelling the next day to Thanjavur to meet Rajendra himself and his sons.

'And if I refuse?' I asked.

He turned grey, poor Bhaskaran, and mumbled an apology. Then he wished me an enjoyable evening and walked away without answering my question. Bhaskaran was like my rainbow, changing colour whenever it suited me. *Vaanavil,* I would call him. I chuckled as I entered my room.

A woman sat on the bed. I thought it was some kind of mistake and walked up to her.

'I believe you have the wrong room,' I said courteously.

'I'm sure I have the right one.' Her voice was husky.

She was dressed in a green sari – a *puduvai* – and wore large golden earrings. A large round shield-like ring covered half her nose. She wore armlets with a single pearl on each of them. Her eyes were lined with kohl and her lips were coloured red.

'They say you're a guest from a foreign land,' she said, her eyes looking up at me, and her lips stretching with the hint of a smile.

I nodded.

'Would you allow me to show you the pleasures of ours?'

Sumitra stuck close to the princess and their horses trudged behind the queen. She did not speak much, blindly obeyed the princess or the queen. Did she have family back in the city? Did she have a husband or a lover or someone she had left behind? The princess didn't know. She found it strange that she was asking herself these questions. They had never occurred to her before.

'Sumitra, do you have a family?'

Sumitra looked frightened. The veil of formality that had shrouded their relationship had been pulled off rather brutally by the princess, leaving her exposed.

'Sumitra, do you have a family?' the princess asked again, her voice gentler, a rope to drag her companion out of the quicksand of silence into the security of conversation.

'Yes. They work in the royal kitchen.'

The princess considered this.

'I'm sure they're all right. The Cholas are only after our gold. They'll leave soon enough. Don't worry.'

Sumitra looked to the ground and nodded.

The princess felt miserable for Sumitra. There were so many times in the past two days that she had wanted to burst into tears at their predicament. The sight of her mother had given her strength. How did Sumitra, who was younger and less sophisticated in the ways of the world, find her courage? If they ever got the chance, she would return Sumitra to her parents.

The queen travelled ahead, alone with her thoughts. The princess called out to her but the queen did not appear to listen, so she cantered up to her mother.

'Ma?' she asked, and probed her mother's face for any sign of insanity. She had never been taught to suspect the worst at first, but the last few days seemed to indicate otherwise, and the princess was already imagining the horrors that might await her if she had to handle both an ailing mother and a silent servant in a strange jungle.

'We'll find a way,' she said, her voice sounding a little unfocused. 'Not all the Medang hate us. Some even believe *Mahapralaya* was a good thing.' She smiled at the princess, trying to look confident. 'We shall reach the tip of Suvarnadwipa in a few days on horse. I've been here before. The forest isn't very large, and there is a village on the other side. We will cross it by the evening and try finding shelter in the village.'

However, she had gone pale just talking about her plan.

'Mama, why don't we just apologize to Srideva and maybe he'll let us pass through?'

The queen looked a little surprised, more perhaps at her daughter for raising a query than the query itself.

'Don't be ridiculous, child. We're safer here. Lord knows how long it will take the Cholas to cross the jungle and trample over Srideva's little dung pile of a kadatuan. Besides, you can't trust a man like that. Lord knows how he became a Daatu in the first place.'

The princess was silent. She looked around the forest now. It wasn't very different from the one separating her kadatuan and Srideva's, except the trees were taller and thicker here, as if they hadn't seen a woodman's axe for centuries. The silence was occasionally broken by the shrieks of monkeys fighting for food or birds calling out to one another.

They went further into the jungle along a rough path hewn, perhaps, by the villagers. The sun rose but its harshness fell upon the tree leaves that protected the travellers without a kingdom. Around midday, they stopped to eat. They tied the horses to a low hanging branch of a tree and sat in a circle. They had jasmine scented rice that had been packed for them and fresh water. The queen told them to eat half of the rations in the day and conserve the rest for the evening. They ate in silence, without much thought or pleasure.

A branch cracked near them. And then another. The princess thought it was probably one of the monkeys and ignored it, till she saw her mother's face looking behind her, puzzled. The princess turned around and saw Pavitran with two men behind him. He smiled at them.

'I'll make it quick. You are no longer queen. This land is no longer yours. You may give yourself to me or let my men have their way with you.'

As he walked towards the princess, the queen stood up and looked him in the eye. 'You've been drinking.'

For a moment, Pavitran stood staring at her without blinking. He crossed his arms and looked down penitently. Then, he burst out laughing.

'Drinking? I've been swallowing oceans, my lady. I've run the river Musi dry. The great revenge they're calling it in the bars. The *Mahapralaya* of madira!'

He looked back at his soldiers who stayed passive.

'In any case that doesn't matter. But I'll tell you what does. I will take you back to the Cholas and they will reward me it handsomely with elephants or gold or what-have-you. You'll all be a little worse for wear, but that is only to be expected from prisoners of war.'

'You're a crude animal, Pavitran. I'm not sure why the Maharajah chose you as his captain of the guard.'

'You're holding your nerve just fine, my lady. Though you'll wish you held that tongue of yours when I'm through with you. And your daughter too.'

He looked behind at his men.

'You two can split the wench.'

Sumitra cowered behind the princess who was partially hidden behind the queen who was now quavering with rage.

'Are there more of you?' she said. 'Or was it just the three of you who decided to betray the king? A special hell awaits those who do. You know about this, Pavitran, and perhaps you've accepted your damnation. But do the soldiers know?'

'Most of the soldiers aren't really men. Can't take what's there to be taken, you see. Only these two proved real men.'

'And what is a real man, according to you?'

Pavitran chuckled. 'Bide for time as much as you want, my lady. No one is coming to rescue you here in this forest. No one's been here for years. Villagers say it's haunted. Maybe it is.'

He looked back at his men who had begun to look a little unsure. 'So we should finish this off before sunset, shouldn't we, boys?'

'Whatever Pavitran has offered you for this unforgivable act, I will offer you double,' the queen declared, her gaze on Pavitran.

Pavitran snorted. 'You don't have a comb to your name to dress your pretty hair, and you're offering these men double? Double of what? Young men like these need sport. And I'm telling them to go and play.'

The queen began to speak, but was interrupted by Pavitran. 'Enough talk!' He took two giant strides towards the queen and clasped her arm. The queen wrenched it away from him. When Sumitra started screaming for help, a soldier strode towards her while another went after the princess.

The princess took two steps back. The soldier loosened the belt that held his sword, unclasped his dhoti and lunged at the princess. The princess twisted away from his grasp and looked around. Pavitran had the queen in his arms and the other man was lying on top of Sumitra and loosening his dhoti.

The soldier jumped on the princess and brought her to the ground. He pinned her wrists to the side and sat on her stomach, overpowering her easily.

'I have never done this before,' he said, almost apologetically.

'Boys! Enjoy it while it lasts. Remember, we take turns,' shouted Pavitran over the rustling of branches. He had overpowered the queen by now and was completely naked.

The queen and Sumitra were screaming loudly for help. The princess did not scream. She spoke to the man calmly.

'You don't need to do this,' she said in an oddly penetrating voice that was devoid of fear. The soldier looked up at Pavitran who was grappling with the queen and then looked down at the princess. 'Sorry,' he said in a trembling voice. His arms reached out to cup the princess' breasts.

Then he fell over.

The princess sat up to see that an arrow was now lodged in his head. The other soldier was also lying on the ground with an arrow in his skull. Pavitran was screaming in pain. An arrow was lodged in his shoulder. A group of six men walked towards them, dressed in shabby grey robes and brown leather armour. All of them wore swords. Four of them had slung bows over their shoulders while two held them lightly in their hands. The queen ran over to the princess to check if she was well while Sumitra sat up and started crying loudly.

One of the men walked over to her and, without a word, slapped her.

6

The lady left my bed early in the morning, a little disappointed perhaps. Most kings are supposed to be endowed with godly virility capable of satisfying three women at a time. At least that's what your book says – the one on love that I have not yet managed to read, but have heard quoted several times. Pleasure thrives on masculinity, and what masculinity can a man who has lost his kingdom provide?

I heard the jangle of her bangles and the soft rustle of her silk puduvai being swept across her frame. She was taller than the women I had been with. The women of my land were fair and short and not endowed with the hips of the women of Chola Nadu.

I feigned sleep, as I had so many times in these past days, and tried to gauge her reaction by the sound of her actions. Her movements were brisk and efficient. I suspect she did not look back at me as she left the room silently.

I'll keep the details of what we did that night to myself. I wasn't at my best, and that's not a detail you need to mention in your story. After she had left, I waited a while and then gingerly got up from my bed, and peeked outside the room. A man was standing with a wash cloth. If he had heard about my downfall last night, it did not show on his face.

I cleaned up, and almost as soon as I had finished, Bhaskaran appeared. He was dressed in travelling clothes – a brown dhoti with a shawl and a turban – and held a large staff. 'We're travelling from Puhar in the next hour. You're being taken to Gangaikonda Cholapuram now, not Thanjavur. It's two days by river and a brief horse ride away. The royal yacht will be taking us.'

The abruptness of my departure was surprising, but also gratifying. I had feared that I would have to wait a very long time to meet Rajendra.

Bhaskaran and I travelled on the royal yacht – one with a snake head and a royal umbrella – for six days. We passed the great city of Thanjavur that used to be the capital city under Rajendra's father Rajaraja, till Rajendra decided he wanted his own new capital city and built one from the ground up.

We reached the city of Gangaikonda Cholapuram, or Gangapuram as the locals call it, after a few days of sailing languorously up the Kollidam river which was not unlike the Musi – wide of bank and rich of fish. A river of plenty. My time – or should I say our time, for Bhaskaran was determined never to leave my side – was spent playing chess on the barge, and listening to a minstrel sing songs accompanied by a *yaal*.

That evening, when we sat for dinner, I told Bhaskaran that I wished to partake of fish. By the look on his face, you would have thought that I had told him I wanted to eat him alive. Nevertheless, Bhaskaran complied. The next day for lunch, I found myself eating some kind of river fish with small bones that knotted into my teeth. He sat with me and watched as I ate, and soon blanched, vomiting the vegetables he had eaten over the side of the barge. I did not press him for meat after that.

The ship docked at a large port in the middle of the river filled with local traders taking their wares out in large earthen caskets, or in large bundles tied in jute and balanced precariously on the heads of a labourer. The scene is something I would have encountered at any one of my cities – Kadaram, Jambi, Palas Pasemah. Bhaskaran, I think, was a little disappointed that I was underwhelmed, for he kept plying me with details about the number of sacks of grain moved, or the amount of camphor sold, or the terracotta sculptures that exchanged hands here.

I smiled and nodded and tried to look impressed, but Bhaskaran eventually gave up. We found a royal retinue waiting for us outside the port area with a horse-drawn open carriage sporting the Chola emblem and a troop of cavalrymen. The carriage was elaborately furnished with silk cushions and feather down pillows. As the convoy set off, the people on the path made way and bowed to the carriage.

We passed through a tree-lined road that stretched for miles, almost like a highway. We stopped at an orchard for lunch that had been packed from the barge and then carried on to the city of Gangaikonda Cholapuram. Or rather the city that would come to be known as Gangaikonda Cholapuram.

Bhaskaran told me that the city was still being built, and I could see strewn carelessly on the road were bricks and huge uneven slabs of granite that would be pulled into the city and hewn into some form.

'The emperor's father, Rajaraja, built a great temple in his capital city of Thanjavur; it was larger than anything anyone has built dedicated to the Lord Brihadeeswara,' said Bhaskaran, for whom anything the Chola emperors touched could not be surpassed by anyone else. He probably thought my city or Jambi or Kadaram were still villages where tribals paddled about in canoes to pluck fish out of the water.

'Gangaikonda Cholapuram will be unlike any city ever seen. The emperor began conquering his way up north a little over six years ago, laying waste to the cities of Vengi, Kalingga, Odda, Kosala and Vangaladesa until he finally reached the Ganga river. He then brought back water from the river in large vessels of gold to fill up the water tank of the city. That's why he will call it Gangaikonda Cholapuram.'

'The city of the Chola who brought Ganga,' I said.

He nodded vigorously, smiling at my recognition of his emperor's greatness.

'So, did the emperor go and conquer these places himself?' I asked, curious. How old could he be? He had a son who was a full-grown man, but if he went around conquering all this territory just over six years ago, he wasn't the doddering old senile I thought he was. Or perhaps the son was an adopted one? Or they had some martial custom where all the generals were known as 'sons' to keep them close to the king?

'Oh no, the Emperor went up to the river of Godavari, just about half way through. The rest of the raid was conducted by Prince Rajadhiraja Chola and General Araiyan Rajarajan. They trampled all over the north, crushing the Palas and the Chalukyas.'

The Chalukyas were a name I would hear frequently over the next few years. They were also known as the Kalyani Chalukyas, taking their name from their capital city of Kalyani. Both the Cholas and Chalukyas would regularly take nibbles out of each other's kingdoms, while occasionally taking a sizeable bite and digesting it into their empire. When he was still the heir apparent to the throne, Rajendra had gone forth and taken one of these sizeable bites, dispossessing the Kalyani Chalukyas of many important cities. They never forgave him after that and were constantly bristling at the Chola borders. Eventually, Rajaraja had realized the importance of peace or, more likely, the importance of having his own man on the throne, so he married off his daughter to the king of Vengi to make a new ally who would act as a deterrent to the Chalukyas. When the king died, the Kalyani Chalukyas tried to get their own man on the throne, and Rajendra took prompt action by defeating them in battle. He then set up his nephew, Rajaraja Narendran, who was a powerful Vengi prince as well as his son-in-law, on the Vengi throne. The Ganga expedition I later learned was retribution against the kingdoms of the north for lending their support to the Kalyani Chalukyas.

These were facts that were dinned into me for years. The Tamil names still don't sit well on my tongue. They are long and wind up and down the throat and twist the tongue, leaving behind their impression long after they are gone.

You laugh at this. What right does a man called Sangrama Vijayatunggavarman have to call our names long, you ask? Perhaps you're right. But it wasn't just one name; I had to learn many new ones when I arrived.

The Chalukyas play a tragic part in my story later on, but for now, all Bhaskaran could tell me was how the Chalukya campaign had filled the kingdom's coffers. Apparently, in the words of the poets, the Chalukya king Jayasimha 'ran away from the battlefield and hid like a mouse', a flight of poetic imagination I considered far from the shores of reality. But there was no doubt that he lost much territory and Rajendra built his great city with the riches he earned from this campaign.

We reached the city at night. Fires blazed atop a large wall made of burnt brick, nearly eight feet tall, which circled the city, much like in my own city. We passed through the gates and entered Rajendra's new township. Under the yellow glow of the torchlight, it looked like a giant child had carelessly kicked over a box of his toy blocks. Buildings were half-constructed, and large square and rectangular stones were littered across the city. The king's royal guard stood at every turn or junction; there were no civilians to be seen. The city was like any other – or rather, would be like any other when it was fully built. Many of the homes had no residents, though I was told all would move into their new homes on the day the king came and proclaimed this his capital city. At the moment, it was a city populated by stone and wood.

We stopped at a mansion, one of the few that had been completed.

'Where are we?' I asked Bhaskaran who had been threatening to fall asleep ever since we entered the city.

'Royal guesthouse,' he mumbled. 'A few rooms have been set up for you.'

I got off the carriage and we were welcomed by a few retainers. Bhaskaran then ushered me into the mansion that had been prepared for my arrival. Brass lamps burned all around us as we walked into a large room with a bed that had been prepared.

Bhaskaran then said, 'I am being put up in another mansion close by. The servants are here if you need anything. Please do not hesitate to ask them for anything.'

'A woman, like the one you procured for me the other night?'

Bhaskaran turned pale and walked out with his head bowed.

I must describe my mansion. It would be my home for the remainder of my time here. It was a two-storeyed building made of brick and painted clay red. It had a large garden in the front with rose shrubs and jasmine and mango trees that flowered in the summer. Six peacocks were also part of the landscape and were fed and watered by my retainers. Two pillars made of polished wood were positioned near the entrance of the house. Inside, there is a small sitting area, where I could meet visitors, though wholly inappropriate for personal guests. The sitting area was like a throat, and it led to the belly of the house – the open courtyard, that was normally busy with activity. Rooms were built around the courtyard and mine was the largest one. No one else occupied the house while I lived in it. A kitchen and a stable were situated behind the house.

My own room, where I spent most of my hours in Tamilakam, had a large bed in the centre of the room. A swing hung a little distance away and there was a writing desk in one corner. The room was quite spacious, and there were several feet between the door and the bed. Four fan bearers stood behind the bed holding large white fans made of yak and horse tails. They would enter the room whenever I did, and stand against the wall a few feet behind my bed, waving their fans till I fell asleep. They were deaf and mute, Bhaskaran told me, and this was a good way for them to earn a livelihood.

He introduced me to a man called Nadan who would be my chief retainer and look after the running of the household. Nadan grinned and bowed. He was a tall, clean-shaven man with curly hair, and a sparkle of mischief in his eyes. The kind of retainer who would not hesitate to filch money from your purse when you were not around. I had no such worries here, luckily. Everything was given to me by your emperor. There were clothes in boxes already available as well as a horse in the stables outside along with a carriage that could seat four, and I did not have to pay for anything since I was the emperor's foreign guest. Your eyes widen, but this is normally the way kings are treated when they visit foreign lands. For some reason I could not fathom at the moment, I was the emperor's guest.

I was too tired to clean myself up, so I asked the retainers to leave. I removed my dhoti and clothes and lay down on the bed and blew out the lamps. The room was cloaked in darkness, and I fell asleep without much effort.

A few hours – or what I felt must have been a few hours – later, a series of soft thumps woke me up. I didn't pay attention to the sound at the time. What got my attention was the fact that I was bathed in sweat. The fan bearers had stopped fanning me. I peered sleepily and tried to see if I could spot one of them and was about to shout when I saw the area in front of my bed being illuminated by a small lamp. I rubbed my eyes to dispel sleep from them and then rubbed them again to ensure that I was not seeing a ghost.

A strange-looking man was sitting on a chair in front of my bed holding a small brass lamp, or a *vallakku*. He leaned forward and I saw his face clearly in the lamp light. It was a long face with a long nose and long ears and long brows. Every feature seemed to be the opposite of mine. He was clean-shaven too – a far cry from most of the Chola men who wore their beards like war flags. His face was lined, but his hair was streaked black, disguising his age. His eyes were laden with kohl and regarded me with no emotion.

I sat up in my bed and waited for my guest to make a move. I wondered if this was an assassin that the Cholas had set upon me. Perhaps they realized they have no need for me anymore.

After a few moments of tense silence, the man said, 'Welcome to my kingdom.' His voice was deep and low and rumbled through the room. It sounded like a mountain had cracked. 'I am the son of Rajaraja Chola, and the emperor of the Chola kingdom of Tamilakam. Rajendra Chola.'

'You'll fetch a decent price. Even the old one.'

The three women sat in front of a fire. They wore dirty grey shawls that covered their tattered clothes. Pavitran had been tied to a tree and his wound had been bandaged. His mouth had been gagged with a cloth.

'I am the queen of the Srivijaya empire. I will not be sold in a slave auction.'

'And I'm the emperor of the Song,' said the man sitting in front of her. He smiled widely and his mouth opened to reveal only four yellow front teeth. He was short but muscular, bald but wore a long grey beard. His visage could have been frightening but for his large eyes that regarded them gently. His name was Balan, he had told them soon after rescuing them from Pavitran and his men.

'I'm a small business owner in search of capital – my trade being slaves.' He had grinned, as if making a joke. 'You three women look like prime real estate in a market that's already overcrowded.'

'I thank you for your services. You will be rewarded by the Maharajah when the time comes. I promise you that. Now take us back.'

'Back where, ma'am? The country is in ruins. We escaped from the Chola raid by the skin of our teeth.' He bared his four teeth as evidence.

The queen was silent.

'You will be auctioned off as slaves. That I promise you. I can do one thing, though,' he said as he removed his knife. 'You three will get the pleasure of carving up your man any way you see fit. You're going to fetch me a lot of money, and this man was trying to tamper with the goods. It's the least I can do for you,' he said, and flipped the knife over to offer its hilt to the queen. She took it gently and looked at it, gauging its edge.

'Girls,' she said softly.

The princess stood, as did Sumitra who had been sobbing quietly to herself since she had been slapped into silence by the men who had feared that her bawling would attract visitors.

The queen motioned to Sumitra who took her position in front of Pavitran and gave her instructions. Balan and his men sat back and looked intently at the proceedings as if they were watching a performance at the theatre. One of them even picked an apple from a tree and began chewing it.

'A far worse fate awaits traitors to the kingdom, Pavitran. You are a lucky man indeed. But I'll do the best I can,' she said. She motioned Sumitra to lift the loincloth that protected his manhood.

The queen looked into his eyes as she cut him slowly. He screamed into the cloth that muffled his voice.

The men behind cringed as they heard his disembodied flesh fall to the leafy ground with a wet thwack followed by a gush of blood. The queen used the loincloth to wipe her hands.

'Sumitra, your turn.' She passed on the knife to the younger girl.

Sumitra picked it out of her hand gingerly and then clasped it hard. She looked at its bloodied surface, shuddered. The men behind her began shouting, goading her on.

'Stab! Stab! Stab! Stab!'

With a scream, she stabbed him in the stomach, over and over again. The men stopped shouting. The only sound was that of the relentless stabbing.

One of the men caught hold of Sumitra's arms and shook her. She looked first angry and then frightened as she slowly realized what she had done. She gasped and shuddered as if coming out of a spell and burst into tears. This time, the man held her to his chest and began cooing to her soothingly.

'Daughter' said the queen now. The princess looked at Pavitran whose body was a bloody mess, but was still alive. Sumitra's blows, though frenzied, had not been hard enough to penetrate his vital organs.

The princess took the knife, wiped the bloodied hilt of the knife on her shawl and clenched it tightly in her first. Pavitran groaned.

She had not been brought up to be cruel. Her father had discouraged it.

But this was the man who tried to assault her mother, the man who betrayed her father.

'Stab! Stab! Stab! Stab!' The men behind her shouted.

Pavitran saw her walking towards him. Petrified, he began to cry but the sound was muffled by the cloth that gagged his mouth. He bowed his head towards her, his eyes pleading for mercy.

'Stab! Stab! Stab! Stab!'

She could cut out his eye, dice his fingers into little pieces, cut out his tongue, who knew what else? Her father had been a great admirer of Chinese torture techniques and had spoken about them on more than a few occasions. Though she hadn't paid attention when her father had rambled on about Chinese ingeniousness, some nuggets of wisdom had stayed with her.

But what was to be served through this cruelty? There was no audience to frighten into servility as most displays of torture were supposed to do. Indeed, the audience here revelled in blood. Torturing him further would take more time. And time was something they had little of. The more time she spent on Pavitran, the less she could spend thinking about how to escape their predicament.

She grabbed his hair and raised his head; with a quick stroke, she cut through his jugular.

He groaned into the cloth and his spirit left his body.

The men behind her were disappointed and began hooting.

She walked back and handed over the knife.

'Thank you,' she said, shyly, more out of instinct at returning someone else's tool. The whole group burst out laughing.

'She's going to fetch a good price,' said Balan with conviction.

7

Much later, I would wonder why he told me about his father and about the fact that he was the emperor of Tamilakam, but, as I later learned, that was Rajendra for you.

He was in his sixtieth year at the time, or perhaps even more. No one could tell, and those who could maintained a studied silence. He was a man of no extraordinary height or girth, but one who commanded the space around him through the imperiousness of his being. I cannot describe it adequately, and perhaps your narrative skills, if any, can do it justice. He had a rare charisma; you could not help but be in awe of him. Perhaps it was his face that could remain still for hours on end yet frighten you with the slight raising of an eyebrow. His eyes followed you, scrutinizing, deconstructing your every move; it was unnerving for many who met him for the first time. Perhaps it was his voice, deep and booming, carved as if out of the depths of a mountain.

To my credit, I remained calm when faced with his unexpected visit. 'It is a great honour. The Srivijaya kingdom offers its greetings.'

He exhaled loudly, the sound echoing through the room. And then there was silence. He looked at me, a tiger regarding its prey, stalking it. I looked back at him, trying not to betray any emotion. There was a slight rustle behind him and I realized we were not alone. A man, possibly more than one, was hidden in the darkness.

We sat in silence for a long while, until I was tempted to lie back down just to see what would happen.

'Once upon a time, a dove was being chased by a hawk. The dove flew till it was tired, and finally came to rest in the court of my ancestor, Sembiyan. The dove begged my ancestor to save it and provide sanctuary from the hawk. Now the hawk flew in and, on seeing the bird cowering behind my ancestor, demanded to have it. Sembiyan told the hawk that he had offered it his protection and would not let it die. The hawk seethed and told the king that if justice was really what he sought, then where was the justice in allowing the hawk to die of hunger since it had been deprived of its prey? Sembiyan considered this and then, looking at the dove which was not very big, offered that he would cut off flesh from his body to match the weight of the dove. The hawk agreed, and Sembiyan brought a weighing scale, and began carving out flesh from his body. First, he carved out the flesh of his thighs and put it on the balance but it was not enough. Then he carved out the flesh on his buttocks but that did not lift the scales either. He carved out large pieces of his body. Slowly. Painfully. Tearing through limb and sinew. All the excess flesh of his body was on the scale now, and it didn't budge. Finally, he sat himself on the scale, and it moved. In effect, he had to sacrifice his life for the dove. Without thinking, so it is said, he took his knife and began hacking away at his neck. The hawk and dove changed into the gods Indra and Agni who restored him back to health. Sembiyan was a good man. A generous man.'

I was a little taken aback. In place of formal pleasantries, he had offered a story. A cryptic one at that. Was there a message here?

I thought for a moment.

'He was indeed. A trait his successors share, no doubt?'

I let the sentence taper into a question.

There was no reply. My back was hurting, and I shifted a little on the bed. Again, a rustling was heard from the darkness behind the king. Whoever it was, was on edge.

Rajendra himself did not move. He continued to watch me. His silence had begun to make me feel uncomfortable.

He took a deep breath and slowly blew out the lamp. The room resumed its garb of darkness and I heard more rustling. Finally, the door to my room clicked shut. The fan bearers resumed their duties, as if nothing had happened.

I stayed awake the entire night, wondering what had just transpired. It was only when light lifted the veil of darkness from the room that I fell asleep.

Bhaskaran let me complete my rest. He was waiting patiently outside my room when I stumbled out mid-morning.

'The emperor. He was here last night,' I said, without caring to offer any form of greeting.

Bhaskaran looked at me curiously.

'Really? Why...why would you say that?'

'Because he was. In the flesh. A middle-aged man who had coloured his hair black and put kohl on his eyes. A deep rumbling voice,' I said, jumbling my words as they gushed out of my mouth.

He chuckled. 'Impossible, my lord. He is in Thanjavur today. He will only return in a week's time for the inauguration ceremony of Gangaikonda Cholapuram.'

'He was here. I'm not lying.'

Bhaskaran looked worried.

'I'm telling you he has not set foot in the city for a week. There are petitions waiting for him that will only be addressed after the city is formally declared the capital of the kingdom. This must be some elaborate hallucination. Shall I get a doctor? There is a *vaidya* nearby, and also an Arab who is passing through. He's very good, I'm told.'

I just shook my head. Bhaskaran had either been told not to reveal anything or was genuinely in the dark.

'I know what I saw,' I said firmly, refusing to believe my mind was capable of fooling itself.

He gaped at me and spread his arms helplessly. Since it was no use arguing, I went to the bathing area and had a bath. Clothes were presented to me, which I wore hastily and joined Bhaskaran for a late breakfast in the mansion's dining area.

'I shall show you the city today,' he said. 'It's very modern. There are wells everywhere and gardens and orchards. This will be the greatest city ever created. One hundred and one poets have been commissioned to write songs of praise for it. *Yaals* have been made, thousands of them, especially for the occasion. When they sound, it will bring rain!'

His boyish enthusiasm for his emperor was tiring. I simply nodded and did not reply, hoping that he would not continue in this vein. We finished breakfast and came out to the stables where the horses were tied. I chose a dark coloured one and he got onto a white one, and we set off, followed by bodyguards. Again, we took a road named after Rajaraja Chola that led to another named Rajendran. Bhaskaran told me that there were highways named after them too. Finally, we came across a street called Madhurantaka

Vedavaru, and when I asked Bhaskaran who the street referred to, he told me, reverentially, that it was named after Rajendra Chola.

The whole city seemed to contain reminders of Rajaraja and Rajendra Chola for the citizens. Even the coins were designed to remind the people of the glory of the Cholas. I remember seeing one with what I later learned was once the Chola emblem – a seated tiger, representing the Cholas, placed alongside two fishes placed side by side vertically symbolizing the Pandyas, and next to them a bow that symbolized the Cheras. All three symbols were under an umbrella which symbolized that the Cholas had vanquished the Pandyas and Cheras and brought their lands under the Chola dominion. The vertical fish, I later learned, symbolized that they were dead, unlike horizontal fish that swam. A macabre little symbol, but effective nonetheless. There were other coins too, I heard, that had been issued by Rajaraja himself that actually had the emperor on one side, and a seated Goddess on the other.

One structure towered over all. It was the tallest building I had ever seen. And, for once, I believed Bhaskaran when he told me it would be one of the largest Shiva temples in the country. I wanted to visit it, but Bhaskaran said that there would be time later on. The streets in the centre of the city were clogged with stone that was being used for the structure. It would be 185 feet tall, he said, and proceeded to compare its height with all the other big buildings he had seen. I was truly impressed. The tallest building in Srivijaya was a temple too – the Buddhist temple at Borobudur that stood at 114 feet.

I wondered bitterly for a moment, what would have happened if my city's battlements had been over a 100 feet in height instead. Our temples are too big and our walls too small. That was true of

Rajendra as well. One day, perhaps, he would realize his folly too late, as I had.

The city is now bustling, but at that time the roads were empty. There were many small ponds and wells across its landscape, most of which were full, owing to the recent monsoon. In addition to these, the Cholas had built a large artificial lake called the Chola Gangam, into which they had poured the water from the Ganga. The Ganga river, I was told by Bhaskaran, enjoys a special privilege when it comes to the rivers of this region, assuming an almost mythic role. It is believed that an individual who bathes in it will throw away the shackles of rebirth and attain moksha. Is that so?

Alright then. Perhaps it would have done me good to take one last dip. Though I don't think there is much possibility of that anymore. The Chola Ganga Lake was, Bhaskaran pointed out, the largest in Chola Nadu … nay, Jambudwipa … no, actually, the world! No one had built anything like it, nor would anyone ever again.

At around lunch, Bhaskaran seemed eager to finish sightseeing, and said that we had to hasten back towards the mansion. I suspected he had something planned for us, and I wasn't wrong. We didn't exactly go back to the mansion but went a little ahead towards another mansion, larger than the one I had been housed in.

The mansion was still being built. Dust flew all over the courtyard, colouring all the workers brown.

We gave our horses to an attendant walked through the garden in which gardeners were digging and planting flowers. Bhaskaran told me that after Rajendra decided to build the city, he had arranged for gardeners from all over the world to provide a selection of the fastest growing trees and flowers, and a selection that would bloom in every season so that the city would change colour four times a year and be full of leaves and flowers and never barren. I took this in with reluctance as I did all his claims. A worker was hammering an iron nail into a granite block, and two others were polishing a large wooden cylinder that when placed upright would become a pillar in the mansion.

We walked inside and found artists painting a mural. It was a painting of Lord Shiva in his dancing form that you call Nataraja. Next to him was a handsome man who offered flowers to the deity and near him were three women of different hues – brown, fair and one almost alabaster. I later learned this man was Rajaraja Chola who had taken wives from many kingdoms. My ancestor, Chudamani Warmadeva, was a great friend of his, and one of our princesses was even sent to marry the Chola monarch nearly thirty years ago. I was a child back then and had seen her crying her way up to the docks, being bundled into a ship, never to be seen again. I believe she must have died for we didn't hear of her after that.

We stood for a moment, admiring the picture. The artist had done an excellent job with it. The king's face was large and lustrous and occupied most of the painting; he was shown bowing towards Lord Shiva and offering him flowers. The women were adorned with heavy jewels and belts and smiled benevolently. The artist, who was putting some touches on the king's crown, ignored us. However, when three men entered the room, he stood up promptly and bowed to them.

One of the men waved at him to sit down and bade him to complete his work. Bhaskaran, too, bowed to them. I recognized only one of them.

'The sons of his highness, the Emperor – Prince Rajendradeva and Prince Rajadhiraja. You, of course, know Prince Virajendra…' he said to me, his voice trailing off towards the end.

The sons of Rajendra. I looked closely at them trying to find any resemblance to the man I had met the previous night. In varying degrees, perhaps. But then, to me, all Tamils look the same.

Virajendra greeted me first.

'I hope your journey was satisfactory. Bhaskaran can be tedious company, but he is a friend of the family.' He looked at Bhaskaran and grinned. Bhaskaran blushed and took a step backward outside the circle of conversation that was now inhabited only by me and Virajendra and Rajendradeva. Rajadhiraja stayed a step behind his brothers.

'We will speak of terms after the inauguration of the city. It would take more than a month or so. Father is in Thanjavur finishing a council meeting,' Rajendradeva said.

It seemed everyone wanted me to believe that he was in Thanjavur. Or wanted me to believe that I was experiencing some kind of hallucination. I kept quiet.

The three brothers were not alike. If there was tension among them, as was normal among princes, I did not see any. Rajadhiraja was the prince regent, chosen to be Rajendra's right hand only two years after his coronation. Not that Rajendradeva and Virajendra were given roles of less importance. As soon as Rajendra had ascended the throne, he had begun to cede certain responsibilities to his sons. They would be blooded into becoming rulers and administrators gradually and not be pushed suddenly over its precipice. All of them handled key administrative roles within the empire and were often at the forefront of any act of economic or military significance. All three of them had been to Eelam, as had Rajendra himself, to cut their teeth. They had all fought the Chalukyas, and had been individually given command of expeditions.

Throughout my stay in your lands, I never saw their wives or mothers. Bhaskaran told me once that Rajendra had three wives, but I never bothered to find out if each wife had borne him one son each, or whether these three strapping men had sprung from a single woman's womb. I heard that the women of the empire wielded great influence behind the scenes of the court, but I was never privy to any of it. If they had, in some way, influenced my own stay here, I did not know about it.

But my story is only a small one in the grand scheme of the Chola empire, so perhaps it did not merit their attention.

We went inside to the kitchen of the mansion where we sat on tiny pedestals and ate a meal. The princes did not seem to want any special privilege, and each of them made it a point to greet the servants by their names.

Virajendra was the most talkative. Perhaps he felt that as my oppressor and conqueror, he needed to be my friend. Rajendradeva himself was polite and spoke little. Rajadhiraja said nothing, and ate his food in silence. Bhaskaran listened more than he spoke.

Virajendra questioned me about everything in my country, and treated me as if I was still its king. He picked my head about everything from taxation levels, excise duties for local produce, and even how royalty spent their leisure time in the kingdom.

'There isn't much,' I replied with smile. I was uncomfortable but kept the mask of serenity glued tightly to my face. 'We are a kingdom of traders, and ships come in at any time.' I thought it wouldn't be prudent to take the same liberties with my condition as a prisoner as I had with Bhaskaran. I did not mention the invasion or my subsequent kidnapping, and neither did any of the princes.

We soon finished eating and took our leave. Bhaskaran and I rode our horses outside the city on a highway – also named after Rajendra – for some exercise and returned to my mansion in the evening, just as the sun crept under the blanket of the horizon. I had a bath and rubbed sandalwood oil on my hair, more for its familiar soothing fragrance than anything else; it reminded me of my home. It was a practice I have continued till this day. I blew out the lamps and lay in bed and fell asleep.

Again, I woke up in the middle of the night, drenched in sweat. The winds had ceased to blow, and the men who fanned me at night were not doing so anymore. I cursed them in my language first, then in Tamil but the air was still. I opened my eyes slowly and saw the yellow light of a lamp at the foot of my bed.

The strange figure from the previous night sat looking at me passively.

I took a deep breath, pinched myself hard and shut my eyes. If this were indeed an illusion as everyone claimed it was, he would vanish. I opened my eyes again. He was still there.

'Are you really the emperor, Rajendra Chola?' I asked, keeping my voice firm.

He did not reply. I could see his face made ghoulish red in the light of the lamp.

I cleared my throat and reminded myself that I was the Maharajah of the Srivijaya empire. His equal in stature. I ruled lands that were richer than his and enjoyed the trust of kingdoms farther than his. I was the lord of the mountains and of the oceans. His ships needed to pay me tax to engage in trade.

'Silence is not a fitting ally of a king. Words make for better companions,' I said, waiting for him to silence me through a swordsman.

He did not reply for a long time. When he did, his voice boomed like a mountain shaking itself out of slumber.

'The Cholas have an ancestor who went by the name Ellalan. Ellalan was a just king, though a strict one who, it is said, never gave himself a measure of doubt when pursuing justice. He hung a giant bell outside his palace that anyone could ring and seek justice. One day, he heard the chiming of the bell and found a cow waiting for him outside the palace. The cow wept as it told him that her calf had been crushed under the wheels of a horse-drawn carriage, and she wanted justice for her dead one. The driver of the horse-drawn carriage was Ellalan's son. When he learned this, Ellalan did not hesitate. He dragged his son out to the street and rode a horse-drawn carriage over his neck, so that he would suffer as much as the calf. The cow later revealed itself to be Lord Shiva, and He blessed him and rejuvenated his son.'

This said, he settled back into his chair. The flames in the brass lamp flickered. I heard him take a deep breath, and a steady rustling began behind him in the darkness. He was leaving. This time I was ready.

'Wait,' I said. 'Before the lamp is extinguished, there is a story of my ancestors you must hear.'

'Bhumi Java was ruled by the queen Shima. She was the bravest woman of her time and, like your ancestor, insistent on honesty and justice and taught her people the same. Once, a foreign king wanted to test the honesty of her people and left a bag of gold at the intersection of two roads in her kingdom. No one touched the bag since it did not belong to them. However, nearly three years later, someone did.'

Rajendra turned his head slightly and regarded me curiously.

'The queen's son. The boy accidentally touched the bag with his feet, while playing. Like your ancestor, mine too did not hesitate.

She ordered her son killed. The people were aghast, and a minister finally reasoned with her and said that since the prince's foot had touched the bag, it must only be the foot that suffered mutilation and not the rest of the boy.'

He remained silent as I completed the story.

'Our ancestors are not dissimilar, so neither should we be.'

I could see that his eyes had widened just a little.

'Like Sudama, I will keep our friendship, if you, like Krishna, send me home to my kingdom. I ask for generosity. Treat me like a hawk, and not a dove,' I added, I admit, a little desperately.

He was silent, and then began to shake with laughter. For a few minutes, the roar of his laughter flooded the room, leaving everything else silent in its wake. He blew out the lamp and left the room just as he came. The fan bearers resumed their work. That night I was again unable to sleep.

They rode for a day through the forest and passed through the village on the other side quite quickly. No one asked why a grubby group of men was briskly leading three beautiful women, whose hands were bound with rope, to the local dock and onto a small, ramshackle boat. Slavers were clearly common here, concluded the princess.

They set sail without resting across the Sunda strait, which was a narrow channel of water between Bhumi Java and Suvarnadwipa.

'Not a place for big fleets. The Chinese hate it, as do the Arabs and the Hindus. They have to almost sail in a column when passing through here. Makes 'em easy prey for us,' said Balan, pointing out the strait as they travelled across. He had taken personal charge of her. She would be sold to a person of his choosing, and his alone, he had boasted. The princess told him that she did not want to be separated from her mother and friend. He replied that that was not good for business. It was a knife in the belly for small business owners like him who were looking to expand their trade if their assets started making demands of their own.

As soon as they reached the dock on Bhumi Java, Balan disappeared to bribe the customs officers. The women and the rest of the men waited. An hour later, Balan returned to the boat and told them to come out. The customs office was a small brick building whose walls were charred. Finding the princess staring at the fire-blackened walls, Balan told her how it was the outcome of *Mahapralaya*, when the land had plunged into lawlessness due to Srivijaya intrigue. They entered the building and walked into a small hall that was filled with people. Balan navigated the women through the hall until they reached the desk of a man dressed in yellow robes. The man was short and thin and looked irritable.

'My highness, here is the cargo,' said Balan.

'Hmm, yes. Three women? I thought you had mentioned only one.'

'No, no my lord. There are three, see. One, two...'

'I know how to count, Balan,' the official snapped.

'We're taking them into the Kahuripan kingdom. We wish to keep everyone happy with this trade, your highness-ship.'

'You had better. So, show me the goods.'

The three women were pushed in front of him.

'These look like noble women,' remarked the official.

'We found them in a forest on Suvarnadwipa, your lordship, wandering like nymphs.'

'I am the queen of Srivijaya,' said the queen firmly.

'This one's quite mad. Don't know what I'll get for her,' Balan chuckled nervously.

The princess saw an opening.

'And I'm the princess. Now kneel before me, you rogue, or I'll have your head!' she glared at the official.

The official looked at her, shocked.

The princess looked at Balan and began to cackle maniacally. She then glanced at Sumitra who quickly followed suit.

The hall was filled with the laughter of the young women.

Balan looked at the official and smiled apologetically.

'We're not running a madhouse here, Balan.'

'My highness, they're just playing. Honest.' He looked at the princess and said, 'Have a heart. I am a small business owner.'

The princess cackled loudly.

'They're either mad or beyond your control, Balan. In either situation, I wouldn't want them on our shores.'

'Please, your sire-ship! I'll pay you double of what we discussed!'

The official nearly fell off his seat.

'Double? Of what? The only payment is your twenty per cent customs fee. And that is of no use to me if you're selling damaged goods. At this rate, we'll become a refugee wasteland.'

'Please, my lord!' pleaded Balan.

'Your items will be confiscated and kept here for the time being. You can appeal for them in court tomorrow morning.'

8

The next day was spent much like the previous one. I wanted to tell Bhaskaran that I had met the emperor, but after his earlier reaction, I realized that it was probably better not to say anything at all. The emperor obviously wanted to keep his interaction with me private.

The day was spent in Bhaskaran's company. He had arranged for a game of chess and we played till lunch, neither winning a game. The afternoon was spent riding around the city that was in a state of chaos. Elephants carrying timber had dropped large trunks of wood on the road and refused to pick them up again despite the urgings of the mahouts. Now no one could get into the centre of the city from the east. The army had been asked to assist in clearing the timber from the roads. The streets were clogged by warriors, who wore their weapons as a mark of their trade, much like ours who carried a ceremonial sword called a *kris* in a band around their waist.

We walked closer to the centre where three elephants still stood stubbornly in their spot as their enraged mahouts tried to goad them into action. The warriors kept the crowd that had gathered around them at bay. One of the elephants trumpeted, and shook itself vigorously, throwing its mahout off. It blared again and charged into the throng of people that had gathered around it, all of whom ran for their lives. The warriors ran after it. Some of them held long spears that they began jabbing into its side. The elephant twisted around in agony; it then picked up a warrior and flung him away with incredible force. It cried out in rage, and trampled through a group of people who were running away from it. Finally, it charged towards the east gate, with a few warriors in hot pursuit. A group of people quickly, gathered around the injured men and women and took them to a nearby *vaidyasalai*.

I had seen elephants go mad before so I explained a range of possibilities to Bhaskaran who looked shocked at the carnage.

'The elephant could be in *musth*. Or it might have gone mad carrying lumber. Or it could have just decided it did not want to be a loyal subservient subject. Who knows?'

A long dark stain ran through the street as the blood of the people mingled and became a river with several small tributaries. The event had shaken Bhaskaran, so we retired to my mansion where he ate areca nuts by the cartload to calm himself down. It was evening by the time he left, still unable to get the picture of the elephant trampling people out of his head. I led him out and, returning quickly, I prepared for bed. The most important part of my day.

I was still alive. Maybe the emperor had listened to me? I felt momentarily ashamed, trying to curry favour with him like this, but quickly swallowed my pride. I would regain control of my kingdom, and pay him back in kind one day.

I lay in bed and closed my eyes but stayed awake, thinking of what I would ask the king. The sounds of the street grew quieter then faded away completely. I lay in bed, pricking my ears at the slightest sound, my body still. Hours passed. The men fanning me continued to do so as I waited intently. Many hours passed, and I heard a rooster crow.

I was exhausted and turned to my side to sleep when I heard a slight click. My eyes, now accustomed to the darkness, searched for the sound until I saw the door to my room open and three figures slide in, lit faintly by the light of a lamp. One was holding a brass lamp and the others quietly walked behind him. The fan bearers immediately ceased their activity.

It was my turn to surprise my visitor.

'Consider this your own room, my lord. You don't need to enter silently like a thief,' I said, trying my luck.

He laughed. Like a storm it came, and blew past us in the room. A deep ululation from the belly.

'A sense of humour, Maharajah Sangrama Vijayatunggavarman, is like God. If you keep your faith in it, it never deserts you in your hour of need. A handy tool to have in these times.'

'Why does the emperor of Tamilakam visit his prisoner at such odd hours? Surely we could trade stories in broad daylight as well?'

He sighed loudly, and then the now familiar rumble of his voice sounded.

'The day is stacked with meetings. *Velaikarrars*, *nayakars*, ministers of every kind. My time is the flesh of a fruit that has been created to warm the bellies of other people. But at night...well, that is when I become my own person.'

'So why do you come here then?'

'To see if my guest is well.'

'Surely my health is of more value to the emperor when I am awake?'

'Maharajah, your health is of value if you wish to return to your land. Other than that, I have little to do with it. Srideva, your feudatory – or Daatu as you call him – has taken your place as the head of Srivijaya affairs. My navy is stationed at Kadaram, Jambi and Barus. All your major ports. We have sacked fourteen of your cities and drained your land of gold. My merchant guilds are now at Barus, preparing new terms of trade for Srideva.'

I felt a great rage surging through me. More than I had felt since I was captured. For a moment I thought I'd risk it all and lunge at him. The people in the darkness were guards, no doubt. Before they killed me perhaps I would be able to take out an eye of the king.

'Don't forget – your greed brought us to this point. Tipped us over the edge of our lands and into your seas.'

For a moment, I wondered what he was talking about. Then it came to me.

A short geography lesson for you, young Ganapathy. The islands of Bhumi Java and Suvarnadwipa are in the centre of the ocean between China and Jambudwipa, a useful location that facilitates trade between not only those two lands, but also the Muslim lands from further north of Jambudwipa. A normal cycle of trade involves ships from your land laden with spices and gems sailing to our lands. Some of the products are traded here, and some make their way to China where they are sold at exorbitant prices. There is a great demand for foreign goods from China, much more than the demand we find from Jambudwipa and the Arab lands. The Song court profits from the expensive tastes of their people. On the return voyage, the ships carry products like silk or incense and stop by our islands to replenish their stocks before heading back to your land. Suvarnadwipa is the gateway to Jambudwipa and, as such, we are the *dwarapalas*, the gatekeepers.

While the Cholas nearly monopolize trade from the Tamilakam, they are by no means the only kingdom that wants to trade with the Chinese. The Palas trade too. And so do many other smaller kingdoms along the eastern coast of Jambudwipa.

Recently, as I've mentioned before, I had increased the taxes for goods entering our waters, a measure that had annoyed the merchant guilds operating in our lands. They came to my court waving documents of petitions furiously. Foremost among them was the merchant guild 'Thousand Directions'. Their name is a little more elaborate – the *Nanadesa Tisaiyayirattu Ainnutruvar*, meaning the 'The five hundred from the four countries and the thousand directions'. Since writing this will take time, I will refer to them as the Thousand Directions Guild. We must be committed, you and I, to the speedy completion of my story. The chief representative of the Thousand Directions Guild was a large man called Vikraman – a butter ball with a moustache.

'Maharajah! Rajan!' he said, his fat quivering and adding pathos to his angst-ridden voice. 'The taxes will bleed us dry. In any case, we are paying a toll on entering these waters and exiting them. Plus the tributes we pay to each kadatuan. Then there is the protection money...' He let his sentence hang.

I had looked on coldly.

'Do you not wish to pay for the protection that my fleet provides? That can be arranged.'

I had some desire to intimidate him. Traders always negotiated hard and Vikraman, I suspected, must have performed with a drama troupe before becoming a trader. I was used to seeing him stomp around my court as if he was going to have a seizure. I knew that his fleets lost up to a third of their cargo on the sea route to China. Pirates swarmed across the ocean like vultures looking for easy pickings. A few years ago, we had offered the Thousand Directions Guild the protection of our fleet and they had been able to trade without trouble. Of course, protection was expensive and only restricted to our waters. Once they were adrift of our lands and closer to Chinese territory they became vulnerable to Chinese pirates.

Vikraman had gone silent then. His bombast quickly drained and he stammered some apology and left the court.

I had raised taxes for Chola traders only because I knew they were monopolizing the Arab trade. More Arab traders had begun to prefer trading with these guilds in Jambudwipa than come all the way here. The Cholas were taking Arab goods and then selling them to us and the Chinese. The loss of income had been profound. I had needed to make it up from the Cholas somehow.

'My kingdom survives on trade,' I said coldly to Rajendra. 'My rates are fair. A king should not listen to the whining of merchants.'

'True,' he rumbled, 'but should he not listen to Chinese emissaries who inform him that you write to him on coarse paper?'

I had no answer to that. In fact, I was surprised he even knew.

It had been a common ruse of ours. The Chinese trade was prized both by us and the Cholas, and since the Cholas did not meet the Chinese as frequently as they would have liked to, we told them all sorts of stories about you. We said that you were our vassals, an overseas kadatuan. Our merchants were instructed to tell the Chinese that we wrote our letters to you on plain paper, as if you were not worth any more effort.

Easy there. Stop sputtering, young Ganapathy. This is as regular as the sun rising in the eastern sky. Your Rajendra has done the same himself, I'm sure. I have heard that he has made the brief occupation of my lands sound like he has conquered them. That's what kings do, young scribe. They tell stories.

Rajendra continued, his voice menacing now, 'Should he also not listen to Chinese emissaries who have evidence that you fund the pirates of your sea and then ask for protection money from us?'

How did he know this? No one knew this except my own Daatus. Was one of them a traitor?

Why does your face turn red again? All we did was to pay pirates to stop attacking your vessels, and replenished our coffers with money taken from you. On occasion, the pirates would disobey us. They're like animals, you know. No self control. Though once protection money had been given, these attacks decreased in number. No Srivijaya ship was involved in these attacks, I can assure you. We can spend the rest of the day debating the economics of the same, though I suspect you would rather speak about the ethics, but I have a story to complete, and little time.

'Show me the emissary, and I will prove him a liar,' I said. 'Srivijaya has always been fair to you.'

He fell silent again. Then, after a few moments, he spoke.

'Largely, yes. But we need to renegotiate terms. The Thousand Directions Guild is not happy at the moment and, like any emperor, I desire the happiness of all my subjects. Vikraman has certain demands which are a little, well, excessive, to put it mildly. I will bring down his appetite for profit, large as it already is, and ask him to introspect.'

He obviously knew more than I had bargained for.

'So why keep me here further? Wouldn't we both be served better by returning me to my land until Vikraman is dealt with?'

He looked at me and did not say anything for a few moments. Then he looked down at the floor, as if putting his thoughts together.

'It is not an easy task being king. Poets have spoken at length about it, as have monarchs. But no one really knows what the throne hides until one sits on it, Sangrama. For once you sit on the throne, you are well and truly alone. My father told me that. And he did as good a job as any king. He always used to tell me that a king is a man who everyone answers to, but is answerable to everyone. It was one of his favourite aphorisms. I never cared for its simplistic construct, but there was truth in those words.'

He paused, and then continued almost tentatively.

'Only a king can understand a king. Until you leave, and long after that, I want you to be my friend, Sangrama. Will you be a friend to me?'

Friendship among kings was unheard of. Surely he knew that. People killed their own family to be kings. I, too, had had to watch my own Daatus so that they would not plot murder behind my back. Now that I was away from my kingdom, they would be tearing each other apart, trying to become king. Yet, Rajendra sounded earnest – like a child desperate to formalize and secure a relationship. And, more surprisingly, he sounded terribly lonely. Men never announce their intent for friendship with each other. Any attempt at formality when securing a relationship with another man is met with contempt. I had never been propositioned for friendship before and beheld it almost suspiciously.

But, there was also the fact that at this moment, he called the strokes in this boat of our relationship.

I was silent for a moment. We had been duelling with stories since I arrived. Now, it was time for me to take the offensive to him.

'The Yavana King Alexander conquered the ancient kingdoms of Athens and Sparta and proceeded to lay waste to the Sassanid empire and conquered the lands till the Indus River. Between him and the conquest of Bharatavarsha stood a single king – Porus. He was a king of rare dignity, who, despite being outnumbered severely by the Greek hordes, stood his ground to protect his kingdom. When the inevitable happened and Alexander defeated Porus in the battle of the Indus, he took the king captive. The prisoner Porus was brought to his court and Alexander, impressed by Porus's grace and valour, had asked him if there was anything he desired. All Porus replied was, "Treat me as befits a king." The great and benevolent Alexander was pleased with the answer and gave him back his kingdom and made a friend forever. Now, I'm no Porus, my lord. But you could still be Alexander. Treat me as a friend then and let me leave your shores soon.'

He sat still, absorbing my words. It was a rather shameless way, I admit, of tickling his vanity. I hoped the idea of being Alexander appealed to him.

'All in good time, my friend,' he said finally. 'Trust me. You will return home soon. But not before my city is born.'

'And when will that be?'

'Two, maybe three months. My astrologers are trying to work out a date for its birth. Yesterday's elephant stampede was not auspicious, and we have had to postpone the date. We will discuss terms after that.'

I nodded in the dark. I had no other choice really.

'Till then you are my guest. I have arranged for a tour of Thanjavur, my father's capital city and currently the biggest in our land, for you. My son, Rajendradeva will take you there tomorrow.'

He said this with finality and I suspected I had no say in the matter. Then he stood, bade me a good night and blew out the lamp. Soon, the fans began flapping again.

The next morning I was on my way to Thanjavur.

The three women were housed in an empty warehouse until the next morning. They were given a small bowl of rice to share. None of them touched the food. They did not speak to each other either. The queen seemed a little distant since the incident with Pavitran. She kept glancing outside the warehouse window and sighing. Sumitra, on the other hand, fell asleep immediately. The princess lay awake for most of the night, mostly out of concern for her mother, but as the first light of dawn peeped inside the warehouse, she too fell asleep.

Sumitra gently shook her awake a few hours later. They washed their faces with a bucket of water that had been provided. None of them had bathed in three days now, but the princess was growing used to the stench. They were escorted by an armed guard to the customs court that was a short distance away from the dock. The customs court was not housed in a very impressive building. It was a rectangular structure with broken windows and a ramshackle roof. Pockets of men huddled together near the building, talking quietly among themselves. The queen and the princess walked inside with their heads straight and backs erect unlike most of the other women who walked with submissive postures.

The official and Balan were waiting outside. The former looked at them and spoke.

'There's no need for a case here. Balan has come to an agreement with me. You can all leave with him.'

He looked at Balan who handed him a small pouch. The official inspected the contents.

'Gold coins? All of them?' he asked Balan.

'Yes, your lordship.'

The princess began to cackle desperately, and Sumitra followed suit, but the official looked at them unimpressed.

'Balan, they're yours.'

Balan took a step forwad and slapped the princess with the back of his hand; the force of the blow made her fall to her knees. He held her by the wrist and began dragging her towards the door. The queen began crying out for help, and Sumitra jumped into the fray and began dragging the princess back towards her.

Suddenly, all the men and women around them began to kneel, falling to the ground with their heads touching the earth. A man dressed in expensive silk robes approached them.

'What seems to be the matter?'

Balan, too, fell to his knees, lowering his head to the ground.

'M'lord, these are my goods. I'm taking them with me. No matter at all. They're just a bit feisty.'

The princess shouted him down.

'No, he's a liar. We're not goods. We're from Srivijaya. I'm the princess, she's the queen.'

Balan growled. 'Will you stop with your lunacy!'

'Interesting,' remarked the man. 'Stand up.'

The princess stood up shakily.

'The girls have bowed before me. It is the protocol expected of a senior minister of state. Yet the elder one does not? Why?'

The princess looked behind her and saw that her mother had not bowed.

'I can have your head for that, you know?'

The queen replied in a firm voice. 'I am the queen of Srivijaya. I bow before no one.'

There was an embarrassed silence before Balan spoke up.

'She is completely mad, my lord. Completely! Been blathering about being queen since we took her.'

The official looked at her keenly.

'Well in that case she needn't bow. If the Gods have removed favour from her intellect, what more can I do?'

The official piped up from the ground. 'You are a most benevolent minister, Dharanindra!'

'I will buy the young one,' he said abruptly. 'And the other one with her. The court needs attendants urgently. The "queen" I leave to you. How much?'

Balan quoted a price and was delighted to hear that the minister did not wish to bargain.

'My lord, please! I cannot leave my mother alone. Please let me take her with me. She's gone mad. I need to look after her,' said the princess desperately, hot tears burning her eyes.

'I have no need for mad women. Lord knows there are enough of them in the court.'

The men around them grinned and nodded.

'Please, my lord,' said the princess and bent to grab the minister's feet.

The minister kicked her away as his attendants lifted her and Sumitra up and pulled them away.

The princess began screaming until a heavy cudgel hit her on the head.

9

I had expected that your emperor wouldn't send me back so quickly. What I hadn't expected was this sightseeing picnic of the Chola lands, with his son, no less. At the moment, though, it provided an almost God-sent opportunity – perhaps my first real stroke of luck since I entered your kingdom. I decided that I would use this time to become friendly with Rajendradeva. Perhaps there were seeds of dissatisfaction in his mind that could be made to flower. He was second in line to the throne. Surely there were some ambitions of overthrowing the emperor, killing his brothers and taking the crown for himself? There had to be. Every kingdom in the world, without exception, had brothers killing each other or their father for the crown.

Your face darkens. Poor Ganapathy. You came here hoping for a straightforward description of last evening's events but instead have a full-blown regicide conspiracy on your hands. This is above your pay grade, you're probably thinking. Wait, there's no need to call the inquisitors or torturers. Not yet anyway. The truth does not need to be extracted from me. It comes at its own pace.

Rajendradeva was not flamboyant. Like most middle siblings, he preferred to be hidden away from the attention, comfortable with ceding it to the eldest and the youngest. He was more of a bureaucrat, comfortable with overseeing the construction of canals in the cities than with their destruction.

And he bored me nearly to death.

He had inherited the quality of earnestness from his father. And he relentlessly plied me with details about every little thing in your empire. Everything, in his worldview, was made of intricate little cogs, and he delighted in deconstructing the world to the smallest one; to my horror, he also insisted on telling me every little detail.

It took us four days to travel to Thanjavur, travelling as we were at a leisurely pace. But it felt like four years. There was little to do but talk. Or, in my case, listen to his ceaseless droning about the state of the land, the quality of the crops, and the system of justice. We travelled in a royal horse carriage through lush farmlands that were growing tall with paddy and then through rocky hillsides washed with red dust and no trees in sight.

For the most part, your administration is similar to ours. At least that's what I understood when I actually listened to his rambles. The kingdom was a parcel of principalities that was under the king but mostly self-governing. Nearly twenty-five years ago, Rajendra's father, Rajaraja, had initiated a land survey and assessment project that organized the land into individual, self-sustaining principalities called *valanandu*s. Each principality was divided into smaller provinces and villages that administered themselves. So far so good. But the most intriguing part of it all was the system of elections in your villages.

Rajendradeva called it the *kuduvolai*. The village would gather to elect thirty members to administer them. Any person could apply to office, but there were restrictions involved. The person had to be between thirty-five and seventy years of age and possess taxable land, among other things. Murderers and thieves were disqualified. On election day, all those who wished to participate would write their names on palm leaf tickets and put them in a pot. A small boy, one of the youngest from the village, would pick up the leaves from the pot, and all those who the boy had selected would be elected. This way all elections were up to chance, and anyone could be elected. Risky, in my opinion, since you want your best men in places of maximum influence, but then it gave no one the opportunity to feel snubbed or slighted, and also preserved the peace. Perhaps a greater advantage.

Like us, Rajendra, too, I observed, was advised by a council of ministers. The revenue officials were the most important, as they were in ours, and their positions were highly coveted but rarely relinquished since offices were hereditary. The main treasury of your empire, I found out, was in Kumbakonam, and land revenue was the biggest source of finance. A third of the produce in the land was routinely taxed, and collection was rather brutally enforced, I was told. No one could escape taxes. There are taxes on everything in this kingdom. Professional taxes, road taxes, mining and forestry taxes, even marriage taxes. The Arab merchants would often complain that the Cholas tax everything – even an ant that settles in an anthill on your lands would be subject to rent if that were possible.

Forgive me for this deviation; my kingdom is one of merchants and any sound of monetary exchange is sweet to our ears.

Along our journey, we came to a village, and Rajendradeva, in his enthusiasm, invited me over to meet its council for a better understanding of how justice was conducted in your lands. I had no choice in the matter so I accompanied him reluctantly. We entered the village premises but there was no one there to greet us. A throng of people were gathered in the village square around a group of middle-aged men who were having a discussion. A young man stood amidst them with his head bowed.

Our retinue was greeted warmly by the middle-aged men who, I learned, were the village council members. They were adjudicating a case related to the young man. As soon as they learned that Rajendradeva was among them, the village council members offered to let Rajendradeva give his verdict on this case.

It seemed as though this young man had murdered a senior official in the village, while trying to elope with his daughter; we had arrived at the point where he was to be sentenced. Rajendradeva considered the story, heard the pleas of both the young man's family and the murdered official's relatives and made his decision quickly. He spoke calmly, but his tone suggested that there would be no room for debate on his judgement. Another inheritance from his father. The only thing missing was the rumble in his voice.

I don't remember what he said exactly. But the punishment that was meted out to the young man was that he would have to maintain a lamp in the local temple for the rest of his life. He was young, said the prince, and he could still change his ways. He would, however, no longer be able to marry his lover. Both of them would have to look for new partners. I'm not sure if the judgment satisfied both parties, but they accepted it without complaint and everyone dispersed.

When we had left the village, I asked Rajendradeva why his sentence had been so light. How was lighting a lamp in the temple any form of penitence? We would have had the man trampled by elephants. He told me that here only treason, or *rajadroham*, was punishable by death while most other crimes, even murder, had less drastic punishments. Moreover, maintaining a brass lamp in the temple was no small feat, he assured me. While the boy had belonged to a wealthy family himself and would be able to bear the costs, he would have to visit the temple and light the lamp every day, a considerable investment of time and effort, and also a source of constant shame. Everyone at the temple would see him lighting the lamp and remember his crime for the rest of his life.

Apparently, it was a popular form of justice in Chola lands. I was not entirely convinced by the argument, but as I knew from ruling a kingdom myself, justice was rarely absolute. Sometimes compromises had to be made, and someone's justice was invariably incomplete.

But I had little time to pursue the justice of others at that moment. I had a kingdom to get back to.

'So if *rajadroham* is punishable by death, does that mean no one would dare plot against the king?' I asked innocently, as I watched his expression closely. His features remained unmoved.

'No, no one has. Yet,' he said curtly.

The carriage rumbled on towards Thanjavur. I wasn't sure, but maybe I had got the answer I had been looking for.

10

When we arrived at Thanjavur, Rajendradeva insisted on first visiting the temple. I had assumed that it would be a large structure, but it turned out to be larger than anything I had seen before.

You've seen the Brihadeeswara temple yourself, haven't you, Ganapathy? It is, without a doubt, the most magnificent structure I have seen in your part of the world, and perhaps even mine. The tallest point, I heard, was well over 200 feet from the ground and the complex was spread across several thousand feet. Innumerable people inhabited its grounds, and Rajendradeva told me that over a thousand people were employed for its maintenance. I could gush about its beauty, but we have not the time. Besides, you know what it looks like.

Temples, I learned, were the centre of life here. People would come here and pass the day listening to the minstrels sing or watching the *devadasis* or temple dancers dance. They would get food at the temple and learn about what was happening in the kingdom. Emperor Rajaraja had even inscribed his achievements on the walls of the complex of the temple and provided minute details of the gifts he had given to the temple. Everything from flowers and jewellery to bronze statues that had been gifted by the king had been featured in the inscriptions. The measurements of each idol were also written in the stone.

I asked Rajendradeva the need for such rigorous documentation.

'So that everyone remembers,' came the reply.

Rajaraja's fingerprints were still all over the land. He lived in this temple and in the daily lives of the people. I had no envy for Rajendra's position. Maybe he had realized early on that the only way he could step out of his father's shadow would be with the conquest of other lands. Perhaps that was why he had expanded his kingdom beyond Rajaraja's dominion. And then, when he had made enough of a name for himself, he had decided to build a whole new city to further cement his reputation as an emperor in his own right.

I remarked casually to Rajendradeva that it would be a difficult job following up on Thanjavur and Gangaikonda Cholapuram for whoever became the next king.

He nodded when I said this, almost contemplating it himself.

'I believe there's more to an empire than a few cities. Its strength lies in its farms and villages. Grandfather knew that, and organized the land assessment accordingly. No one in the world has done the kind of complex yield measurements that we have. Father, I suppose, knows it too, though he is currently obsessed – well, I shouldn't say obsessed – *occupied* with building his city of victory he said.'

'You're absolutely right. Most of your people live in the villages. It stands to reason that they should be lavished as much attention as the cities. What do your brothers think?'

He thought about this for a moment.

'Virajendra wants war. Rajadhiraja wants glory. Both ultimately are important in creating the legend of a king. More, perhaps, than canals and roads,' he said with a shrug.

'So if you became king, you would not wage war but spend the treasury on public works?'

'I don't think about becoming king. If I ascend the throne, I will do what I believe is right,' he said coldly, signalling that he did not want to take the conversation further.

I was silent for a few moments, and then began asking him about some new farming system that had been devised in your land, and he was happy to explain the whole thing in great detail. I didn't really listen to it, you see. Rajendradeva had given me some new information to deconstruct.

Virajendra was clearly unhappy at being made to travel to distant lands and conquer them, as I had learned earlier. Rajendradeva was clearly unhappy at the disinterest shown to his land development projects. It seemed neither of the two princes was certain of his position as heir to the throne. Perhaps the sons had come to terms with the fact that Rajadhiraja would be the next king. He was, after all, the eldest. It would be interesting to see what was going on in Rajadhiraja's mind, I thought at the time.

As it turned out, I didn't have to wait long.

We spent a day at the temple and, in the evening, made our way back to a royal guesthouse where a messenger was waiting with a missive. There had been a skirmish near Vengi at the northern borders; the Chalukya army were marching towards the city, and Rajadhiraja had been asked to take a regiment of the royal guard there and put them down decisively. Rajendradeva, meanwhile, had been asked to travel to Kumbakonam to take over some treasury matter Rajadhiraja had been dealing with.

'Father says you can join me at Kumbakonam or you can join Rajadhiraja and see our army at war, if you so please,' he said without much ceremony. It did not seem to matter to him either way.

I told Rajendradeva that I would like to accompany Rajadhiraja.

He nodded, and replied in his earnest manner, 'He leaves tomorrow two hours before dawn. You must get some sleep.'

Her head hurt when she awoke. It was placed on Sumitra's lap and Sumitra was stroking her forehead gently.

'Sumitra,' croaked the princess.

'Don't speak my princess.'

'Mother…'

'We're in the Palace of Kahuripan. We're now servants to the Raja Airlangga. Please rest for now, my lady.'

The princess closed her eyes and began to cry even as a voice croaked from behind, 'Shut up! Let us sleep.'

Sumitra held the princess close and gently rocked her back to sleep.

The next morning before dawn, a bucket of water was emptied on both their heads.

'Wake up you lazy animals.'

A stout, matronly figure holding a bucket appeared before them. 'Get out of your dirty clothes and into uniform!' she shouted, and threw two white threadbare robes at them. Sumitra and the princess stood up and began to undress, throwing away their dirty clothes and put on their new ones.

'You only have one pair for the year. Keep it clean. And don't ask me for more,' she barked.

The princess soon found out that no one knew the older woman's real name – everyone just called her Mama. She was the matron in charge of housekeeping for the palace. Rumour had it that her husband was a General in the Kahuripan army and, inspired by his example, she ran the girls like her own personal army.

The princess and Sumitra had to wake up every day before dawn and clean the royal hall. They were given a square piece of cloth with which they, along with the other girls, had to dust the pillars and the walls of the room. This done, they had to sweep the floors with brooms until it was time for the court to assemble.

The girls would eat breakfast and then put in a shift in the kitchen where the royal chefs would get them to cut and clean vegetables and chop meat for the cooks. They would then serve the royal household lunch and wait until they had finished eating to clear the banquet hall. Then they would clean the royal hall again and prepare the bedchambers of the Raja. Only once the Raja had fallen asleep did their day end.

The princess was miserable. She was useless at assisting with the cooking and had cut her fingers and bled over food more times than she could count. She was no good at dusting or cleaning. The other girls would laugh at her and call her 'Lady Thumbs'. Sumitra, for her part, tried to help her as much as she could and stayed close to the princess.

A month passed in hard labour. Harder than anything the princess had seen. She would burst into tears at least once a day, and was either consoled by Sumitra, or slapped into silence by the matron. After a month, the matron had had enough. She told the princess in no uncertain terms that if her work did not improve immediately, she would be sold to a brothel, or back to the slave traders, whichever paid more money. And the slave traders would have no use for a slave who did not know how to cook or clean. One more mistake, she told the princess, and you're out.

That mistake came sooner than the princess had anticipated.

The princess was cleaning a vase in the royal hall, a large porcelain one from China. She had resolved to be doubly careful at all her tasks. There was no way she could emulate the briskness of Sumitra and the other girls when it came to doing housework. But if she was careful, at least she wouldn't commit so many mistakes, and perhaps then the matron would not notice her lack of speed. The princess tilted the vase carefully towards her chest to wipe its underside but it was heavier than she expected it to be. As she fumbled, the vase rolled down from its pedestal and fell to the ground with a crash. The princess froze. There was no one else in the hall except for Sumitra who beckoned her to leave the room quickly. The kingdom of Kahuripan could cut off her hands for this. The princess ran up a staircase and into the Raja's room and made an act of cleaning the furniture there. Her heart beat wildly in her chest as she began to imagine the consequences if she was found out.

A palm leaf manuscript lay on the desk. She looked at it, and began to read it without thinking. It was a story written in epic form. A *kakawin* about the Hindu prince Arjuna.

'Yes?' a voice enquired from behind her. She turned around, startled, and saw the Raja. She immediately leapt to the ground and prostrated.

'Apologies, my lord,' she stuttered.

'Can you read?' he asked.

'What? No, my lord…A little…my lord,' she said, not sure about what would happen to her now. It had been a terrible day.

'Can you read?' he repeated, gently.

She took a deep breath, buoyed by the gentleness in his voice.

'Yes, my lord.'

'Show me.'

The princess stood up, and turned to the desk to read, 'Suprabha and Tilottama were sent to seduce Arjuna out of his penance by Lord Indra…'

'Excellent!' cried the Raja. 'Where did you learn? It's an uncommon skill in our lands. More so for women.'

'I learnt at home, my lord,' said the princess, red-faced now. Would the Raja believe her if she said she was from Srivijaya? If he did, would he help her or have her put to death?

'What home is this that teaches its women to read? Tell me so I can congratulate your father.'

'He is no more, my lord. I'm here alone,' she said, desperately searching for a way out of this conversation.

The Raja seemed to consider this for a few minuts.

'Your father did well,' he said sympathetically. What did you think of my *kakawin*? I've commissioned a poet to write it. This is an early draft.'

She remained silent, so he continued.

'Arjuna is a favourite character of mine. I feel a mystic connection to his life. I can't really explain it. There is a desire in him to do what is right, more so than his other brothers. Of course, he also has the skill to do it. That's another reason I admire him…' he smiled to.

As he spoke, her eyes snuck up to catch a glimpse of him. She had seen him several times before himself in court where she would stay hidden behind curtains as he delivered his verdict on matters.

Justice was important to him and he would spend an inordinate amount of his time trying to settle matters fairly between parties. He was a man of medium height with striking features – a long nose, small ears and large eyes. All the women in the palace adored him. He spoke calmly, as if every word from his mouth needed to have the weight of a royal decree.

'Have you read about Arjuna?'

'I've read both the Mahabharata and the Ramayana, my lord.'

'Really? What else? You could put half the people in the kingdom to shame.'

She was about to answer when the matron entered the room.

She saw the king and bowed to him, before spotting the princess. 'There you are! My king, could I take the servant away? There's much work to be done, and a broken vase in the throne room that needs an explanation.'

'Really? Which vase?' asked the Raja.

'The white one from China.'

'Never liked it anyway. Good that it's gone. All is forgiven. This lady won't be working in your employ anymore. She is to be my personal attendant and secretary. I need a new one since the other one passed away.'

The matron looked startled but bowed and left the room.

'You know how to write, don't you?'

The princess nodded. 'And keep numbers,' she added for good effect.

'Will wonders never cease! You can occupy my old secretary's room down the hall. See that the palace seamstress gives you an appropriate uniform.'

The princess bowed, not believing her good luck, and immediately thought of Sumitra.

'My lord, would it be possible for me to take someone in my employ. As a sort of help?'

'No, of course not,' came the clipped reply.

The princess felt a little deflated, but walked over to the seamstress marvelling at how her life had changed in the past few minutes.

She went to Sumitra and told her about the events of the morning. Sumitra was happy for her; she knew that the princess wouldn't have been able to survive as a maid for much longer.

The princess slept in the old secretary's bed that evening – his death bed, she had been told. But she slept more soundly than she had had besince they had left home fore.

11

Neither the chants of the priests offering prayers to the Sun God, nor the cacophony of roosters roused me. I had to be awakened by an attendant who shook me by the shoulders until my eyes opened. I haphazardly swung a dhoti around myself and, putting on a tunic that had been provided by Rajendradeva, got on a horse.

We went down a narrow road outside the city till we came to a vast plain upon which the army was getting its final orders. The army then turned around and began marching slowly as the first rays of the sun sparked the skies. We galloped to the head of the troops where Rajadhiraja paced on his horse and reached him after a few minutes.

'You may accompany us. But don't get in our way,' was all I got as a greeting.

I rode side by side with Rajadhiraja and swivelled in my horse seat to see the troops march behind me. They marched in a disciplined manner, each of them wearing the red dhoti and coats that I had seen them wear while invading my lands. They had strapped their shields on to their backs and held long spears made of ash and pine wood.

'So are you your father's favourite? I was an only son so there was no question of not being the favourite, really,' I said lightly, trying to provoke Rajadhiraja into conversation. There was no point making small talk with him like it had been with Rajendradeva who had to be coaxed out of his shell. Rajadhiraja was a man who pulled no punches. He spoke when he was spoken to, and always said what was on his mind.

'We are all our father's favourites,' he replied curtly.

'But aren't you next in line to the throne?' I asked, wondering if I could get some reaction from him.

He glared at me in response and I fell silent. After a few moments, he spoke.

'There is no heir to the kingdom. I am co-regent because I was the eldest of the brothers. Father may well decide I am not capable and put one of my brothers on the throne.'

It was unusual for a co-regent to say that he may not be crowned king. I wondered if he actually felt insecure, or had somehow read my motives and was trying to throw me off.

'I remembered what it was like when my father had departed. It was quite sudden, more than six years ago. He went to sleep one night and never woke up. I was away at the time and received the news in the middle of my morning ablutions. The rest of the morning was spent trying to communicate the news to the rest of the kadatuans and inviting them to swear an oath of loyalty to me. I had acted quickly, since any hesitation on my part could have resulted in a coup. We concluded all the ceremonies with as much grace as we could. It was only much later that I felt his loss.'

I had spoken spontaneously. It was rather like uncovering an old wound that hadn't yet healed.

'Enjoy your time with your father. When he goes, your friends and brothers will cease to be yours. You will all be rivals for the same throne. And only one will not be a pretender.'

He was silent.

'I had no brothers. As such, I made all the Daatus swear an oath of loyalty to me, but it has done little good, as you can see. It's no different anywhere else in the world. Ask the Arabs or the Chinese. It is the ones who are the closest to you that you have to be the most suspicious of. The ones who claim they will never let you down. I have seen enough of the world on my shores to know that.'

'We aren't like that.'

'You're probably right.' I left it at that.

We were silent again. After a little while, he spoke.

'Father was an only son too. The kingdom was served up to him on a platter. Yet, I think he knows more than most how ambition works. Part of the reason was his own father, my grandfather, Rajaraja. Father knew the weight of being his son. Some kings are warriors, others administrators. Some poets and patrons of the arts. Some are patrons of religion. Emperor Rajaraja was perhaps the only ruler to combine all of these aspects. So everyone in the kingdom had a reason to love him. Perhaps more than any other man, my grandfather realized that to be king was almost akin to being a God. He had to be everything to everyone. A father and a mother to his people.'

He paused, as if considering something, and continued.

'Father learned very quickly that he would forever be in grandfather's shadow. But he also learned that he needed to be his own man. A king cannot rest on his father's laurels, can he? So my father began to conquer kingdoms of his own. He beat off the Rashtrakutas and our western neighbours, the Chalukyas.

He pushed them off our territories so emphatically that they were only able to respond twelve years later. Grandfather had only conquered the north of Eelam, but father conquered the entire island. He even captured their king, Mahinda, and brought him back to Thanjavur.'

'And what happened to Mahinda?' I asked, intrigued.

'He lives in comfort at Thanjavur as our guest,' was all Rajadhiraja said.

So Mahinda had been housed in one of these mansions as a 'guest' of the king like me. We had heard about Rajendra's conquest of Eelam. At the time it did not mean anything to us. As long as trade was good, it made no difference to us who was paying.

Mahinda's fate worried me, but the king had told me that he would allow me to return. Besides, I was no threat to him. Yet.

'Father went on to beat the Cheras and Pandyas to the west and south of our empire and strengthen his hold on the kingdom. He now wants to create an army and put the Chalukyas under his yoke once and for all.'

He took out a leather pouch and took a sip from it. He offered it to me but I declined.

'It can be done. A few years ago, we had taken our army right up to Vangaladesa. There is no army in Bharatavarsha that cannot be beaten by us.'

It was almost as though I was talking to Bhaskaran. Again that cloying earnestness, that almost utter contempt for any opposing will. As if every other army in Jambudwipa would fold up in front of them when they arrived.

'A few years ago, we fought our way to the Ganges going through the Odda, Chalukya and Pala kingdoms. Their armies are not very different from ours. Elephants, horses, infantry. Nothing that really differentiates us on the field. At times, we've even been outmanoeuvred.'

'So what separates you?' I asked, genuinely intrigued.

'Luck,' was all he said, and smiled.

'Surely there's more to it,' I said, a little outraged at the simple answer. I was hoping for some insight I could carry back to my shores.

He shrugged. 'Father surrounds himself with competent men but no more or less than anyone I've seen.'

He paused for a moment, and then continued.

'A shared sense of purpose, perhaps. Grandfather put up all these inscriptions on the walls of his temples. Each time he made a conquest, he got the court poets to write something called a "*prasasti*" – a song of praise that described the conquest in the most glowing terms. It is not a new practice, I will admit. But grandfather became renowned for them. And father too. The people of our kingdom read them, and learn that the Chola kings are always restless. Always looking for new conquests. Everyone in our kingdom learns about every victory, every gift or donation, as you saw at the temple at Thanjavur, from our *prasasti*s and other inscriptions. This makes them feel as though they are part of an empire that is expanding. A part of history.'

I was silent for a few moments, not knowing how to react. Again I got the sense that Rajaraja had ensured his influence was felt long after his time. Rajendra was merely following his lead, and expanding on his work.

'You do not agree?' Rajadhiraja asked, noting my silence.

I considered the question. 'The Arabs have a saying, which I believe they've taken from the Franks: "The world is a bridge. Pass over it, but do not build your house upon it." Your inscriptions are monuments to eternity. I don't see the purpose.'

Rajadhiraja looked quizzically at me but then a general interrupted us and monopolized his attention.

Every king makes his greatness known to the people. We were no different, and we carved our greatness on stone through elaborate inscriptions. But I had never seen it done to this scale. The Chola emperors were bent on ensuring posterity would always know of them, if not live in awe of them. I wondered if this was sheer paranoia. To keep telling the subjects how good their rulers were. If you control what is in the heads of the people, you control them.

Or perhaps my days here had made me cynical. Rajaraja and Rajendra were extremely rigorous in their administration. If they could survey all the land in the kingdom and reorganize it, then maintaining records of every victory, donation or gift was also something to be expected.

Rajadhiraja was busy for the rest of the journey. Some of his supply wagons had broken down, and the troops had been forced to march to the nearest barrack so they could eat dinner.

After marching for two days, we learned that the Chalukya troops were marching towards us. We would meet them at a red plain, which was more dust than grass, just a little distance from the border.

I have been in battles, Ganapathy, though we tend to fight mainly on the rivers that garland our land and on the ocean that girdles it. The few land battles I have seen have mostly been decided by the brute strength of elephants. We're not a civilization that enjoys long, protracted sieges so our walls remain unharmed most of the time.

I stood on a small hillock with a bodyguard of four that was supposed to whisk me back to the Vengi capital of Rajahmundry if your troops were routed. The Chalukyas were arranged in three large squares of infantry, behind whom were two lines of cavalry and a single line of elephants. There were roughly the same number of troops as the Cholas, perhaps a few hundred more.

The army, Rajadhiraja had told me before the clash, was called a '*munrukai* sena' or a 'three-limbed army', the limbs being the infantry, cavalry and elephants. There was also a regiment of archers, placed discretely behind the lines of cavalry, called *villaligal,* he explained. These were protected by spearmen called *sengundar*. He seemed particularly proud of the regiment in the centre and front. He called them *velaikkarar*. All of them were masters at *silambam,* a martial art that was actively promoted by your rulers. More names followed that would have twisted my tongue out of shape had I attempted to practise them.

Rajadhiraja was down amidst his beloved *velaikkarar*s. I could make him out in the distance. Sitting on a gold and red caparisoned elephant with the leaping tiger emblem of the Cholas emblazoned on it. He wasn't content to sit behind and direct the proceedings – a strange practice for a prince, especially an heir designate. If he died on the battlefield, succession plans would have to be changed. Not that it would have made too much of a difference to Rajendra, who had three sons.

The sound of conches and the dull rhythm of war drums pulled me back to the present. The men from both sides slowly started walking towards each other, then began jogging and, finally clashed headlong. I heard your troops shouting '*Vetrivel! Veeravel!*' as they had done on my shores.

The battle was swift and bloody. The Chalukya elephants waded into the centre but were halted by the spearmen. The *villaligal* archers had instructions to bring down all the elephant troops and focused their fire on the elephants. The Chalukya cavalry crashed into the left of the square of the Chola *velaikkarar* infantry that was fighting back the elephants and Chalukya foot soldiers from the front. The Chalukya strategy, it appeared, was to concentrate all their force in the centre – quite similar to what we tried to do with the Cholas at Kadaram. I was curious to see how they would escape this.

The *vellaikkarar*s were magnificent. They did not yield an inch. For every one of them that fell, another took his place immediately. Their forward lines did not waver. There was no question of retreat, and though the Chalukyas hit them with all their strength, the *vellaikkarar*s withstood them heroically. Rajadhiraja's elephants soon entered the fray and bolstered the ranks.

Conches sounded over the din. Rajadhiraja's cavalry swung around the right and tore into the Chalukya flanks. Battles are decided in moments like these. Where the *vellaikkarar*s were able to withstand the pressure of cavalry, the Chalukyas melted. The troops began to panic, and the Chola cavalry was able to cut through to the heart of the army. The battle did not last for long after that. Rajadhiraja sounded an elephant charge, and they broke clean through the front line. The Chalukyas retreated haphazardly and Rajadhiraja sent his cavalry chasing after them.

You can use all the familiar clichés to describe the scene. Blood-soaked ground, vultures circling overhead etcetera. They still don't do justice to the tragedy of death on a battlefield. When all the killing was done, one of Rajadhiraja's men came by and asked me to meet the prince at the camp that had been set up a short distance from the battlefield.

In the camp the mood was sombre. Wounded soldiers were being tended to, and men were counting the friends they had lost. I was led to Rajadhiraja's tent. He had been injured in battle; an arrow had pierced his armour between the shoulder and collarbone. It was only a light wound so it would heal in a few days. When I walked in, he was rapping out orders to his commissariat, telling them to get lunch ready and not to give the soldiers toddy.

'There's no point getting their blood up,' he said as he stood up to greet me.

'Congratulations on your victory,' I said.

He regarded me for a moment. 'It was far too easy. I expect another attack soon.'

'My lord, our cavalry is just returning. Almost all their forces have been slaughtered. We can rest easy,' said a general with a bandage across his eye.

Rajadhiraja shrugged but his response was curt. 'I'd rather not.'

An awkward silence spread across the room like noxious gas. Invisible but unpleasant. Everyone was mindful of it except Rajadhiraja, who did not seem to care about the discomfort he was causing others.

In any case, the expected counter attack did not come. A day later, a regiment of the Vengi army came and took our place, and we began marching back to Rajahmundry to replenish our supplies. It was a two day march to Rajahmundry and, on the first evening, we got a missive from Rajendra instructing Rajadhiraja to return with me to Gangaikonda Cholapuram. The astrologers had found a muhurat somewhere in the early hours of a day next week. Rajadhiraja and I were to rush back for the ceremony. We left just two hours after receiving the missive, giving charge of the army to the general with the bandaged eye. The feast that had been prepared at Rajahmundry in our honour had to be forsaken. Instead, the king of Vengi, too, had to attend the inauguration of the city.

After three days of hard riding, we reached the city early in the morning. I was escorted to my mansion while Rajadhiraja went straight to the royal palace for a meeting. I was exhausted and slept for most of the day, and would have slept through the night as well but for Rajendra's visit.

In just a few weeks, she had become the Raja's eyes and ears. Her knowledge of languages and numbers was better than the old secretary's, and she soon became a mute spectator to the council meetings where she sat in her corner, taking down notes. The ministers, though initially sceptical, soon came to accept her quiet presence in the room.

A constant refrain of the ministers was that the Raja refused to get married. He had held off for far too long, they complained. The Kahuripan state was new, he would tell them. It has blossomed out of the dried out pod of the old Medang state. It needed stewardship desperately. He had, after all, only been ruling for five or so summers. His prime minister, Narottam, would disagree vehemently with this point and insist that he get married. How would he show his face to the dead king and queen in the afterlife otherwise? The Raja would spend the rest of the council meeting trying to mollify Narottam.

Then, one day, the Raja told the princess why he had not yet married.

It had been a reasonably quiet day. Narottam had come brandishing a piece of manuscript. Srideva had taken over Srivijaya, he proclaimed. And laughed.

'Serves them well. And may the empire drown in blood,' he said gleefully.

Then one of the noblemen from Bhumi Java casually stated that Srideva had a daughter. Perhaps there was some scope for a match?

'Never in his next hundred births!' Narottam roared and proceeded to flay the minister for even suggesting union between the Srivijaya and Kahuripan.

'The king who crossed water will sooner be drowned before he marries a Srivijaya Daatu's whore!' he roared again, and walked out of the room, scattering the ministers in his wake.

That night, the princess recited the day's itinerary to the Raja. When she finished, she bowed her head, waiting to be dismissed. Instead, the Raja began to talk.

'I am sure you have noticed that my people call me the king who crossed water. It's an odd name but it has stuck. I was not born here in Bhumi Java, you see. I was born in the neighbouring island of Bali Dwipa. I "crossed the water" between Bali Dwipa and Bhumi Java, and received a new name for my troubles. My father was the ruler of the Isyana kingdom of Bali Dwipa. He had married Dharmawangsa's sister and, consequently, Dharmawangsa was my uncle. I was probably closer to him than many in my own family, and he wanted me to marry his daughter and rule the Medang empire one day. I was sixteen when we were betrothed. You probably know the rest. The *Mahapralaya*...'

He paused and spoke softly.

'I remember the redness of the walls that day. Blood was spattered everywhere. Man, woman, child. Pieces of human flesh floating in the blood that was ankle-deep in the royal hall. And laughter. Not the kind you would hear at the wedding. It was a harsher one of hatred and triumph. I hid in a store room in a large cask of rice, too frightened to do anything.

'Narottam had been a soldier in Dharmawangsa's army. He had entered the store room. too, hiding from the Srivijayans. We were almost about to kill each other. Well, he was about to kill me. I had little proficiency with weapons. But he recognized me. We put on the clothes of dead Srivijayan soldiers and escaped through the back door into the heart of Bhumi Java. I was too ashamed to return to my father. What would I tell him? That I had been cowering in the dark, unable to protect my future wife or her family? If I returned alive, it would be seen as cowardice. And my father would not be able to confer his kingdom to me without opposition. It was best, I decided, to let everyone think I was dead. I did not deserve a kingdom. So I became a hermit in the Mount Vanagiri with Narottam in tow.

'It was a quiet life. I spent my days reading Hindu and Buddhist scriptures and wallowing in self-pity. Then, one day, Narottam confronted me and said plainly that to live like a hermit was no life for a king. He had secured meetings with some of the warlords that had sprung out of the debris of the Medang kingdom and some from the Isyana kingdom of Bali Dwipa, my original home.

'I was scared, you understand. All the stories they tell you about the palace raid are true. I remember walking through a pathway of the palace with Narottam that was littered with dead men and women. Littered. I use the word deliberately. The way they had been killed, so casually. It seemed as if their life had no meaning to the men who assaulted them. The thought of it still chills me. I refused at first. I told Narottam that I did not have it in me to be king. I could not pick up a sword and protect Medang then. Why did he believe I could do it now?

'Narottam glowered at me, and told me to pick myself up and be a man. But I only wept and buried my head in my arms, refusing to look at him. Narottam then came and sat next to me and spoke gently, for perhaps the first and only time in life. I still remember what he said, for the kingdom of Kahuripan stands because of those words.

'He told me, "You may never win your kingdom back, your highness. But you, more than anyone else I have ever known, deserve a chance to change the way you look at yourself. You are not a coward. And you owe yourself a chance to believe it."

'And so Narottam convinced me, not so much to take back my kingdom, but my own self-esteem. I met the warlords. They offered to help me stitch a kingdom together. There were many battles that were fought in those days. The land was parcelled out among chiefs who wanted to re-establish the Medang kingdom in their own vision. Narottam and I put together a kingdom and called it Kahuripan meaning "To life". The kingdom represented a second life for both of us.

'Narottam will never forget what the Srivijaya empire did to my uncle and the Medang kingdom. Perhaps I have a different view. You can't be enemies with everyone all the time. A wise man has no enemies. A Chinese or Hindu philosopher once said that. These words have have trickled into our island and stayed with me.'

He sighed. 'Perhaps I desire a normal life now. One not spent waging wars for my survival, but spent making my land larger and prosperous. A male heir or two to surrender the kingdom to when my time has come. Is it too much to ask?'

The princess remained silent.

'Kahuripan cannot afford war any longer. It is draining us of wealth and people. We need allies quickly. Srideva maybe our only hope. If nothing else, a marriage alliance into the Srivijaya legitimises our claim to the throne. It makes us nobility. That itself may bring some warlords to our side. Narottam will never understand, but the Srivijaya empire may be the only way Kahuripan can survive.'

The princess had heard enough.

'I have something to tell you, my king,' she said quietly.

12

The next night, Rajendra came to my room and sat with his lamp; consequently, the fan bearers stopped their work so that I could awake. I woke up to see the emperor sitting patiently at the edge of my bed. In my mind, I cursed his lordship.

'A few hundred years ago, there was a king,' began Rajendra, speaking more to himself than me. 'His name was Amoghavarsha. He was not a Chola, but a Rashtrakuta. He ruled for precisely sixty-four years and expanded the Rashtrakuta empire in the south and the north. The records we have from those days tell us that the Muslim, Jain, Buddhist and Hindu subjects of the day were happy. He let all his subjects worship their Gods and even funded their own individual practises. He patronized Sanskrit scholars and mathematicians and theologians. Even the Arabs began calling him the greatest king on earth.'

He continued, 'And, yet, they say he never wanted to rule. That he left kingship midway to become a Jain monk. He was more intent on breaking through the structure that his life imposed on him than letting its boundaries dictate his life.'

He paused for a while and then resumed speaking, his voice a low rumble.

'People spend their entire lives praying to become kings and fantasizing about the lives they could live. Yet, who does a king fantasize about becoming? A monk.'

His words drew me out of my sleep.

'Many years ago, Ashoka of Magadha also went in the same direction. A man with everything, who eventually learned that he desired nothing. Who is the more successful man then? A man with riches, women and progeny, or a man with nothing – with no responsibility to anything except himself?'

He fell silent, ruminating on his own thoughts.

'According to some people, renunciation of desire is the beginning of enlightenment. The first step on the road to nirvana. Or moksha, as you call it. Yet, the desire for renunciation is a desire in itself, is it not?' I asked the king, curious to know whether he had considered this aspect in his own spiritual quest.

'Perhaps,' he rumbled. 'Or maybe it is a state of not having desires. A void, an emptiness. *Shunyata*, as the Buddhists say. A state of mind where it doesn't worry or fear anymore. The mind is married to greed. It covets things and ideas. When it is single, it is truly free.'

'So real renunciation is not the lack of desire, but the lack of fear?' I ventured. 'Isn't that dangerous? If a man loses fear, he loses a sense of responsibility to the people around him. Fear is what stops us from killing other people … and taking their land without consent,' I added, hoping he would get the message.

'No,' he declared. 'If a man needs to kill other people, he does so because he fears what they will do to him. He does not truly live without fear. A monk lives without fear because he lives only for himself.'

He took a deep breath.

'Structure is our opium. Order is our drug. What have we without them? Laws – some human, others divine – define our lives and decide the extents to which we can lead our lives. To break out of that structure imposed on us, from the day we are born, is all that anyone really wants. Those of us who benefit most from the structure are responsible for its upkeep, and cannot escape it. Unless we are brave like Amoghavarsha.'

'Do you plan to escape your structure?' I asked him. I couldn't make out his expression, but his voice sounded wistful.

'We all escape our structures, sometimes by choice, otherwise by design. The Lord has given me fifty and more years to escape my structure. When he realizes I am incapable of it, he will pull me out, like he does every human.'

I was silent, and so was he. I got the sense that the conversation was over. He stood up after a few moments, and blew out the lamp. As the rustling behind him began, I heard his voice again.

'One more thing. I need to ask a personal favour of you. As a king, do I have your word that you will keep this to yourself and not bring this up ever again?'

I was intrigued.

'Yes,' I replied, after thinking for a few moments. 'You have my word.'

'You have met all three of my boys now. Each of them has their virtues, and all of them have their supporters. As an outsider – someone who sees us outside the structures that define us – which of them should be king after me?'

Airlangga had never stayed silent for so long in his life. The woman, his secretary, an able woman who knew business better than some of his merchants, who understood literature, language and statecraft, had now pulled another surprise. Like a magician releasing a dove from an empty cage.

'A princess? Of Srivijaya? What are you talking about? Dharanindra had told me there was something wrong with your mother. I had no cause to believe it was hereditary.'

The princess was in tears. The Raja did not seem to believe that she was the heiress to the Srivijaya throne. She began reciting the names of the Sailendra kings to prove her claim but Airlangga stopped her.

'You can get that from any history book or storyteller.'

'Then take me back to the capital city, my lord,' cried the princess. 'I still know the Daatus. I played in their laps while growing up. I'm not lying.'

Airlangga was quiet.

'I will accept Srideva's invitation to visit his palace in the capital,' he said after a while. 'The one that you say had been burned down by the Cholas. You will accompany me with Narottam. If what you say is true, then you could yet be useful.'

They left for the capital the next day. Narottam travelled with them and glowered at the princess whenever he got the chance but did not say a word. She had dressed like a noblewoman in silk lilac robes along with a veil, and had two women attending to her. Sumitra was not among them. If she was successful, she would be able to get Sumitra back into her retinue. If she failed, and was put to death, Sumitra could at least live out the rest of her life in Kahuripan.

They arrived at the capital the morning after, and the princess nearly burst into tears when she saw her city again. They passed through the walls, and the princess noticed the *vidyadharatorana* had been removed from it. It must have been Srideva, she thought bitterly as they entered the palace. It was exactly the way the princess had left it. Every trace of her last vision of it with plumes of smoke stretching up to the sky and cries renting the air were forgotten. Srideva met them in the throne room. He embraced the Raja warmly, and Narottam too who responded with a stiff pat on his back. The princess, in the meantime, stood with the rest of Airlangga's retinue, her face covered with a veil.

This was her father's room, she remembered sadly. Gold pillars and floors painted regal blue. The walls filled with paintings of the Srivijaya kings of yore. She recognized many of the ministers in the room. It was as if nothing had changed.

Except that Srideva sat on her father's throne.

After the formal niceties were complete and they had praised each other to the heavens, Srideva began talking like a trader.

'The Kahuripan kingdom is a fledgling one, but one we see potential in. We will support you in your wars and join our families together. I see us as being one large family ruled out of two branches. One in Bhumi Java, the other from here.'

'What assistance would you provide?'

'Elephants. Archers. Spearmen. At a nominal cost, of course.'

'Cost?'

'Yes, well we can't give them out for free, can we?' snorted Srideva.

Airlangga was silent.

Srideva continued, this time in a harsher tone.

'The Maharajah of the Srivijaya empire seeks an alliance with your kingdom. It is not an offer to take lightly.'

Airlangga nodded.

'If I marry into the Srivijaya kingdom, will all the Daatus support my claim to my land?'

'Yes, of course,' said Srideva.

'Will I get access to Srivijaya trade?'

'Yes, but a nominal amount.'

Airlangga stood up. Srideva did too and embraced him.

Then Airlangga looked around him and, addressing the room, said loudly, 'Allow me to introduce someone to the court.'

The princess stepped forward and removed her veil.

'My consort. The Queen of Kahuripan!'

13

Why would the most powerful man in Tamilakam, with hundreds of ministers, philosophers and poets armed with the wisdom of the ages at his disposal, ask such a question of a complete stranger?

I admit it threw me off initially. But as I sat the next day and tried to work out if he was springing an elaborate trap for me, I realized that I was perhaps the only person he could ask in the whole of Chola Nadu. Yes, he had ministers and many wise advisors. But he had no one whose life depended on telling him the truth.

Let me explain. The ministers or whoever he sought advice from would not dare answer him, for what if the prince they did not bet on came to the throne and had their heads crushed for treason? They probably had already told him in various ways that all three sons were fit for the crown and it was not possible to make a choice. His wives? The mothers of the princes or the aunts would obviously be biased towards their own child. Who was left?

How about an outsider who could provide an answer, and then leave just as swiftly as he came?

It all made perfect sense then. Why else would he try to befriend me? Why else would he make me meet all his children? And, more importantly, why else would he keep me alive?

Why me, you ask?

Perhaps because I was a king just like him. Maybe because he saw some kind of kinship between us as kings who did not have the support of brothers growing up. Maybe our nightly trysts trading stories had convinced him that we shared the same values, and that I could be trusted. Or maybe he just liked my face.

I could not tell. Still can't. Your emperor remained a closed book to me till the last time we met.

My plans to ally with a prince and overthrow the king were put on hold for the moment. It would be easier to negotiate a way out of his kingdom by providing an answer to his question than by plotting to overthrow him.

He came the next night as well and sat like he had done the previous ones on a chair at the foot of the bed. This time, I was prepared.

'If I give you an honest answer, will it have a negative influence on my prospects for freedom?'

'No, none at all. You will be a friend of the Chola nation, and have my everlasting gratitude,' he said without any pause.

He was silent for a moment and, just as I was about to begin, he said, 'Virajendra is brave. And not in a foolhardy way. The generals like working with him. They see him more as a little brother who needs to be indulged, than a prince of the realm. He has his own ideas, but is willing to be convinced otherwise. Rajendradeva is calm. No less in battle than his brothers. I've seen him in conflict. But he sees the less glorious aspects of kingship that perhaps the rest of them don't. He is less obsessed with posterity than the rest of them. Which leaves Rajadhiraja. Rajadhiraja combines the virtues of Rajendradeva and Virajendra. He is ambitious but he will never let the common people get swept away by his ambition. But he can be hot-headed and impetuous. My father lived a long and healthy life, and I only attained kingship after I had passed more than forty years. The time I ascended the throne was precarious. As always after the death of a king, all the other kingdoms were circling around like hawks around a dying beast, waiting for it to fall so they could take pieces of it. I knew the fate that befell kingdoms without rulers, so one of my first acts as king was to groom Rajadhiraja as my regent, should I fall. I invested him with the title two years after my own coronation.

'It was an act done for the survival of the kingdom. Rajadhiraja was the eldest, and as such the logical choice. The situation as it stands is different now. Rajadhiraja can be reckless with his life. He still insists on leading his men into the fray – for what reason I know not. A king needs to worry about all his subjects, not just the ones on the battlefield. The generals of our forces need to worry about soldiers. I seek stability in my empire. I have not built this kingdom for it to break asunder when I'm gone.'

'Do you fear civil war after your time if your princes don't agree with your decision?'

'We will cross that bridge when we get there. There is no point building homes on it now, no?'

So, Rajadhiraja was talking to his father about me. This presented a dilemma. Would Rajendra talk to his sons about what I had said? I had no allies in this country. I could ill afford to make an enemy, that too one of the princes. Was he testing me?

'So, which one of my sons should be king?'

I detected a hint of menace in his voice. Or perhaps it was just my own fear colouring everything I heard.

'All of them,' I said in a panic. But the moment I said it, I knew it would not be accepted.

'That is the answer of a minstrel, not a king,' replied Rajendra, and was silent.

If I couldn't get out of the situation, I decided I may as well spread discord.

'Virajendra, then. Any prince who can defeat my navy can defeat any kingdom in the world. Let the others guide and support him. But let him rule the land.'

Rajendra was silent. After a while, he blew out the lamp. Our meeting was over.

Rajendra's nightly visits were depriving me of sleep. So I slept in the day and avoided Bhaskaran scrupulously. He had come in the morning to enquire after my health and had been told by my attendants that I was sleeping. He had wanted to tell me about the pooja and celebration that would happen tomorrow for the inauguration of the city and told the attendants to inform me when I awoke and send word to him so he could visit again. I had no real desire to attend to the pooja so I conveniently forgot to tell the attendants to summon him.

I spent the day doing little except wondering whether Rajendra had been upset by what I said. He did not appear agitated last night and if he truly was upset, I could have been beheaded at his behest any time over the day. I waited impatiently for the night and, when it came, I lay down in wait with my eyes open. I had an answer prepared. One that he would hopefully like.

I waited till the cocks crowed at dawn, and it was only when the bright sunlight had completely flooded my room did I come to terms with the fact that he was not coming.

There was an uproar in court. Maharajah Sangrama Vijayatunggavarman's daughter? Alive? The Daatus of the kingdom got in each other's way trying to see her face. The older ones prostrated before her and wept. The younger ones kept a respectful distance. But many of the Daatus went up to Srideva who had now returned to his throne and stood with him in mute solidarity. The colour had drained from his face.

The princess's voice filled the hall. She reminded the Daatus of the oath they had pledged to her father. She told them about how Srideva had refused protection to them and about her subsequent adventures. She made sure to speak well of the king of Kahuripan, who had generously offered them shelter. Many of the Daatus were scandalized. They said they would secede from the kingdom and support the princess. But though a number of them supported her claim, they could not relinquish support of Srideva who, unpopular as he was, had negotiated with the Cholas and brought peace to the land.

A compromise was reached. Srideva would govern the Srivijayan empire, but the Daatus would help the Kahuripan people. Some of the Daatus, who were disgusted with Srideva's actions or were jealous of his ascent to the head of the Srivijaya state, even announced their intention to become vassals of the Kahuripan kingdom.

Thus, the princess returned to Kahuripan a queen.

14

Bhaskaran entered my bedroom just as I was falling asleep. 'It is time, my lord,' he said. 'The pooja is at the palace. I had come earlier to inform you to be ready. The time has come.'

'What possible use am I during your pooja? For heaven's sake, let me sleep, man.'

'Your presence has been requested by the emperor. He has asked me to personally escort you.'

The words shook me awake. I was still in the emperor's favour.

I had a bath, rubbed sandalwood scent over myself, and wore a white silk dhoti and angavastram that Bhaskaran had bought for me. I had wondered at the time as to why Bhaskaran would bring me a crisp formal white dhoti for such a festive occasion, but put it down to the occasion being a pooja. Perhaps a more formal tone was necessary.

We walked towards the palace. I had insisted on it rather than take a carriage. It would help shake the slumber from my eyes. The palace was, perhaps, the third largest building in the city after the temple and the granary. As we travelled, some of the people on the street began to look at me. A squat, brown man with different eyes from them. For the people of the coast, I was not an exotic specimen, but here inland, there were folk who had never seen my kind before. They stared at me curiously, not conscious of the embarrassment they could be causing. Bhaskaran seemed to notice this and quickened his pace.

We soon entered the palace premises. Apart from the palace building, which was a beautiful structure made of stone four floors tall, there was also a large open courtyard where the king could greet people. Bhaskaran left me inside the palace with one of the servants and told me he would join me later. The servant took me to a dining area where I was served breakfast.

Soon after, Bhaskaran appeared. It was time to go to the courtyard, he said. I followed. We did not take the main exit that led outside to the courtyard, but a side exit that led to an area behind the palace. There were some people gathered there. Some fair, some dark. Some like me, brown. None of them spoke but looked glumly at one another. Bhaskaran took my leave, saying he would be back. There was something odd about the gathering. All of them wore similar white dhotis and angavastras as I had. A while later, a guard came and told us it was time for the ceremony. We were asked to assemble in a line.

Another guard came up to me and asked me if I was the king of Srivijaya. I replied I was. He took me to the end of the line and made me stand there. One of the men in the line caught my attention. He was a dark man with a thin, black moustache. His eyes darted around like a caged animal. When he saw me, he took a step forward but was stopped by a guard. Something was not right here, I could feel it in my bones.

We walked into the courtyard in a line. I could hear loud cheering followed by a voice that was drowned out by the noise. Bhaskaran joined me after a few minutes.

'What's going on?' I asked him as he came.

'The emperor is performing a *virabhishekam*,' he said nonchalantly, as if it would mean nothing to me.

I suddenly understood why I was there.

'Who is the dark man who keeps looking at me?' I asked, hoping my suspicions were wrong.

'Lord Mahinda,' he said without emotion.

We were all conquered kings standing in a line. All of us perhaps taken by force from our kingdoms. This was a parade of the emperor's victories and I was to walk in among them as a trophy of war. Behind the facade of treating me a guest, they were treating me as a prisoner of war. I felt embarrassed. Not because of the humiliation, you understand Ganapathy. I had lost a war and been taken prisoner. I had expected to be killed or tortured. But because I had trusted them, I did not see this coming. I swore at myself for being so naive. Bhaskaran must have guessed what was going through my mind. He spoke gently.

'Conduct yourself like a guest, and you will be taken care of. Like Sudama. My humble advice, my lord.'

I remember not comprehending what he was saying at the time. Bhaskaran left me and went back inside the palace. I walked up to Mahinda. He seemed almost relieved to see me. Another foreign man among the Tamils.

'Not the best place to meet,' he said wryly in Tamil, his eyes darting about. He looked awfully nervous.

'I am Maharajah Sangrama Vijayatunggavarman,' I said, hoping his eyes would stop leaping about across the white sky of his eyeballs. He was beginning to make me nervous.

'Maharajah...' he said, with a pause that underlined the hollowness of the title. 'Your presence fills my heart with joy.'

'As does yours.'

A formal statement of greeting. Protocol, amongst royals. It wasn't much, but somehow it was an affirmation that we were still kings. Rulers of our lands, even in this state of imprisonment. It did both of us some good.

'The emperor says he will meet me and discuss terms for my release. I hope to see him today.'

I nodded.

'It has been more than five years since I was taken from Anuradhapura. I haven't seen the emperor since then. I hope today is different.' He ended the statement with a short, nervous bark of a laugh.

'I hope it is too,' I mumbled, now getting increasing clarity about my own fate.

One of the guards came up to me, and requested me politely to stand at the end of the line. I could have had made a commotion at that moment, and tried to storm off. But that would have served no purpose. No, I decided. I would bear my humiliation, and pay it back in kind if I ever got the chance.

Each of the kings walked into the courtyard accompanied by a deafening roar. Moments later my turn came and I was escorted by guards to the stage, where the priests were anointing the king at a sacred fire. A group of priests stood around the fire and chanted sacred mantras, while the main priest poured ghee into the flames as he chanted. A large crowd of more than five hundred people was assembled in the courtyard, witnessing the event. Several more stood outside the palace premises.

A man bellowed over the din.

'Chakravarti Rajendra Chola, blessed be his name, having conquered the Chalukyas of Kalyani, now proceeded across the ocean where he defeated the empire of the Srivijayas and brought back bound in chains the Maharajah of Kadaram.'

For a moment I marvelled at the inaccuracy of the statement. I was not the Maharajah of Kadaram. There was no Maharajah of Kadaram. Just a Daatu who pledged allegiance to me, the Maharajah of the Srivijaya empire. A careless error. And where were the chains this man was talking about?

'Fourteen cities and many riches were plundered, including the *vidyadharatorana* – the famed gateway of the fort of Srivijayas ...'

So, they had brought the *torana* back. I looked around wondering if it was here, almost desperate to see something that belonged to my home. Some link to my past.

The crowd cheered as the priests continued to chant. Rajendra and his sons sat around the sacred fire, clad in dhotis without any upper garment. The sons were seated behind Rajendra in the lotus position, their arms resting on their thighs, their palms facing upwards, deep in meditation. Rajendra's bushy eyebrows and moustache were coloured black, as was his hair. He sat with his eyes shut and his palms joined together in worship, lips moving to the chanting of mantras. I kept looking at him, hoping that our eyes would meet and I would nail his treachery. He finished saying his mantras and stood up.

The head priest chanted some more mantras and addressed him with a series of titles – 'Gangaikonda Cholan, Irattapadi-konda Cholan', 'Mannai-konda Cholan'. These, then, were the titles that he could lay claim to now. He was the emperor who had brought the Ganga, and all these distant lands including mine to this ground. I looked around. Apart from the conquered kings, there were also a few men who were dressed strangely in garments of leaves and women's anklets.

The priests stopped chanting, and Rajendra stood in front of the crowd, arms akimbo.

The announcer made a proclamation and the crowd roared. One of the men in garments of leaves came and bowed his head and touched the feet of the king. The crowd roared ecstatically again.

'Talaikonda! Talaikonda! Talaikonda!'

You know the meaning, Ganapathy. 'The king who has brought the head.'

I gathered that this man was also a king, or a chief of a tribe if nothing else. Rajendra could now claim that he had brought back the head of this rival king and subjugated him completely.

Something about the crowd roaring its approval of the poor king's humiliation angered me. I decided that, if I was called upon, I would not bow to your king. Even if it meant my end. As it happened, only the kings dressed in the garments of leaves were called upon to do this.

The conquered kings stood on the stage for the remainder of the ceremony that went on for an hour more, followed by another brief ceremony where the generals of the realms were anointed. Rajendra's generals were anointed by him personally and given a royal title that, not surprisingly, derived from Rajendra's name, or if they had served his father, Rajaraja's name. Some of them had even served three rulers and were called 'Muvenduvelar'. I saw a familiar face among them – the general who had kidnapped me from my palace. The announcer called out his name and told the baying crowd how he had put my city to the sword.

'Rajendran Brahmarayar!' He roared, announcing the general's new name. The title was a reward that would live with him forever; a symbol that he had performed his duty towards Rajendra admirably.

The ceremony continued for another hour. Rajendra did not even look at me. He finished anointing his commanders and walked off the stage without even a glance towards the defeated kings. All part of the act, I suppose. After the ceremony, I told Bhaskaran to take me to my mansion.

There, I wept.

She thought about her father and mother a lot that day. Sumitra was her bridal companion, and she cried all the way to the wedding, and then through the ceremony.

'Someone needs to cry from her parent's side. I'm playing the role of both parents,' she declared when someone tried to comfort her.

The princess did not know whether she was in love with the Raja. But both the Raja and she knew that their marriage was a way of securing the future of Kahuripan. And, most crucially, a better life for her and Sumitra. Perhaps that was what marriage was – a contract for the mutual benefit of two parties. The king did not set her heart aflutter, a condition she had heard afflicted the love-lorn. But she felt safe around him, and free to express herself. That was enough. But, perhaps, that was what love was now. And maybe, like everything else, the idea of love too changed as you grew older. From being a storm, it becomes a harbour. She felt happy at the thought.

The couple took their vows in the Buddhist way for the princess, and the Hindu way for the Raja. All the ministers were delighted with the match, including old Narottam, who had finally come around and was now claiming that he would never have allowed her to marry him if she hadn't lived as part of the Kahuripan household first. A princess with Srivijaya royal blood added legitimacy to the new kingdom of Kahuripan. They could now count themselves among the royal families of Suvarnadwipa. With an heir, they could even create a ruling dynasty.

BOOK II

BOOK II

1

I see something akin to sympathy on your young face, Ganapathy.
Your eyes widen like the sun after an eclipse. Your lips have pursed
themselves into a slit on your face. Your hand has ceased moving
and, with it, the sound of scribbling, our worthy companion for the
past few hours has left the place. Be cold, young scribe. Don't feel it.
Not for me. There is much of my story still to be told. And maybe
you will add a page too, to my life.

Two things happened as a direct consequence of the
virabhishekam. I refused to see Bhaskaran for the rest of the day,
saying that I was unwell with fever. He offered, via the servants,
to send a *vaidya* to check on my health, and I declined. I locked
myself inside my room with strict instructions that I was not to be
disturbed. At meal times, a man would bring various items of food
wrapped in a palm leaf and leave them at my door after knocking
three times. I would emerge after a few moments when he had left.
This way, I spent the whole day without seeing anyone.

At night, the fans stopped their motion again, and I lay still.
Rajendra sat at the foot of my bed again, holding his lamp. I closed

my eyes and pretended he wasn't there. He must have sat there for a long time. In the end, he just stood up and left.

Bhaskaran sent me frantic messages nearly every two hours the next day. I refused to meet him citing my ill health as an excuse. Finally, he barged into the mansion with armed guards, and got them to kick open the doors of my room.

'Thank God, my lord! I feared something had happened.'

'Why would you feel that, Bhaskaran?' I asked, coldly.

He stuttered and looked sheepish mumbling something incoherent.

'Please, leave now. I'm unwell,' I said.

'Tell me when I can return,' he pleaded.

'It's your kingdom. You can come and go as you please.'

'My lord, I'm sorry if you are distressed. I had come to inform you about the ceremony but you refused to meet me.'

'Do you think I would have been happy being paraded around like some spoil of war had I known about it earlier?'

'My lord, I'm sorry. The emperor desired it.'

He was as helpless as I was. A prisoner to his emperor's whims. There was no point being angry with him.

'So am I to live here for the next five years like Mahinda?' I asked instead.

'Lord Mahinda has been accorded the highest respect. He has his own mansion and even has his own troop of armed guards.'

'Are they to keep him safe or to keep him in the country?'

'What? No, my lord, you misunderstand. He is free to roam around Chola Nadu as he pleases ...with the emperor's permission, of course.'

'And yet he can't return to his own country?'

'The state of Eelam is very complicated right now. It is best if he resides here.'

'Is that what you're saying about the state of Srivijaya these days?'

He was silent, and then spoke haltingly.

'My lord, I beg you, be patient.'

'Did your emperor ask you to come and tell me this?'

'No, my lord. I come as someone who wishes you well...as a friend.' He uttered the last word slowly, as if he wanted to test if the word applied to our relationship.

'I've seen the strength of your friendship, Bhaskaran. Begone now and do not disturb me again.'

Bhaskaran looked at me sadly and nodded.

'I'll return again tomorrow and again till you agree.'

I spent the rest of the day in my room in a silent rage, wondering what my next course of action would be. Could I escape to my lands? Gangaikonda Cholapuram was too far inland from the port. Besides, who would give me passage back home? The monsoons were upon us, and ships were not plying their trade.

At night, the fans ceased to move again. I closed my eyes and waited for the emperor to leave. He sat for a longer time than usual. When he stood up, the chair he sat on creaked. He seemed to know I was awake, for he spoke.

'You are my guest. This land, and all its pleasures, are open to you.'

I did not react.

When he blew out the lamp, I spoke, 'And what if I desire to return to my own home?'

He was silent for a moment. 'That cannot be. This is your home now.'

I sat up on the bed.

'You told me we would discuss terms for my freedom. That you would treat me as befits a king.'

'You are being treated as a king. You are not imprisoned. The royal exchequer funds your existence. You have the freedom to move around as you wish within the city. If you would like to leave and visit any other part of my empire, it is possible to, with prior permission from me. There are many who are treated far worse. Did you see the *virabhishekam* and the subsequent ceremony? Be grateful that I did not have you put in a cell, dressed in leaves with anklets made from your own crown and made to beg for your life at my feet. Your dignity is intact. Your life and limbs too.'

I was quiet. Had our positions been reversed, he would probably be dead by now. His head would be strung up on a tower as a warning against my enemies.

'I suppose there's nothing left to speak of then,' I said, coldly, and, perhaps, a little ungratefully.

There was a rustling sound and the fans began to move.

The queen would wonder where the next two years of her life went. It seemed as though there was a meeting with some dignitary or the other elderly statesmen – or Rakai as she had learned to call them – every day. Haughty men who would look at the offerings of Kahuripan, smile sympathetically and never respond to any invitation again. There were warlords that peppered Bhumi Java who guarded small tracts of land with their lives and bristled at the slightest disrespect. There were also Rakais who did not want to come into any fold as they felt that their own independence would be at risk it they did. Who knew anything these days? First the *Mahapralaya* of Medang, then the Chola invasion of Srivijaya: no kingdom could bear the weight of time these days. Best to stay neutral, they would tell the Raja of Kahuripan. Who knew which enemy you'd make by allying with someone?

During these days, two things occupied the queen's mind. The first was protecting her kingdom, for it was hers as much as it was Airlangga's now. Walls needed to be built, an army needed to be armed and fed, and the ports needed to be safeguarded. At once she became architect, general and farmer. Burnt brick walls taller than any that Srivijaya had ever seen were commissioned. She personally haggled with the contractors to buy bricks at a discount. She tested blades and arrows from the local arms suppliers and found them wanting. An order was promptly sent to China and, within three months, the army had steel that none in the island kingdoms had seen. Engineers from the Arab land and China were employed and academies were built to raise the next generation from Kahuripan soil. Elephant farms and horse stables came up in every nook of the land. It seemed no man or woman in the city was found wanting of a profession. The queen also persuaded the Raja to build canals across the land. Every inch of land that was not rock or dwelling place for man would yield food, she decreed.

Once this was done, she embarked on her most ambitious project.

A river is like a wild stallion, her father once told her after the Musi River had flooded the kingdom. It needs to be tamed. If you allow its wild nature to take over, this is what will happen, he had said, stretching his arms across the panorama where fields were buried in water and dead bodies floated on its surface.

That day, the Rakai of Kamalagyan came to see the king. He was a worried-looking man, whose face seemed so morose when he met them that the queen had thought he was going to confess to treason. Kamalagyan was in the delta region of the Brantas River that flowed through the Kahuripan kingdom, just like the Musi in Srivijaya lands, and was one of the most fertile areas of the kingdom. Bowing before the king, the Rakai had burst into tears and said he would not be able to pay taxes that year since the local dam had broken and the river had flooded the region. The Raja managed to console him but what was to be done? If he waived the taxes, it would set a dangerous precedent. On the other hand, the region's entire produce was wiped out. There was little left to pay taxes with. He thought, as he always did at these points of moral dilemma, what the other kings would do. Certainly many of them would insist on the payment of taxes and even execute the Rakai if he couldn't deliver. But many of them would take it as an opportunity to show their magnanimity too. Which one would he want to be remembered as?

A wise man has no enemies, reminded his wife.

Hence, engineers were despatched to the region and, after a lengthy analysis, they told the Raja and his wife that a *dahuwan* or a dam, needed to be built upstream. Several small dikes could be built across the river to redirect its flow and spread the bounty of its water across other lands. The trouble, though, was that the surrounding villages did not have enough money to pay for it.

The Raja considered this. Any kind of public building was built by the resources of the people it would directly benefit. That was how kadatuans functioned. But they did not need to, reasoned the queen. Kadatuans were fickle, she reminded him. And people were more loyal to their Daatus and Rakais than their Maharajahs, often with good reason. However, if the king himself could show that he was concerned about the livelihood of his people, then perhaps one day, when he needed them most, they would remember.

And so a dam was built across the mighty Brantas river and, in the Kamalagyan area, a large stone pillar was erected that told the people that Raja Airlangga was looking after them. The people believed him; after all, did he not pay for the construction of the dam from his own coffers?

The rice-heavy lands of Bhumi Java became heavier still and invited more people from all lands to come stay within it. Waterways were built across the rivers and trade benefits were given to all who passed through them. The land grew rich, even as Srideva fought to keep his alive.

Even as the kingdom prospered, the queen would feel a small pinch of sadness. Ever since she had become queen, she had rounded up all the slave traders, and tried to get as much information about Balan from them. He had simply disappeared, they told her. The minister had given him enough wealth to disappear off the coast of Bhumi Java. He may yet return, they said; the world was large, and his money could only last so long. The minister who had bought the princess from him had also died before she had become queen. He had been ambushed by thieves as he was collecting taxes, she'd heard. She had given up any hope of seeing her mother again.

And then Balan arrived.

2

There's little of interest in my story for you over the next two years,
Ganapathy. Just that I developed a fondness for wine.

After your emperor's visit, I had woken up the next morning,
feeling dull and hopeless. Nadan, the rogue who also played the
part of my chief attendant, took pity on me, and procured some
toddy in a cup.

'It will ease the pain,' was all he said as he handed me the cup.

And it did, young Ganapathy, it did. I quaffed it without
thinking, and let its bitterness flow deep into my belly. And
then I asked for some more, and he brought it for me in a dark
green bottle that the Franks used to peddle on these shores.
There was some kind of figure etched on it – a man with a crown
of grapes surrounded by two naked women. I ran my fingers
across their bodies and then poured the wine into the cup and
lifted it to my mouth. A liquid salve for my invisible wound.
Bhaskaran came that day, and I told my attendants not to let him
inside and to tell him that the lord was asleep until I gave them
instructions otherwise.

I told Nadan to procure me a bottle of the stuff everyday. Soon, a bottle began to appear at my bedside every morning without fail. There was no mention of money or costs of procurement. It was well matured toddy, for sure. Nadan told me it had been buried in the ground in bamboo barrels for a very long time. Precisely how long, I never bothered to find out.

Your blank expression tells me you don't understand what I am saying. Most of you city boys, mollycoddled by expensive wine, don't know how it comes into your bottle. They call toddy – *ooral*, in your lands – 'that which drips'. A reference, perhaps, to the way it oozes into pots while being procured. In my lands, as in yours, a toddy collector climbs a coconut tree and strikes the crown of the tree with knives or hooks. They tie their pots underneath to collect the sap that flows from these wounds. The pots, when full, are taken down and stored underground. The sap matures into toddy. The toddy that was procured for me went in smoothly, and if I had enough to eat, I would even avoid the customary headache that came with its consumption.

Ten days later, Nadan asked me if I would like to try something different. Since he was perhaps the only person I trusted even to a small degree, I agreed. The next day, a pot arrived. A round, red clay thing more suited for water than intoxicants. Upon it was written in white chalk – *Munnir*.

Munnir, or the 'three water liquor', contains milk from a coconut, palm fruit and sugarcane, and is matured till it becomes liquid fire, without the unpleasant bitterness of toddy. It is a drink you can have for flavour as well as escape.

Munnir became my weapon of choice for beating despondency. On days it was not available, toddy would make its appearance – an important supporting actor in my star cast against misery, a play in a single act of my life.

Bhaskaran kept coming. Every day. Without fail. Every afternoon, when the sun was at its highest, he would call on me and wait in the portico outside, and every afternoon he would be told I was sleeping, that I would not be able to see him. He could have entered at any time but chose to wait until he was invited. After a month, I called him inside, weary of my solitude, and perhaps a little more drunk than usual that day.

He saw the empty bottles of toddy and said nothing. I opened a new one, and began drinking in front of him. He declined a drink, and sat in front of me, watching me polish off an entire bottle without saying a word. When the bottle was complete, he escorted me to my bed.

Loneliness is an itch. The more you scratch it, the worse it becomes. I had indulged it by letting Bhaskaran back into my life, such as it was. And now I began to desire more company. The wine or toddy made me feel garrulous. I longed for the company of men, and especially the company of women.

And so I began preying on social events. Dance performances, plays, musical concerts, I went to every place I possibly could, any place that would have me. As a guest of the king, there were no restrictions to the places I could visit, as long as they were within the confines of the city. I travelled with two armed guards most of the time for my 'protection', but they were rarely a nuisance and would try staying outside my personal orbit as much as possible.

I gagged every memory of my wife and daughter and kingdom with the help of the wine. Made prisoners out of them, to be locked away in the recesses of my mind never to be set free among my thoughts again. My daughter's toothy smile, the way her eyes lit up when she saw something she liked, her morning music lessons, the sing-song way she memorized her alphabets, the way she wanted me to tell her a story, the way she wanted me to help do her hair in a bun when she was little, the way she would be afraid of thunder and lightning when it rained, the way she curled up when she slept. The glint in my wife's eye when she said something mocking, the way her hair fell over her shoulder in the mornings, the birthmark on her left cheek, the way she would silently disapprove when I cursed in her presence. So many more memories, all of them locked away.

They began to call me *Suvarna*, or the golden one, not just a pun on my origins but also for the fact that my arrival meant gold for them. With the emperor's purse looking after my expenses, my hedonism was unfettered.

Suvarna would wake up, wash his mouth with toddy, perfume himself with sandalwood and wear garlands of fresh jasmine and champaka to hide the smell of grog. He would eat areca and betel nut and wear a freshly laundered dhoti, one of many provided by the emperor, and make his way in the morning to the theatre school where he would see the actors at play. When it came time for lunch, he would spend it at the mansions of some of the other noblemen or women who would host elaborate banquets and show him off to their friends. In the evening, Suvarna would watch a dance performance funded by some nobleman no doubt wanting to make a name for himself as a patron of the arts. And, in the evening, Suvarna would visit one of the younger blades about town and make a nuisance of himself at their homes, or would go visit a courtesan at the Avenue of Pleasures.

Does it sound like paradise to you, young scribe? On the contrary, it was just a distraction from the void that seemed to grow deeper within me. As soon as I awoke, I would try to addle my wits. I would inebriate myself to enter another *loka* between this and the next one – without the worries of this one and without the fear of infinity of the next. I would remain in this state all day until I stumbled back home and fell asleep. Nadan was complicit in my plans. Bhaskaran would reproach me and soon I began avoiding his sanctimonious company again. This time, however, instead of being locked inside my home, I used the entire city of Gangaikonda Cholapuram as my refuge.

Somewhere in the mist that had I willed over my senses, I met Paravai.

The dancer? Yes, she was a dancer. A great one, courted by nearly every prince or nobleman from this side of the Vindhyas to the north; she of the waist that could fit in the palm of one's hand and collarbones that smiled over her breasts. Would you like to hear of her breasts, cheeky boy? I have no doubt you would.

I met Paravai at a private *sadir* dance performance at some noble's house. Perhaps it was Arulvarman, the minister of finance, who was coveting a position in the external affairs ministry and felt it was best to be seen with a foreign king wherever possible. I spent a lot of time with him in those days and was promptly forgotten once his lobbying proved successful with the emperor. But that happened later, and has little bearing on the course of my story, save for now. A stage had been erected in Arulvarman's home for Paravai's performance. You may remember that at the time she had come to the end of her dancing career and was starting a school of dance for girls. The performance at Arulvarman's home was a goodbye of sorts at his request.

The home was lit like the city during Diwali. There were lamps all over the main hall where she would perform. The pillars of the house were entwined with lotus flowers, and marigolds lined the corners of the room. Men came and sprinkled rose water every few minutes and incense was burned all around the stage, further adding to the heady mix of fragrances.

A thin man sat in front of a fat *mridangam* and a fat man held a thin *nadaswaram* in his hand. Both of them wore expensive silk dhotis and vests. A far cry from many other performances I had been to, where the accompanists of dancers were the worst paid of the performers and had to wear threadbare dhotis.

I entered the hall with Bhaskaran, who was also invited. He had recently been chosen as a council member on the Commissariat and was overseeing grain deployment across Chola Nadu. Never a man to toot his own trumpet, Bhaskaran had not told me the news himself. I had heard about it at one of the lunches I had attended at the home of one of the outgoing council members. Bhaskaran was rising up the ranks rapidly on his own merit. I was happy for him. His stupidity of the past had been forgiven.

Paravai and an apprentice of hers began their performance. She was enacting a story from the lives of the Nayanmars, the sixty-three saints of the Lord Shiva. The story she told was of Siruthondar. You know the story. Paranjothi, a general of the Pallava king Narasimhavarman, becomes a monk after defeating the Chalukya king Pulakeshin and dedicates himself to the glory of Lord Shiva. One day, the Lord visits his house in the disguise of a holy man. Siruthondar and his wife are devout and make it a point to feed holy men. The holy man comes to their home and says that he desires the flesh of a five-year-old child who is readily given up by his parents. Siruthondar and his wife have a child of the same age; without hesitating, they kill him and serve the meat to the holy man, who restores the child after seeing their devotion.

Some years ago, a Jewish merchant who was trading with the Arabs told me a similar tale from the Jewish faith. One of the great holy men of the Jews, Abraham, too, was commanded by God to kill his son Isaac and was prevented from doing so through divine intervention. The Gods of every faith test the courage of their devotees by threatening the ones they love.

But my thoughts were not on theology at that moment. Paravai played both the roles of Siruthondar and the holy man. When she straightened her back and puffed her chest as Siruthondar, she seemed twice the size of any man. When she strode across the ground, she looked like a general in control of his terrain. When she bent her back and stood on the balls of her feet and wrinkled her face, I honestly thought she had become the holy man. And, finally, when she ended the performance as Nataraja, the lord of the dance, with one leg in the air and the hands initially a blur till they stilled themselves, I thought the Lord himself had arrived.

'Not one of her better ones,' grumbled Bhaskaran as the music winded down, and the audience started cheering. I ignored him, my eyes seeking the dancer as she made her way to the centre of the stage and bowed for the audience.

I had been with women since I had arrived in an attempt to imprison the memory of my wife in the recesses of my mind. But I had never wanted to be with one as much as Paravai. I intruded into a conversation between her and Arulvarman and introduced myself.

'Your performance was truly magnificent,' I blustered.

She regarded me with a smile and continued her conversation with Arulvarman.

'Could I have a word with you when you're done?' I interrupted again.

'Most certainly,' she said politely and turned back to Arulvarman.

She came to me when she was done. I was ready.

'They say you can hear God's heartbeats in a dancer's footsteps. I can safely say that is true tonight.'

She laughed – a warm, throaty sound that flooded through my body.

'They say the words of kings are hollow. Good for the sound they make, but little else.' Her eyebrows arched, challenging me.

'I'm no king here, my lady. You can trust that these words are not empty of meaning. They are a bridge. Strong at every link.'

'A bridge to what?'

'To the citadel of your desire,' I said, rather shamelessly.

She smiled at me. 'There are many who lay siege to the same, my lord. Some are actual kings. Others use armies of words. You had best give up now.'

Her mocking tone spurred me on further. 'I don't give up. I merely get captured.'

She burst out laughing, and I smiled at her.

'Most people use words as shields to protect themselves. You use yours as a sword. Even at the risk of damage.'

'It is better to be wounded in the quest for love than to spend your days hiding behind a wall of what-ifs.'

'I'm afraid there is a lot of wounding in store for you.'

'It is a cause I will gladly martyr myself to.'

We smiled at each other and did not resume conversation all evening.

I pursued her all over the city after that. I got myself invited to each and every one of her dance performances – for it was not just Arulvarman who wanted to see her perform one final time – just to get the chance to meet her. Soon, our meetings grew from just the performances to rendezvous at gardens. We began taking picnics at nearby orchards in the city and soon were attending performances together.

Paravai's was an interesting story. She was not a *devadasi*, or a servant of the Gods. She had not committed her life to the temple and the furtherance of the arts from there. She belonged to the Parathaiyar caste, the dancer community, as you know. She had earned enough from her performances to not worry about money for the rest of her life and lived alone in a mansion with a loyal old manservant and a coterie of maids. There were at least fourteen villages across the country to her name that paid her an annual income. She also supported temples and dance academies across the state.

Tamil society spoke about us in uncomplimentary terms. She, a dancer, entertaining a foreign, even barbarian king. A perfect recipe for scandal. Bhaskaran would come and tell me the lascivious gossip about us. She was using me to access the vast riches of Srivijaya. I was using her for sport. They couldn't have been further from the truth. There were no vast riches of Srivijaya; in fact, she would regularly buy me clothes or beautiful objects to keep in my mansion. As for using her for sport, I would only say this to you, young scribe, that the sentiment was mutual.

There is a part of me that, in keeping with my Buddhist traditions, indulges prudery. So I will skip the details, bounce lightly upon its surface at intervals, like a stone thrown upon water. It was perhaps the happiest time of my sad existence in Chola Nadu. Festivals every day, dance, music, drama, and Paravai occupying the centrepiece of my life.

Then, one day, Indravarman arrived, and everything changed.

'I always knew you would be lucky for me,' said Balan, looking at her like a long-lost daughter.

He had arrived at the royal palace and asked to see her. The guards had laughed at him and were about to throw him off the premises when he told them he knew where her mother was. The king and queen were busy, and appointments for their time needed to be made months in advance. Yet, Balan was brought to the court almost immediately and presented to the queen.

'Do you now believe I was a princess?' she asked coldly.

'Let bygones be bygones, princess. As someone once told me: A wise woman has no enemies.'

He prostrated himself before her.

'Stand up. Tell me where my mother is, and all will be forgiven.'

He stood up and dusted himself off. 'Your mother is safe. I kept her with me after you were sold. I did not have much to offer her, but I protected her and gave her food. I always knew you would come back for her. We went away to Suvarnadwipa and started a farm. After your sale, I lost all interest in the slave business.'

'Bring her to me then, and you will be rewarded for your service,' said the queen, trying to hold back the tremble in her voice.

The next day, he came again, this time accompanied by the former queen. She had aged many years in the past two. Lines criss-crossed her face. Her hair was greying, but her eyes were still defiant. She refused to bow to the royalty of Kahuripan while entering the court, but the entire court bowed to her when their queen did so.

The two queens embraced and wept in front of the court. The elder queen was announced as the queen mother; she would live with the couple in the palace, it was decreed.

After the court retired, the queen of Kahuripan summoned Balan for a private audience. 'Why did you not sell her? The truth this time.'

'No one wanted her. She was old and did not know how to cook or clean. And she kept saying she was queen. After a while even I started believing it.'

'She says you treated her with dignity.'

'I did a little searching of my own, and found out what she was saying could be true. I kept her, hoping that someone would pay a good ransom to have her back. Luckily, it was you.'

She nodded. 'Now what?'

'I'm setting up a business in the area of goods transport.'

'I see.'

'Mildly illegal goods transport.'

'How mildly?'

'Oh, it comes down to definition. Some people would call me a pirate. I would prefer to be a privateer. I have men and ships. All I desire is that the state of Kahuripan looks the other way when I plunder ships.'

'You will plunder my ships in my waters?' she asked incredulously.

'Not at all, my queen! Chinese, Tamils and Arabs.'

She would think about it, she said.

His words came back to her when the Srivijaya merchant arrived at Kahuripan.

3

Paravai had called me for a musical performance at her home. A singing minstrel had entered the city and was in great demand among the nobility. Paravai had paid him a hefty sum to have him perform to a private audience at her house that evening. There were no guests. There rarely were. Despite her many achievements, Paravai was somewhat of an outcaste in Tamil society, hovering between acceptable and non-acceptable. She could endow temples and land and patronize artists, but her own presence in society was restricted; a strange hypocrisy, but not unheard of in a world where attractive single women were perceived to be more of a threat to the institution of family than a philandering man.

'I have a surprise for you,' she said. She led me inside one of the inner corridors of the mansion to the storage room, where grain was packed in jute gunny sacks. She smiled mysteriously at me, and said that she would return for me once the minstrel had finished his piece.

I walked inside, curious about the surprise in store for me. The last time she had surprised me with a jade elephant that came up to my waist and was so heavy it needed to be lifted on a trolley to be hauled around. I walked inside the storage room towards a flickering torch at the far corner of the room.

A man stood dressed in white flowing robes and a similar white turban. He was scraping some dung from his heels on the stone tiles then examining the sole of his foot up to see if the dirt had been removed. He tilted his face towards me at the sound of my footsteps and I saw his face in the yellow light.

He was the first Srivijayan I had seen since I arrived.

I was nearly moved to tears. After being around you Tamils for so long, his features looked almost otherworldly to me. I wanted to stand there and gaze at him for the rest of the day. His face coloured brown by the sun, devoid of hair, and his eyes, narrower than the Tamils, and more beautiful than they could ever countenance. He noticed me looking at him, and bowed low. It took me a moment to remember that I had to give him the command to rise. I had not done it in so long.

'My lord, I come from Suvarnadwipa,' he said, by way of greeting.

I wanted to take him in my arms and not let him go. Instead, I asked, 'How are my people?'

It came out more like an apology than a king inquiring about his subjects. I had not spoken like a king for so long; the natural sense of entitlement, of ownership, did not come easy.

'They're still coming to terms with the loss of their king. Srideva has assumed the throne and is now Maharajah. He has provided great concessions to the Thousand Directions Guild. Trade has resumed between the two nations.'

I felt a strange anger. I find it hard to describe even now. The anger was directed at Srideva for countering my trade decisions and capitulating to the Cholas. Yet, it was disembodied anger.

I was no longer in my kingdom, and I hadn't felt that it was my kingdom for a very long time. I pined for the land and the people, but the idea that I was king had been stripped away from me since I had arrived.

'Our traders are not very happy,' he said, a little sourly.

I nodded. 'He is stupider than I thought. Suvarnadwipa is a gateway through which the Chinese and Tamils must pass. They can afford to pay their way through.'

'He blames you for the war and tells the people he would not have to take such drastic measures had you been reasonable in your dealings. The Chola navy was stationed there for nearly two years, but left just recently. I came in bearing spices and camphor, which we sold at a loss on Chola shores. But the main purpose of my visit has been fulfilled. It is good to see you alive, my lord.'

'It is good to know that I am remembered.'

There was a pause.

'Apologies my lord, for not introducing myself. My name is Indravarman. I am a trader in camphor primarily, but wood and spices on occasion. My ships normally ply to China.'

'I have never seen you in my court before.' Mistrust was second nature to me as a king, and it kicked in after days of being dormant. Was this some kind of Chola ploy?

'I'm one of the thousands of smaller traders, my lord. Though I have every desire to grace your court, today I am merely an emissary. A representative of a group of merchants that believes your return would be more beneficial to the kingdom. And our cause,' he said smoothly.

'I see.' My heart was thumping louder than a war drum.

'There are risks, my lord. Would you be up to taking them?'

'What kind of king would I be if I didn't?'

Indravarman smiled with relief and quickly explained the plan to me. His group of traders had paid a fleet of pirates to attack the port of Puhar. The timing of the attack would be communicated to me. A raiding party would enter the dock and fight their way to a designated house where I would be staying. They would bundle me back to my ship and take me home. Indravarman was returning to Puhar that evening. He would tell his partners of my agreement and send word back to me. I had only one thing to arrange, but it was a crucial part of the plan: permission from Rajendra to visit Puhar.

Paravai joined us as soon as our conversation was completed and led me back inside to listen to the rest of music. I maintained a calm exterior, but was doing somersaults in my head. How was she involved in all this?

The concert ended, after what seemed to be a long while. The minstrel sang a cheery piece about the summer and how the sun was happiest during those months. The song, however, did nothing to help my pensive mood. The minstrel sang for an hour and was showered with gold coins and enough cloth to cover his body for the rest of his life. After he finished, we ate dinner together, and once the minstrel left, Paravai chatted with some of her maids for a little while before dismissing them.

When we were finally alone in her room, I brought up the subject.

'What do you know about Srivijaya?'

She smiled at me. 'I know little. Indravarman paid a reasonably good sum of money for an opportunity to meet you.'

'You know it could have been risky for you. And for him. I haven't seen another person from my land, much less heard news from the outside. The emperor is keeping an eye on me. All my freedoms are afforded to me, but curated by him. I suspect he has even run the rule over you and deemed you worthy of my company.'

She laughed, a generous scattering of mirth that spread across the room. 'The emperor has more to worry about than the private life of an old courtesan. I suspect he knows of our relationship, but I doubt he is bothered by it. Like you said, I am a worthy companion for you. Enough of a distraction, but not much beyond that.'

I stood silent, not knowing what to believe. Was she a spy for the kingdom? Was this a trap to make me go to Puhar, and have me assassinated there? Why would Rajendra need to go through such elaborate lengths?

She seemed to sense my discomfort and said reassuringly, 'A single woman who cannot earn for herself and does not wish to rely on patrons has few sources of income. I welcome all with open hands. When Indravarman's servant came and requested an audience with you, I agreed only because he had two large chests of gold with the promise of more.'

The thought made me more uncomfortable. She sounded like the pirates Indravarman was going to hire. I was nothing more than her chattel, her keep. To be disposed of when things got dirty, I thought bitterly. Again, she read my discomfort correctly.

'Come now, I would never do anything to get you killed. You're too dear to me. I don't know what you discussed and I do not want to know either,' was all she said, and passed on to other topics of conversation.

A month passed like a century.

I did not speak to Paravai about it anymore. We maintained the outer façade of the relationship, but everything had changed. At least for me it had, so much so that she confronted me one day.

'You don't trust me, do you? You think I'm a spy for the emperor. A fantasy of little boys who love listening to stories.'

I did my best to maintain a stoic expression.

'I can see right through you. Hear your thoughts. There is nothing you can hide from me,' she said, angrily.

I nodded at her unconvincingly.

'What do I have to do to convince you I'm on your side, Sangrama?' She seemed exasperated that she had to ask the question.

I took her in my arms and kissed her forehead. 'I believe you. It's just that all of this is happening very quickly. I just need some time to mull over everything,' I said, clumsily.

'Are you leaving me?

'What?'

'Is that what the merchant and you spoke about?'

'Why would you think that?'

'A journey of a thousand miles begins with a single step. A Chinese philosopher once said that, though I think his intended meaning was more inspirational. I believe it can refer to the state of relationships too. Before a man leaves a woman forever, he is always a little distant at first.'

'Your imagination is working overtime like the labourers in this city. Your mind is filled with dust.' I said, trying desperately to lighten the moment.

I was barely exaggerating. The city had grown by unimaginable proportions in a very short amount of time. More mansions, taller and taller, had sprung up all over it – two storeys, three, and even five-storeyed buildings had come up in orderly blocks around the city. The streets were choked with building materials as usual, but instead of the great blocks of granite that were used to build the first buildings of the city, smaller slabs of stones and teak were being heaved through it. The unfortunate consequence of this was a pall of dust had descended over certain quarters where construction work was heavy. A host of citizens fell ill everyday with allergies, crowding the only *vaidyasalai* the city had. Bhaskaran had been given charge of locating land for a second one.

She smiled sadly. 'I know it sounded callous of me to say that the only reason I let Indravarman meet you was that he had two chests of gold. The truth is that I panicked when you asked me about the Srivijaya kingdom and Indravarman. I wanted to convince you this was not a conspiracy to have you murdered. Believe me, I would not have let you meet him if there was a threat to your life. I orchestrated the meeting at my house to ensure your safety. My men were watching you all the time.'

I did not know if she was telling the truth. But I smiled at her and took her in my arms.

'I believe you. I'm sorry I ever doubted you.'

A few days later, I was walking back through the city from her place. Two bodyguards were walking behind me. We were near the farmer's marketplace and were trying to navigate through a sea of people who were elbowing each other, trying to get the freshest vegetables for their home. In the rush, my bodyguards and I got separated. A beggar suddenly leaped at my feet. I was about to push him away when he looked up at me. His face was covered in a shabby hood, but I could make out that he was from my land.

'My lord, sorry for this intrusion. I have little time. The pirate attack will happen on the twenty-third of Aadimaasam. Tell Lady Paravai where you will be staying in Puhar so that Indravarman can arrange for your pickup.'

He began grovelling at my feet, as if he had committed a grave crime and wanted forgiveness. I kicked him away for good effect before my bodyguards arrived on the scene.

The next morning, I went to Bhaskaran's house at dawn and asked to meet the emperor. 'He's a very busy man. Even I don't see him these days, despite carrying out construction of the *vaidyasalai*. All my bills are pending and I've started paying from my pocket,' Bhaskaran said, wretchedly.

'I'm sure there is a way. Please ask him. I grow tired of this place. All I want is some time in Puhar.'

I sounded desperate. His eyes softened and he said he would try. That afternoon, I was summoned to the palace. I hadn't visited the palace complex since my earlier humiliation. It was the first time I was entering its great hall. I was ushered in past a number of eager petitioners who stood outside on the vast porch and made to sit on a couch until my turn came. After a little while, the large wooden doorways to the palace hall creaked open, and a man announced my name inside.

I walked inside the hall and looked around. There were guards stationed near each pillar and archers on the gallery on the first floor. I walked to the centre of the hall and was asked to stop and speak from there. I looked at the emperor and bowed. He drummed his fingers impatiently on the armrest of his throne and looked around. The sabha was silent.

A man began talking, stating my name and case. Rajendra heard him patiently. There was no recognition in his eyes. I had never existed for him. 'Maharajah Sangrama Vijayatunggavarman of Srivijaya wishes to go to Puhar? Are the pleasures of my city not enough to interest you?' the mountain voice rumbled.

The court burst out laughing in unison. A little excessively perhaps, as is the nature of sycophantic courts. Mine used to do the same.

'I yearn for the sea breeze, your majesty, having been weaned on it since I was a child. I humbly request an opportunity to reinvigorate myself there.'

He scratched his chin. 'What do my ministers advise?'

Nearly all of them shook their heads and declined.

He scratched his chin again. 'My ministers, all of whom have offered me valuable counsel over the years, do not think you should be allowed to go.'

As he fell silent, I knew that it was time for some quick thinking on my part. 'They say when the Yavana King Alexander defeated Porus in the battle of the Indus, he had Porus brought to his court in chains. He asked Porus if there was anything he desired, as a final request. All Porus replied was, "Treat me as befits a king." The great and benevolent king was pleased with the answer and gave him back his kingdom. Now, I'm no Porus, my lord. But I request you to be as Alexander.' I hoped that he remembered the story I had told him.

He looked at me, puzzled, and then began to laugh. The room echoed with his harsh laughter. He looked at his ministers. 'Does my court consider me Alexander?'

The ministers realized it was banter, and pleaded that he was greater than Alexander ever was.

'Very well then. There are other matters to attend to. I will overrule my ministers this time only to fulfil my duty to my guest. You may go to Puhar. But under our watch. A troop of men shall accompany you, and bring you back when you have had your fill of sea air, which should not take more than a month. You will live in one of the royal palaces by the ocean. Now begone, young Porus.'

There was no uproar or murmur of discontent. The court quickly moved on to other matters.

I went to Paravai's house after that and told her I was leaving for Puhar the next morning and would be staying at the royal guesthouse in the Yavana quarters. She asked me when I would return and I replied, within a month. She said nothing. We embraced and she bid me farewell without any mention of meeting me when I returned. This was the end. Even she knew it.

I returned to my mansion and began putting together some clothes in a large trunk. I told my servants to pack enough clothes, along with Munnir, and retired to bed early.

The emperor visited me that might, sitting at the foot of my bed, as he hadn't for two years.

'So, you talk only when you need a favour?' he asked quietly.

I was silent.

'Alexander and Porus. A good story, though a little dry for my liking. I prefer the one you had told me about your ancestor. Alexander has been sung to death by the bards.'

He cleared his throat. 'I will miss these little stories. Return soon, Maharajah.' With that, he blew out his lamp and left the room.

'My name is Indravarman. I represent a faction of merchants from Srivijaya,' he said. 'I have news that would be of interest to you, my queen. It is regarding your father.'

The queen heard his story without interruption. Her father had been captured by the Cholas and taken back to the land of the Tamils. A kingdom conspiring against the Cholas – called the Chalukyas – had brought the information to Indravarman. They would be interested in any plot that would weaken Chola sovereignty and would be happy to help bring the monarch back to his lands if a preferential trade agreement could be worked out. The merchants of Srivijaya were unhappy with Srideva. They were also unhappy with the fact that he had given Tamil traders better trade privileges following the Chola invasion.

'If Maharajah Sangrama Vijayatunggavarman ever was to come back, he would receive our support,' Indravarman said.

He had smiled after that, and looked at her intently. 'We will be able to finance an attempt to bring him back to his lands. A coup, however, is an entirely different proposition for beleaguered merchants without armies. If an army could be arranged to attack the Srivijaya kingdom by the time he lands on these shores, it would help our cause greatly.'

The queen nodded grimly. 'It will be arranged.'

'One more thing,' said the merchant. 'Srideva has cracked down on all kinds of piracy. It has been hard for us to find able men who will be willing to conduct an audacious raid into Chola territory. Perhaps someone from Kahuripan can help with this? Money is no object, of course.'

'I know just the man,' said the queen.

4

I set off for Puhar the next day, accompanied by a troop of light cavalry – ten soldiers led by a man called Beemasenan who did not speak much. I sensed he was annoyed about having to babysit a potentate and would rather have been carving up Chalukyas at the front. The journey passed in sullen silence.

We reached Puhar after three days where I was taken to a guesthouse in the Eastern City that overlooked the ocean and an armed guard was placed around me. I would wander out into the Yavana quarters where traders of all lands hawked their wares. I did not see any Srivijayans, though. I took this as a sign. Perhaps they had been told to keep away before the pirates attacked. I stayed at home, and took the time to exercise and loosen my muscles. There would probably be running and fighting involved.

The day of the rescue finally arrived.

I woke up that morning with a fluttering in the pit of my stomach. For the first time in nearly two years, I did not have my toddy. Instead, I had a bath and went straight back to bed, feigning illness. I had to be well awake for the night. Around late evening, when I awoke and took my customary stroll down the

Yavana quarters, I noticed a great clamour taking place. I asked my guards to ask a vendor what was the matter.

'It's only pirates making a raid. Don't worry, my lord. The coastal defences will keep us secure.'

I nodded.

'Where are the pirates from?' I asked innocently.

'No one has any idea. Maybe from Eelam or from Kalingga. These are the only kingdoms that are close enough.'

I looked around. Traders were lifting their goods and removing them from the port area by horse or elephant or even hand. 'No one wants to take a risk,' my guard informed.

I nodded and we returned to the mansion. The sky went dark and fires began to get lit at the port. I looked towards the lighthouse where the fire had been extinguished, perhaps to not draw the pirates in. I sat on the bed, waiting for something to happen.

And then it did.

A loud crash was heard outside. I leapt up and ran towards the window of my bedroom. In the horizon, I could see three ships on fire followed by several more speeding towards the port, lit by torches on their stern and in their back. Like fireflies in the night. Trumpets began sounding and the beat of war drums filled the sky.

The war ships cut through to the dock that was surprisingly poorly defended. A few ships had sailed out to repel the attackers but had been brushed aside. The ships arrived at the dock with little resistance. I went back to my bed and waited.

My bodyguards – all ten of them including Beemasenan – rushed into my room. Beemasenan then spoke to me for the first time. 'It appears the coast guard has not been able to deal with the pirates. I'm stationing two guards here to protect you. The rest of us will be outside until the situation has been resolved.'

I nodded as I sat and looked at the faces of the two guards; they looked back at me impassively. The sound of war – the breaking of wood, the cries of men, and the sound of metal clashing – started getting louder. I stood up and walked over to the window. In the distance, a group of pirates rushed outside the dock and fanned out. A few armed Tamils were easily hacked down.

Then I heard the sound of thumps coming from below. The guards took their swords out from their sheaths and looked uncomfortably at me as they stood outside the door, waiting for an attack. The thumps were getting louder. All of a sudden, the door was kicked open and four men covered in blood ran inside and attacked the guards, who put up a brave fight. One of them wounded a pirate but was cut open by two of them. The other one took out one pirate with a heavy blow to the head. He swivelled around to kill the other pirate assaulting him, but was run through with a sword.

Panting heavily, one of the pirates came up to me and spoke in Malay; he was one of my people – an ugly man with a bald head, a grey beard and a mouth that had only four of his front teeth.

'Your lord highness, the ships await.'

I nodded, and we charged down the stairs and outside to the street where I saw Beemasenan's body lying with a spear stuck in his torso. As we passed him, I saw his eyes open, wide with anger and shock. We ran up to the docks that were quite close and met with another group of pirates who were waiting to take us back.

An arrow flew from above and sunk into the neck of one of the pirates. Another one caught a second one in the forehead. The pirates put up their shields and we began retreating to the docking area.

A voice rang out into the night. 'Surrender now, and you can expect clemency. The Imperial Chola Army does not offer it frequently to pirates.'

I heard the pirates laugh harshly under the shields. I could smell their salty sweat and the garlic on their breath.

'Does he speak Chinese? I didn't understand a word of what he said.'

'I repeat!' said the voice once again. 'No leniency or forbearance shall be offered if you do not forsake your arms.'

'Does he want to use all the big words he knows?' cackled the voice from behind me.

'Posh boy playing at soldier,' growled another.

Arrows thudded into our midst. One of the pirates slumped on me with a groan. His body was taken out of our group that then huddled closer together. A voice spoke from behind me – it was the bald man from before, who seemed to be the leader of this band of pirates.

'Fear not, my lord. You're getting on that ship. I've promised the queen. All together now!'

I had no time to reflect on which 'queen' he was referring to. We rose as one as the arrows fell among us, killing the pirates. Even as our group thinned, we rushed into a warehouse with deer-eye windows, the last before the docking area began.

The voice sounded from above.

'You are surrounded.' And then with a hint of urgency, 'Please give up.'

'Well, I understood that,' said a pirate, cackling again.

Three Chola soldiers charged into our midst. There was a brief sword fight, and they fell, but took a pirate with them.

The ugly pirate leader turned me around to face him.

'My lord, we have to make a dash for ships.'

I looked in the direction in which he was pointing. A ship was trading arrows with the forces on the ground while three more were behind it.

'Right, one, two... go now!'

The pirates ran out of the warehouse shouting and hollering and waving their swords around. I heard the arrows scythe through the air and hit the pirates running by my side. An arrow caught the ugly bald man through his skull, and I saw him collapse. Miraculously, I was unhurt. I charged towards the ship, running faster than I ever had in my life. An arrow clipped the ground next to me. I weaved to one side and then the other and prepared to leap on to the wooden bridge that extended from the dock to the ship. I saw a pirate on the ship beckoning me towards him as his comrades fired arrows into the army on the dock.

A whooshing sound came from above and crashed into the ship. Wooden splinters hit me in the face and I fell down. I looked up dazed, and saw that a huge stone blazing with fire had been flung into the ship. Two more stones flew through the air; one hit the ship, and the other fell into the water. I looked at the ship. There was a large hole on its deck and one of its masts had been cut down. It was only a matter of minutes before it sank.

I sat there, not knowing what to do. The ship had floated away from the dock and was keeling over to its side. A fiery stone flew overhead and smashed through the deck, setting fire to the ship. I saw the remaining two ships a short distance away. They were beginning to head back out into the ocean. If I jumped into the water and swam, and if they did not let their sails loose to catch the wind, I could still make it. Three arrows hit the ground next to me, and brought the life back into my limbs. I rolled away and found refuge behind some large wooden crates. Behind me was the ocean, and in front were the Cholas. To both my sides, left and right, were warehouses. The ships began moving away from the docks even as two stones fell howling into the ocean behind them like wild dogs stalking prey.

I had to make a choice now. I could risk my life trying to reach the Srivijaya ships, or, if I stayed there, risk being captured by Chola troops and probably executed for attempting to escape.

As the arrows briefly stopped, I ran back to the warehouse I had left. From there I took another glance at the ships that were speeding away from fear of being catapulted with stones. Four ships from the Chola coast guard immediately gave pursuit.

My great escape had failed.

I hid in the warehouse for a few minutes trying to collect my thoughts. I had to get back to my house somehow. I looked around, trying to find something that could aid my escape. There was nothing in the warehouse except for two large crates placed next to each other in its centre. I went up to one of them, and pushed open the lid. It was empty.

Should I hide there? But then if someone discovered me in the morning, I would have to put my skills of storytelling to good use.

It was then that I saw the prone bodies of the Chola soldiers. My way out presented itself.

I dressed myself in their bloodstained clothes. Well, in the least bloodstained clothes I could find. I tore a piece of bloodied cloth and wrapped it across my face till only my eyes were visible. No one would question a wounded man or ask him to take off his bandage. I walked slowly out of the warehouse without being recognized, just as Chola troops flooded in. I proceeded calmly down the docks towards the mansion. When I finally reached home, I headed for the bathing area and washed my face with a pot of water. Taking off the clothes, I bundled them up and threw them away into the street. Then I sat on my bed and waited for someone to come.

They came an hour later. I told them the truth.

BOOK III

1

Well, most of the truth anyway. I told them that pirates had come to kidnap me and my bodyguards had fought to defend me and died in the attempt. I had hidden under the bed until they had left. The Cholas were not convinced. Why had the pirates left without taking *anything*? they asked me. I shrugged and replied that maybe there wasn't anything of worth to take – a rather mean allusion coming from a foreign king. They desperately tried to convince me that the bronzes in my room were very expensive. However, I simply told them that they did not appear so, infuriating those patriots further.

And so I returned to Gangaikonda Cholapuram and fell into despondence again. I shaved off the hair on my head and refused to see anyone. Most significantly, I stopped drinking toddy and Munnir, much to the anguish of Nadan, who suddenly lost his milch cow. Paravai came enquiring about me a few times, as did Bhaskaran, but I refused to see either of them.

Then, one night, Rajendra visited me.

'How was the ocean?' he asked.

'Salty.'

He guffawed. 'I heard there was some trouble. Pirates?'

'I suffered not a scratch, your highness. Your soldiers performed their duty commendably, at a terrible cost.'

'Indeed.'

'Perhaps it is time to leave for my home now. The ocean reminded me of the magnitude of my loss.'

'It is not yet time.'

'My people are without their king. They need someone to guide them.'

'The people are not sheep. They will find their way. Indeed, they already have. Your Daatu, Srideva, has taken command in your absence. He has requested aid from us to counter the kingdom of Kahuripan that has already made inroads into your kingdom, I am told.'

'That is truly tragic news. Srideva is incompetent. Who is the Lord of Kahuripan, who torments him so?' I said, a little buoyed by his misfortune.

'A man they call Airlangga. A recent upstart. Our details are scant as of now, but I will tell you the rest of his story as and when I learn of it.'

'So I am to be your prisoner for perpetuity here?'

'Perpetuity is too long a term.'

'What purpose do you have in keeping me here?'

'Friendship. You are my guest,' he replied, a little coldly, almost as though he was hurt that I wanted to leave.

'Some friendship, this. I am being kept against my will. You may as well just kill me and get it over with.'

He leaned closer to the light until I could see his face. His craggy features stared out angrily at me.

'I offer you my friendship. It is more than most conquering kings do. I leave you free to move around in my kingdom, and even a chance to visit Puhar.'

'You've put me in a prison. It's a golden cage, but a cage nevertheless. Better to die hungry in a dirty squalid one than live a prolonged, meaningless life.'

Something seemed to dawn on him. His features softened. He stood up and blew out the lamp.

'If you do not want my friendship, you need not take it. It is all I have to offer you right now. There is a *prasasti* being carved into the temple walls in my honour tomorrow evening. I would like you to be there as my friend.'

With that he receded into the darkness.

It was then that I realized I had only two options in front of me. The first – in which I killed myself – would end my suffering. A sword, a spear or even a rusty tool wouldn't be hard to find. The second option – staying in this golden prison – would prolong it indefinitely. But I would stay, live and die as a king. Without bending to Rajendra. With as much grace and dignity as I could muster within these circumstances. I would act with all the wisdom and strength of a Srivijaya Maharajah who could count the great Dapunta Hyang Sri Jayanasa among his ancestors. I would consider the Chola emperor as my peer, and not my better, and forgive him with the magnanimity of my people even if he tried to humiliate me.

This time, Porus would act like a king regardless of how Alexander treated him. It sounds simplistic, but the most profound awakenings often are.

Needless to say, I wouldn't be talking to you had I not chosen the second option.

The next day, I dressed in the finest silk garments that had been provided to me. I sprinkled rose water on my body, wore a garland of fragrant jasmines and went to the temple. Its tall *gopuram* loomed imposingly against the sky, like a beacon towards which people were drawn. The royal guards at the temple, perhaps recognizing me, cleared my path to the emperor who looked a little surprised to see me.

I went up to him and whispered in his ear, 'I will treat you as befits a friend.'

He smiled and nodded at me in acknowledgment. And that was it.

Four years passed.

You seem annoyed. Four years of my life, just brushed away like that? Perhaps, but dawn approaches, and with it my execution. I must finish telling you this last and tragic episode of my life, so that you can record it for posterity.

I feel for you, young Ganapathy, you came here for a simple task – to record two lines for your emperor – and found a sack of stories instead. Nevertheless, this is my story. The only thing I own. When I give it up to you, it will become yours. You may do with it as you please. I doubt if it will be very complimentary, but the reason I tell you this story is so that it will, hopefully, be less uncomplimentary.

Let's march four years on then. We still have much ground to cover.

I opened up to both Bhaskaran and Paravai again. I needed the warmth of friendship in my life, and so I turned to them, like a sunflower turns towards the sun. Bhaskaran had risen sharply to become a minister in Rajendra's court. Paravai, well, she never mentioned my departure, and we carried on as before, without commitment but with great pleasure.

I did not suppress the memories of my wife and daughter anymore. I let them wound my mind instead, and found that the pain did not become less intense, but it did become more bearable as the days went on. Instead of stifling it with alcohol, I let it speak to me, and its voice, though clear, became less loud as time went by.

I would meet the emperor at official functions, and occasionally when he wanted to talk to someone at night. Now, however, instead of coming unannounced, he would tell me the morning before he would come. He even started visiting the mansion during the afternoon, though he would be accompanied by his own courtiers and noblemen. It was more to show that I was in the emperor's favour than anything else, I suppose. He would only talk about himself when we were alone at night.

Most of his conversations would be about his legacy – Virajendra, Rajendradeva, Rajadhiraja. The names would circle around like hawks over a carcass in his mind, picking at it whenever he got some time off from the affairs of state, which were many. As you probably remember, Ganapathy, those were lean years. The Cauvery had been stretched to its limit, and there was drought in some areas. There was even talk of famine – so much so that the Chalukyas, who had assembled an army, thought it more prudent to not march into Chola territories till there was food available. They did not want to contend with a rioting population, I heard.

Rajendra was growing old. He was well into his seventh decade by now, from what I had heard. Somewhere over the past year, he gave up dying his hair, letting it take its natural course. He began favouring a walking stick privately, though he would never be seen in public with it. More of the kingdom's affairs passed onto his three sons, who were building allies within the kingdom on their own. The soldiers and generals who had fought the Chalukya wars preferred Rajadhiraja; those who had fought in Eelam and Srivijaya preferred Virajendra; and the bureaucrats wanted Rajendradeva on the throne.

The northern part of the empire was under Rajadhiraja's hold, the southern part under Virajendra's and the central part and the major urban cities like Gangaikonda Cholapuram, Thanjavur and Puhar were under Rajendradeva's grip.

The past was with Rajadhiraja, the present with Rajendradeva and the future with Virajendra.

Each of them had assembled their own coterie of ministers, and even the emperor's most loyal ministers were beginning to drift away from him and towards one of the three. I suppose the emperor knew his time was coming to an end, though we never spoke of mortality those days. He would, however, debate the various strengths of his sons, though mostly to himself – Rajadhiraja was too haughty, Virajendra was too eager, Rajendradeva was too placid. I was, many a times, just a pair of ears in the room.

He asked me once again, one night, who I felt was an able successor to him.

'They all possess qualities,' was all I said. To be honest, I did not want to put my eggs in any one basket. All the three princes were cordial to me, but it was quite evident that my status would change once the old king died.

Then, one day, Mahinda died.

It was a peaceful end – his heart had simply stopped beating while he was asleep. Rajendra ensured that he got a proper funeral attended by the most important dignitaries of the kingdom. It wasn't quite a state farewell, but it was close enough. I had not seen him after the *virabhishekam*. He had left for Thanjavur, and I had heard his name being spoken only once or twice again when he had come to petition the emperor for his release.

After the funeral was done, Rajendra came to visit me at night.

'He was hardly fifty, no age for a king to go. Though, perhaps, I'm biased; my father lived until his seventies. Mahinda's son, a man called Kassapa, is rebelling against our occupation in Eelam.'

He sighed.

'A king should have only one son. More than that makes everything complicated.'

I felt a pang of anger at this. He was not letting me return to my kingdom to secure my throne and yet he wanted me to comfort him about his own legacy?

'You don't need sons to have heirs. We've had several queens of the realm in our island. If I were home, I would have prepared my daughter to be queen.'

'Daughter? Oh yes, I received news some days ago, and it slipped my mind due to Mahinda's death. Your daughter, my dear Maharajah, is the queen of Kahuripan. Airlangga's wife. That is all I know for now, though I promise I'll find out more and tell you.'

The news took me by surprise. I had assumed by now that she was dead. Even the few traders from Srivijaya I had met in the kingdom had told me that they had little idea what happened to the royal family. Some said Srideva had taken them in, others that they had left the kingdom. No merchant told me they were dead, and I took hope from this, even if it was meant to soften the blow.

I couldn't hold back my tears. Understanding my need for privacy, Rajendra stood up and walked slowly out of the room, leaning on his cane.

For the first time in six years, I wept joyously.

After the attempt to free her father had failed, the queen wanted to put all her energies towards bringing him back.

It was the queen mother who had dissuaded her. 'If an opportunity presents itself, by all means bring him back. But you're no longer a princess. You have a kingdom of your own, fragile as it is. Build your kingdom, and talk to the Cholas from a position of power. He is a prisoner now. And your might has not yet extended enough to be able to reach across the seas and bring him back. Until it does, be patient.'

And so the queen resumed building her kingdom with Airlangga, this time with even greater determination. Trade improved, crops improved and their people prospered. Airlangga now controlled most of the land in Bhumi Java, and had even brought parts of Bali Dwipa under his control. The Chinese and Arabs had begun trading with Kahuripan ports. The kingdoms of Jambudwipa would too. A delegation from the Thousand Directions Guild had met their minister of trade. Airlangga's dream for a kingdom was being slowly realized. All that was left now, he would tell his wife, was an heir to the throne. The queen was often amused at the image he so earnestly tried to create. A king and queen with their prince ruling a land where all its people were happy. He would speak about it endlessly, formulating laws and practises for his land, and creating a hive of wisdom for his yet-to-be born son that would sustain him through his life.

Then, one day, the queen gave him the child he so desperately wanted.

2

I met Paravai the next day and told her all about my daughter. She was genuinely pleased.

'One day, you may even see her. Keep hope. The emperor may yet relent.'

We attended a performance at the temple that evening. The rains were arriving and there was a sense of anticipation in the air. A singer sang a hymn in praise of Lord Shiva and another song composed by the emperor. When the crowd gathered in the temple courtyard learned this, they went into raptures and demanded he not leave the stage till he sang an encore.

That was when Rajendradeva came up to me; he looked tense but we greeted each other civilly. Paravai, sensing his tension, excused herself for a few moments on the pretext of buying some jasmine for her hair.

'Father has been talking a lot to you these days.' He came straight to the point, sounding bitter. 'Mahinda's death has made him anxious about his kingdom. He thinks we'll tear it apart unless he appoints a successor immediately. He's been holding long interviews with us. All the courtiers are getting jittery. If the

Chalukyas or Kassapa in Eelam hear of the emperor's desire to appoint an heir, there will be war.'

I was a little surprised at this admission to me, a rank outsider.

'We know of your meetings. What has he been telling you?' he demanded.

'Our words are between us alone,' I said coldly. Were the princes spying on their father?

'Look. All of us want to be emperor. But we can't all be emperor, we know that. We need to resolve this immediately before the kingdom needs to go to war.' He then bowed in *namaskaram* before walking away.

So much for Rajendradeva being the placid one.

Paravai came back and asked me what the matter was. I told her the story of Rajendra and his confusion regarding his successor.

'There would be a lot of people in the Chalukya kingdom who would pay a handsome sum for such information. They've been holding off attacking for some time now,' she said with half a smile.

'Don't you dare!' I said sharply, surprising even myself at how quickly I was willing to defend the Chola kingdom.

She simply smiled and shrugged.

The next evening, I went to a wrestling match at the local academy. A prize fight. The champion Veerasena was fighting someone from China. I met Veerasena and put my money on him through the punters. The wrestlers squared each other in the pit, and then pounced upon each other; the crowd around them roared. The contest was fierce, and I was following it keenly when a man came and stood next to me. It was Rajadhiraja.

'Father is frail,' was all he said.

I nodded.

'He is not speaking to us as a father these days, but as an emperor.' He paused for a moment, and then continued. 'If there is any information he is telling you that will be beneficial to the state, it would be wise for you to tell me.'

I shrugged; we did not speak of such things, I told him. He nodded, unconvinced, and left almost immediately.

I half expected Virajendra to come and ask me for information. Instead, Bhaskaran came.

He asked if we could go on a walk in one of the gardens.

'The emperor is old. Some say seventy-three summers. Others, sixty-nine. For someone so obsessed with rigorously documenting his life's achievements, he has certainly not been very particular about keeping his age in the public memory. His sons are growing old too. At this rate, none of them will be emperor.'

I groaned.

'Not you too, Bhaskaran. I don't have any idea who the emperor favours. He speaks to me of other things.'

Bhaskaran was silent.

'What do you know about me, Maharajah? We have been friends for over half a decade now.'

I looked at him and smiled. 'You are an able minister. A good husband and father. A solid, dependable man. That is the best I can say about you.'

'A loyal servant?' he asked gently.

'Yes. Yes, of course.'

'And for all that, I'm still a minister in court.'

'Well, yes. A very senior one I might add,' I said, not understanding the question.

'If you had the opportunity to rise above your station, Maharajah, would you?'

The directness of the question caught me by surprise. I looked at Bhaskaran, expecting to see him blush; instead, he met my gaze without flinching. 'Let me put it to you in another way. If you had the chance to return home, and renegotiate the settlement with the Cholas, would you?'

'Of course.'

'I have been in contact with the Chalukyas. For some time now. They've asked me to reach out to you, and ask if you would be willing to strike a deal.'

'A deal?'

'Yes. Don't look so surprised. Help us kill the emperor, and you can leave as Maharajah.'

I looked at him, shocked, but Bhaskaran did not avert his gaze. His shy demeanour was gone, and he looked at me keenly, impatient for a reply.

'I hadn't pegged you as a traitor, Bhaskaran.'

'Traitor? I'm merely one who wants what is best for my kingdom: a new ruler.'

'And what of the emperor's sons?'

He smiled at me. 'Let's just say they won't be too disappointed if their father dies.'

'Which prince do you speak on behalf of?' I asked. Who was the son who wanted his father dead?

'I'm speaking on behalf of someone who promises to let you leave, and will ensure that you regain your rightful place in the Srivijaya kingdom. Srideva does not have a very solid position these days.'

He smoothed his *angavastram*.

'I've heard promises in this land before,' I said. 'Forgive me if I'm a little hesitant about trusting you.'

'Indravarman will be disappointed,' he replied quietly.

I looked at him sharply.

'After the failure of their snatch and grab, your trader guild has been coming up with more outrageous ways of bringing you back.'

'How do you know Indravarman?'

'How do you think he arrived in the country? And how do you think he snuck into Paravai's home? Make no mistake: there are spies watching your every move. They only stop watching you at two places. Your own home, where Nadan, who is a state agent, has the run of things. And Paravai's, where her celebrity compels them to look in the other direction.'

He slowed his pace to a stop and turned to face me. 'Indravarman knows the Chalukyas well. They do good business. Better than the Cholas. Srideva has cut off trade with the Chalukyas completely because of Chola pressure. It is in your interest to work with them.

'You only have one thing to do. Call the emperor to your room one night. We will murder him then. After the murder, you will immediately be taken to Puhar, and a ship will take you home. The Chalukya army has been mobilized and will enter the Chola borders the night of the murder. A coup will take place the next day.'

'The emperor's dead body will be found in my house. I assume this is to make everyone think I murdered him?'

'You will be nearly at Puhar by then, protected by an imperial decree stamped by the emperor, forged, of course, by me.'

I was silent as I let this sink in.

'And who becomes emperor?'

He smiled. 'You'll just have to find out, won't you?'

I went to Paravai's house that evening. She asked me what was troubling me and I said nothing. I couldn't trust her, that was certain. I sat by myself, my mind in a frenzy.

I could not trust any of the princes.

I could not trust Bhaskaran.

I could not trust Paravai.

I could not trust Nadan.

I could only trust the emperor.

But I couldn't trust him to send me back home. Could I trust Bhaskaran and the Chalukyas and the mysterious prince or princes who were plotting their father's death?

I was facing two difficult options once again. The first was to trust Bhaskaran and go along with his plan. Escape to Suvarnadwipa, or get executed for murdering the emperor. If Bhaskaran could betray his emperor, there was no reason he would not betray me. I had much less to offer. The second option was to confide in the emperor. His life would be safe. But there was no guarantee he would let me go back home. I remembered the body of Mahinda on its bier. Foreign and lonely in a strange country, his soul forced to wander a land it did not know as home.

They named her Sanggramawijaya. In the months that followed, it seemed that if the queen could not have her father back, the Gods in their infinite wisdom had given her, if not a replacement, then a suitable distraction. If the king was disappointed, he never showed it. He showered the girl with as much affection as he would have a boy. The affairs of the state seemed to pale in front of the needs of the little one. It seemed as though she had been born with an abundance of energy that never seemed to abate. Much like the ocean tides, her enthusiasm came in never-ending waves that often battered her parents' stamina and, very often, patience.

But she was a happy child. Like her father, she was able to find joy in what was given to her. Like her mother, she found joy in being able to give.

When she grew older, they affectionately called her Honeybee, since she was always buzzing around, trying to know everything under the sun. There was no question too large or too small for the new princess. And she collected little bits of knowledge, storing them in that honeycomb of a mind to use at a later date. Like her mother and father, she enjoyed reading and being read to, and would read stories from Hindu and Buddhist scriptures. The world was large for the young one, not broken into the boundaries only the minds of men saw.

The first few years were the happiest of the queen's life. The kingdom grew, her daughter grew, and it seemed everything that was good about life was in abundance.

Then, one day, a visitor arrived with a proposal. He came from Bali Dwipa, a representative of one of the large kadatuans. His Rakai, he said, sought an alliance for one of his daughters with the kingdom of Kahuripan. It was not uncommon for Rajas to marry and expand their kingdom. Airlangga considered it. If he accepted, he would have a kingdom that stretched from the centre of Bhumi Java to the entire Bali Dwipa. For the first time in many years, a kingdom that was not Srivijaya would be the strongest in the region.

His uncle would have been proud.

But, first, he needed to speak to his wife.

The queen was not happy with this decision, but relented. The extra land from Bali Dwipa was welcome and it would make him happy to surpass his uncle, she thought.

The Raja married his new wife a few months later with all the pomp of a royal wedding. The poets said that elephants laden with gold and jewels rode into the city in never-ending lines. Every flower in Bali Dwipa and Bhumi Java had been plucked clean and sent to the royal palace of Airlangga. The smell of camphor and sandalwood hung in the air for a good year after the wedding. Celestial beings themselves gathered in the sky to witness the wedding. The Raja was dressed in luxurious silk robes that were golden in colour, with many garlands of yellow flowers around his neck. He wore a golden mukuta encrusted with the largest ruby the islands had ever seen. His new wife, too, wore golden robes and an *upavita* body ornament made of golden chains. The people feasted as they never had in living memory on rice, fish, meat and jaggery-laden sweets. When the wedding was over, the poets said, many a citizen died of a broken heart.

Of course, who trusted the poets? But even the queen bitterly admitted that the wedding had been spectacular. It had been the first major celebration since he had begun his reign. The first since she had joined him.

Soon enough, the new wife bore her husband two sons.

3

I met Bhaskaran the next day and agreed to go along with his plan. He gave me a small bag of coins for my trouble. They were gold and had the Varaha, the celestial boar, depicted on them – the imperial symbol of the Chalukyas.

'What good are these?' I asked.

'A small addition to your treasury. A *shagun*, as it were. To our partnership. May we rule land and sea forever.' His smile was warm.

'You didn't think I would run to the emperor and tell him everything?'

'Not for one moment. This practise of holding kings is barbaric. The Chalukyas understand how much you have suffered.'

'So how is this going to unfold?'

He smiled. We had met at his home and were seated in his bedroom. His wife and parents were outside. 'Call the emperor over at night in one week's time. Two of my assassins will hide in your room. They will get the job done. I will meet you in the room soon after with the decree for your departure.'

I looked at the two men who had accompanied him. It was clear that they were not from here; they looked like Arabs, with blue eyes, olive skin and angular faces but they spoke a language I had never heard before. We then went to my room, where they looked around every corner and spoke among themselves. They knocked on the walls and tapped on the floors and the pillars. The one in front of my bed turned out to be hollow. They spoke to themselves and then to me in broken Tamil.

'Break pillar. Hide. He bed.'

Bhaskaran interpreted it. 'That's a splendid idea. The pillar is hollow. We'll break it open, and one of them will hide inside. The other will lie under your bed.'

There was no point objecting. The next day, a workman broke the pillar open and fitted it with a door that could be opened from within the pillar. The two men instructed the workman as he worked, and got the pillar redesigned to their specifications. When the pillar was ready, one of them tested it by entering and exiting it. They were overjoyed when it worked.

That night I went to Paravai, troubled. She pestered me again, trying to understand what was bothering me.

'I know about Bhaskaran,' I said, hoping that she would understand.

'What about him?'

'He's not who he appears to be.'

'And who does he appear to be?' she asked. Was there a hint of nervousness in her voice?

'Stop the act, Paravai. I know that he contacted you about Indravarman. I also know that you're both traitors to your emperor.'

It came out a little more bitterly than it should have. Perhaps I was still upset by Srideva and his betrayal. Now I was conspiring with traitors myself.

'Maybe we are, Maharajah. But not everyone is born to inherit a throne. Some of us have to work through an entire system to achieve our own ambitions. You seem more loyal to him than to your own throne. Or is this a case of cold feet?'

I glared at her. 'Never mind.'

Her face softened. 'Look. Tell me what he plans to do. I know that the Chalukyas are getting restless. I can confirm his plans.'

I wasn't sure whether to tell her. Was this a ruse on her part? Wasn't she already allied with Bhaskaran?

'Look. If anything goes wrong, you need someone to stand up for you. I will do it. Just tell me,' she pleaded.

I was silent.

'I can't bear the thought of anything happening to you. I cursed myself when I trusted him enough to let you go with Indravarman. I don't want that to happen again.'

She looked like she was genuinely pained. 'The future of the Chola kingdom is in Chalukya hands. Of that there is little doubt. Your own future is better off with them as partners. But Bhaskaran does not look at details sometimes. That is what worries me.'

Her pleading finally got through to me and I told her the entire story. She listened calmly. When it was over, she spoke.

'It's a good plan. But there is too much risk involved at your end. Ask Bhaskaran to arrange for the decree before the task. That is all.'

What she had said made sense so the next day I went to Bhaskaran and told him of my demand.

He looked a little annoyed, but shrugged. 'As you wish.'

He came the next day with the decree that stated that all roads and highways were open to me by order of the emperor. All aid in my journey was to be provided free of cost. All ships in the port of Puhar were at my disposal to take wherever I wished.

I was to tell the emperor to come home in two days. The rest would be arranged.

I met Rajendra at the palace orchard that afternoon and asked him to visit me in two days time at night. I had a special request that I wanted to discuss with him privately, away from the palace's eyes. He thumped me on the shoulder, smiled and said he would come.

I was restless throughout the day. I don't remember what I did but I do know that I had told Nadan and the other servants to take the day off. There was a carnival in the city that they were keen to attend. There was no need of fan bearers in this pleasantly cool season so I had given them the day off too. Soon, the evening came, bringing with it Bhaskaran with his two assassins. It was only the four of us in the house.

The two men stripped naked till they were only in loincloths. They each carried four knives.

One of them stepped into the pillar and shut himself in. The other slid underneath the bed. Bhaskaran left soon after. As he was leaving, he smiled and told me he would see me after midnight.

I sat on my bed and waited for the emperor.

4

The door creaked open at around midnight. A lamp led the way. Rajendra had arrived, and this time he had come alone. He sat on the bed.

'Your bodyguards are not with you, my lord?'

'Tonight I come alone,' he said. 'I have one question to ask you before we speak of your request.'

'Continue, sire.'

'Were Porus and Alexander friends? Could they ever be?'

'I believe they were, sire. Not before the battle, but perhaps after.'

He nodded.

'And yet Porus was killed by Alexander's general, Eudemus, not long after Alexander's death in the wars that followed.'

What was he talking about?

'The friendship was between Porus and Alexander, my lord, and not between Porus and his general. After Alexander's death, that friendship was nullified,' I replied.

'So what should Porus have done after Alexander's death? Become friends with Eudemus?'

'Why not? Friendships are only as long as lives. And there is no telling how long one will live. Friends are like stories. The more you accumulate, the richer you are.'

He guffawed, even as I heard a soft click. The pillar door opened and its occupant stepped out silently, his body partially visible to me in the soft lamplight. Rajendra's back was turned towards him. He approached silently clutching a knife in his hand.

I took a deep breath.

'There were many kings Alexander showed clemency to. Why is Porus so special? Why do we hear his name over and over again in our stories?' he asked.

'I don't know, sire,' I murmured, mesmerized by the sight of the assassin silently taking step after step towards Rajendra.

'I have a theory. Porus is remembered not only as a king, but as a friend. The world may or may not respect kings, but it always respects friendship.'

The assassin was within striking distance now. He raised his knife and prepared to sink the blade into the emperor's neck.

'Are you Porus to my Alexander, Sangrama?' Rajendra asked.

'No, Rajendra,' I replied, 'I am not.'

Two sons. One year after another. If Airlangga wanted, he could have gone on producing an army, the poets said. The new wife was always pleasant to the queen and, initially, they occupied different ends of Airlangga's life. If the queen was responsible for the kingdom, the new wife was now responsible for Airlangga's legacy.

After the sons were born, the new wife began taking an interest in the kingdom too. She began by overseeing a small project – the construction of an academy of dance and poetry that the king wanted to set up. A growing kingdom needs people who can manufacture beautiful lies and spread them across the world, he would say. The new wife would nod and smile and agree with his bidding. In time, she successfully managed the granaries and farms as well and soon began looking after multiple portfolios. The ministers marvelled at her skills.

She's just like you when you had come, they told the queen.

In her position, thought the queen bitterly, even she would do the same thing – snatch little pockets of power until she had the whole bundle. The new wife did not rest. She won over the ministers, including the gruff Narottam, who had initially been wary of the match. 'You don't need a new wife. You need a new army,' he had told the Raja before the wedding, before going into a tirade about the frivolity of expecting gains through marriage.

Yet, after she had proved herself every bit as capable as the queen and also had (not one, but two!) sons, she occupied a space in the minds of the people that the queen never had.

The Raja began preferring his new wife's counsel, and the queen began to recede into the background of what had become their lives. He began to dote on his boys, and even brought them to court with him on occasion. While he still lavished his love and attention on his daughter and the queen, his new wife and children began occupying more of his time.

She had married him out of necessity, of course. He had needed an ally to build a kingdom. She had needed another chance to regain her old life. Together, they had forged a wall. Made of brick, stuck by mortar. One mind. One thought. One action.

Yet, now, the greatest pang she felt was not the loss of a kingdom, but the loss of her friend and husband. Marriage involves two pairs of eyes. After you've seen the world through the eyes of one partner, it becomes hard to see it through those of another.

5

I leapt off my bed and pushed the emperor down, shielding him with my body against the knife's blow. It scraped my back but I held on to the emperor.

Then the room exploded into motion. The doors burst open and men poured in. Leading them were Rajadhiraja, Virajendra and Rajendradeva.

The assassin was surrounded. He was about to take his knife and plunge it into his own heart when two burly Chola troopers seized him by the arms. 'There's another under the bed,' I shouted, and looked down to see Rajendra. He was unhurt but looked a little dazed.

'Guards, seize the man!' I heard Rajadhiraja's voice.

The next thing I knew, I was being lifted up roughly and marched out of the mansion into the cold night.

I was taken into this prison where I've been sitting since yesterday. And most of my time has been spent talking to you, Ganapathy. If you remember right, the man who left me here came back in the morning with one of Rajadhiraja's officials, who told me that I was being convicted for *rajadroham*, to be sentenced to death today.

He had brought you along to record a final statement. My version of the events, as it were. I had asked him (if you remember) whether my version would make any difference to the sentence, and he looked at me and told me that the only version that mattered was the emperor's and his sons. I had been sentenced to death almost immediately after the assassination attempt had been foiled. I tried to protest my innocence, but the man left, leaving you behind to record my story. Parts of it have been rushed. Some of my memories may be sketchy but, on the whole, the story is true. Only one last detail needs to be added.

Why did I save your emperor when I had every reason not to?

All I can say is that I had a change of heart, Ganapathy. When he asked me whether I was Porus to his Alexander, it all became too much for me. As much as it surprises me to say it, I have, over the years, developed a liking for my foe and fellow king. A grudging respect even.

Perhaps I lost faith in Bhaskaran too. A man who could betray his own people would not hesitate to betray an outsider. I admit, tempted as I was by the thought of leaving your land, this realization did not hit me until it was too late. So when it did, l leapt up and pushed Rajendra away from the assassin's knife. It's as simple as that.

Why do I tell you all this? Do I believe you have Rajendra Chola's ear? No, but someone should know my side of the story.

I hope you believe that I wasn't involved in the conspiracy to murder the emperor.

One day, Narottam met her on the palace grounds. He said he had come to enquire why she wasn't seen in the courts these days. She told him she wasn't well. It was because of the change of seasons, he declared, and gave her a prescription of herbs to strengthen her immunity.

He had given the same to the Raja's boys since they had to be healthy to rule the lands one day.

Why would they inherit the throne? Because that's what boys did. And the Raja had decided to designate an heir soon. To prepare him for the kingdom from an early age, said Narottam heartily.

And so, thought the queen, this was the final sign that she was going to be edged out of the kingdom she had helped create. Her daughter would be married off to a noble family. Airlangga had wanted a male heir for so long that he would never dream of making his daughter monarch. The queen and her mother would probably be relegated to the back of the palace where they had little role to play in the functioning of the kingdom. She had survived an attempted assault, slavery and the perils of building a kingdom. But she would not survive this.

The Raja called both his wives to his bedchamber that night.

'You are both dear to me. But I need to appoint an heir to the kingdom. One of my children will serve as prime minister during my reign and then progress to becoming the ruler.'

'Your boys will be delighted, my lord,' said his new wife. 'They look forward to it.'

He nodded at her but looked at the queen for her response. The queen merely looked at the ground and nodded; she felt a hot flush of anger. This was as much her kingdom as his. How could she let it go without a fight? She had already lost one kingdom. She would not lose another simply because the Raja did not want an heiress.

For a moment, she contemplated getting the wife murdered. With a little money, the right people to do the job, the wife and her children would sleep one night, and not wake up the next. She was almost gleeful at the thought when she raised her head and saw the Raja looking at her with an expression of concern.

In that moment, she realized that the kingdom was not worth fighting for, not if it meant hurting the person you loved most in the world. Airlangga had wanted this perfect life for so long. A male heir and a wife to bear him one. A picture worth painting on the walls. A family unit of king, queen and heir. He had yearned for what he believed was normalcy his entire life. And he now had the opportunity to have it all.

She would not stand in his way.

6

A man entered my cell to summon me so I took leave of the scribe who continued scribbling on his palm leaf parchment, and walked through the dark prison and out into the light. I was blindfolded and made to step inside a carriage. I took a deep breath and tried not to think of my impending death. The carriage stopped, and I was marched into a building of sorts, then up a set of stairs and finally made to sit on a chair. I blinked as the blindfold was taken off me.

I was in what had been my room. On the bed lay Rajendra.

'The situation has been reversed. I lie on the bed now, and you sit in front of me,' he spoke in his rumbling voice.

I sat silently and let him speak.

'The first thing you learn about being a king is there is no room for error. Do my *prasastis* speak of my mistakes? Do anyone's? I've had you spied upon for over six years. God himself probably doesn't know as much about you as I.'

He picked his fingernails as he spoke. 'Not all spies are men who lurk in the shadows. My ablest proved a courtesan who stayed hidden in broad daylight. You know her, of course.'

'Paravai?' I asked, disbelievingly.

'You look surprised? She's been working with me for some time now. Courtesans get access to places most men do not. In this case, the life of a foreign king who found it difficult to make friends away from home.'

'What of Bhaskaran?' I asked.

'When Paravai told me about your great deception, I was genuinely hurt. Bhaskaran had ceased to hurt me. We had suspected his movements for some years. He is the son of my father's minister. Somewhere along the way, he thought he could be king and started engaging with the Chalukyas. When Indravarman finally reached out to him, and Bhaskaran brought him and the Srivijayan merchants together with the Chalukyas, we knew something significant was being plotted. Bhaskaran seemed to be of the impression that he would govern Chola lands once the Chalukyas came to power. It sounds incredibly naive, but I have little doubt, judging by the scale of his ambition, that he intended to use them as a mere stepping stone. There has never been a better time for upstarts in this land. Some years ago, the marauder from Ghazni in the far north near Persia came and laid waste to the lands up to nearly central Bharatvarsha. Since then, that entire region has been fermenting. The Chalukyas were inspired to follow suit, and so was Bhaskaran, by the looks of it. If a marauder from the outside can cause so much havoc and displace so many empires, what could an insider do with some outside interference?'

He cleared his throat and continued. 'Predictably enough, the first plot involved an attempt to rescue you. There was very little chance of that happening, I can say now. We had catapults ready to shore up our meagre coastguard. The only time things got a little problematic, I am told, was when you started moving with the pirates in the night. My men were terrified their arrows would hit you.'

He chuckled to himself. 'But you returned safely of your own volition. After the Indravarman incident happened, we decided to use Bhaskaran as an asset against the Chalukyas. We put him in important departments and gave him the responsibility of projects that looked significant from the outside, but really were not fundamental to the safety of the kingdom. We nurtured him without his knowing.

'He became a truly exceptional asset. We avoided a Chalukya war in the year of the famine when we convinced him that the villagers were threatening to riot against us and would riot against them if they came into power. When he decided to commit *rajadroham* openly by trying to murder me, we all sighed heavily.'

He looked at his fingernails and then looked at me. His eyes were sad. 'But when he brought you into the fold and told you he had a son of mine working against me, I felt vulnerable for the first time in over fifty years. My sons, I knew, were dissatisfied with the way the kingdom was being run, each in their own way. I had not expected them to want to kill me for it. The feeling made me numb. But another kind of pain afflicted me when I heard that you, too, were behind it. I thought we were friends, Sangrama.'

He pursed his lips, and looked disappointed. 'I have been worried about the issue of succession for some years now. You know that. I decided to use the occasion of my murder to learn which son wanted me dead – and if Porus would treat Alexander as befitted him. I sent a message – indirectly, of course, through Paravai – to each of my three boys to hurry to the mansion at midnight since there was to be an assassination attempt on me by you. If one of my boys wanted me dead, I was reasonably certain they would call off the plan and my impending murder once they knew I had learned about it. Imagine my joy then, when it was just the two of us alone in the room at midnight with the assassins. I was prepared, in that moment, to die if my boys had not come in time to rescue me. And they nearly didn't. Another elephant had gone mad in the streets, I was told, and had died on the path to your house, which delayed them.'

'Later, after the assassination attempt, I found out that Bhaskaran was lying about allying with my sons. We did not even need to torture him to reveal it. He told you that one of the princes was involved to gain your trust in the endeavour. After the assassination, he planned to head towards the border and join the Chalukya army there. I believe he was counting on the fact that the princes would be too busy fighting each other for the throne to notice the Chalukya invasion. As it turned out, they didn't.'

He looked at me and smiled. 'The moment they heard that you were going to assassinate me, both Virajendra and Rajendradeva sent word to Rajadhiraja assuring him of their support should I fall.'

His smile grew even wider.

'When I heard about this later on, it was the proudest moment I had ever had as a parent. The decision of who will be king had been taken off my shoulders by my sons themselves. Rajadhiraja will rule, supported by his brothers. And he will be succeeded by his brothers when the time comes. And I couldn't have learned this without you.'

He paused here for a moment, and his smile evaporated for an instant. 'I should have fallen to the assassin's blade. What I wasn't prepared for was what happened next.'

He looked down at the mattress and then at me. 'You saved me, Sangrama. Why?'

I took a deep breath. 'You are my friend.'

He grunted and looked down at the mattress. 'Thank you,' he said, his voice soft for the first time in our acquaintance.

The queen went to the Raja the next day and told him of her decision to become a *bhikkuni*, a female monk. She wanted to leave the kingdom and meditate on life.

'Isn't that a little drastic?' he asked her.

It was what she wanted, she insisted. Besides, she said, there was no room for her in the palace, with the new wife. She could fight for her position in the kingdom, the place she had helped build, but she had decided against it.

He gaped at her. At least stay for the announcement of the heir to the throne, he pleaded.

A week later in the royal hall, the announcement was made.

7

Rajendra Chola apologized for keeping me in prison after the assassination attempt. He needed that time, he told me, to get all the facts from as many sources as possible. I told him I understood, and to let the past be. When I asked him about Bhaskaran's fate, he told me that there was much to be investigated on that front. Chances were that he wouldn't make it out alive, unless he could conduct a plot against his former employers, the Chalukyas. I had little doubt that he would have any problem with that.

The Cholas are sending a trade mission to China. The docks are filled with spices, gold, wood and pepper that will be loaded onto ships and never see their home again, and will probably occupy pride of place in another man's home or dinner plate.

One of the items travelling with this cargo is, however, going home. Me.

I met Rajendra and his sons for the last time. We spoke little, but Rajendra embraced me, and thanked me for my friendship. I would like to think there were tears in his eyes as I left, but that could have just been the dust. Gangaikonda Cholapuram is expanding rapidly, and the dust cloud around it has become an almost permanent feature.

The trade mission hosted by the Thousand Directions Guild will go to China – from Puhar to Eelam to Kadaram and then Barus, unloading cargo along the way. It will then twirl around the Sunda straits and then pass through the Melaka straits and towards China.

I will complete my voyage at a port in Hujung Galuh, a port city in the state of Kahuripan. Not home, but close enough. I will see my daughter and her husband. From there, I will find a way of taking back my kingdom.

A sudden dread seizes me. It has been nearly seven years since I left those shores. Will they remember me fondly?

Worse, will they have forgotten?

The men on the boat are getting visibly flustered. Storm clouds loom in the horizon. The deck is a blur of activity as the Tamils lash the cargo in the hold and on the deck to different parts of the ship. I should be worried. I have sailed through storms before, and they are never easy to negotiate.

And yet, I feel serene. The storm is outside me for once.

I go down below the deck and find a stout piece of rope to tie around my waist and fasten it to a pillar. I begin humming a tune, and end up singing the song. It is a cheery one about the summer, and the sun that seems happiest in those months. I am at peace as we enter the storm.

All the ministers of states and the chiefs of different regions had gathered in the great hall of the palace. The king sat on his throne flanked by his wives. When the silence in the room became almost deafening, he stood up and addressed them all.

'They say I never got what a Raja should get. I was born of another land, and spent my early years wandering the forests of Vanagiri with old Narottam here. Then I spent the early years of the kingdom fighting wars and negotiating petty and humiliating treaties with more kingdoms than I can count. I was never treated like a Raja and I had no official investiture. We grew from a few villages to this prosperous land to which you can all claim allegiance. This ceremony, as it were, is perhaps the first regal one of my reign.

'For many years, I sought to be like other kings. Perhaps because it was taken away from me so brutally when I was young, I needed to regain it for some kind of closure. I wanted an empire of my own and a male heir, because other kings had one or desired one. But, over the years, I've learned that a king alone does not make a kingdom. This kingdom has become what it is because of the people who have loved it and worked hard to build its glory.'

He paused for a while, looked at his audience and then continued. 'We have always been a kingdom that has done things a little differently, guided by love rather than the dynastic norms that govern other kingdoms. Most of you think that I will make one of my boys the next ruler-designate of the kingdom. I love them dearly, and when the time comes, I will ensure that they get their due. But this kingdom has been guided to its current zenith by not one but two extraordinary women. I see no reason why there should not be a third.

'I have no hesitation then to announce that my *rakryan kanuruhan* – my prime minister and heir to the throne – will be my eldest child, my daughter, Sanggramawijaya. Her mother, the queen, shall monitor her progress with me, and we will make sure that she is fit to rule the kingdom by the time she attains maturity. I also want to announce that my daughter's mother, the queen, will, from now on rule with me as Queen Regent and, in the event that something happens to me, will be the new ruler of the kingdom. She has seen Kahuripan from its earliest days. No one knows more about the kingdom than her.'

Even as the audience in the hall – ministers, Daatus, Rakais and warlords – cheered loudly, the queen's first instinct was annoyance. Why hadn't he told her before? They had always taken all the decisions together, hadn't they? She almost glowered at him in front of all the ministers. But before she could dwell on this further, the crowd began chanting her name and drew her attention back to the court. The new wife smiled at the queen but did not say anything. Before he resumed his speech – where he said that his two sons will eventually also learn how to govern so that when they attained maturity they, too, would help administer the kingdom, and then began a long diatribe on what fiscal policy needed to be followed that year – he glanced at the queen and smiled at her. She smiled back and resolved never to doubt his love for her again.

'Thank you, Airlangga,' she whispered.

'Thank you, Dharmaprasadottunggadewi,' he replied.

A HISTORICAL NOTE

All stories are lies. And storytellers? The less said about them the better.

In 1025 AD, Rajendra Chola sent a naval armada to invade the Srivijaya kingdom. An attack of this nature had never been perpetrated before. The Srivijayas were all-powerful in their part of the world. As the epigraph at the beginning goes on to say, Rajendra Chola conquered fourteen cities, including the capital that was located in the area occupied by the current city of Palembang. A city without a name makes for an interesting narrative device, so I have eschewed any identity for the capital city of the Srivijaya empire in this book. Timelines, too, have been tampered with but only a little. The Chola raid did happen around 1025 AD. And, in 1033 AD, a mission of theirs did reach the Chinese. I have taken some liberties with the artefacts of the age too, which a keen historian might be able to spot. Also, the use of the Gregorian calendar and the use of 'Europe', and 'China' as an entity (rather than referring specifically to Song dynasty territories which only included a part of what is today modern China) is more for the convenience of the reader than anything else. I have also, in this spirit, taken the liberty of referring to Rajendra Chola's son, who was also called Rajendra Chola (or Rajendra Chola II), as Rajendradeva, to distinguish him from his father.

Other than that, the sources are suspiciously silent on the matter of Rajendra Chola's age. One source said he was born in 960 AD, but there is no verifiable proof that I could find on this. However, he was closer to middle age than youth when he ascended the throne; that much is certain.

The books of Nilakanta Sastri and the excellent compendium of essays 'Nagapattinam to Suvarnadwipa' have been invaluable aids for information about the Cholas. The translation of the fragment of an epigraph at the beginning is also Nilakanta Sastri's.

Much like Airlangga, the historical fiction writer 'crosses the water', and takes a leap across the gaps that invariably come up in our knowledge of ancient history. He makes certain assumptions that he hopes don't fly in the face of commonly accepted historical fact. And, if they do, he tries to make the rest of the story enjoyable enough for the reader to forgive them. In the end, the historical fiction writer just wants you to read. Not just more fiction, but also more history. Any liberties I have taken that may offend the student of history are my own, and not the fault of any of the sources I have mentioned. I have, at times, disregarded certain details or accepted certain assumptions over others for the purpose of creating a more cohesive story. Human life is messy and unstructured, and left without the pruning effects of narrative, is virtually impossible to render into a story.

So why did the Cholas raid an empire in Indonesia? Many historians believe it was probably a trade dispute. The Srivijaya monopolized trade to China, and even at one point made the Chinese believe that the Cholas were their vassals, as exemplified by the use of 'coarse paper' in correspondence mentioned in this novel. The 'Thousand Directions' were a real merchant guild, and probably benefited from the Srivijaya invasion.

Sangrama Vijayatunggavarman was the real king of Srivijaya. His life is lost to history after the invasion, and all we hear of him is that he was captured by the Cholas, a practice not uncommon. Mahinda, the king of Sri Lanka, was also captured, as I have mentioned in the book, and kept at Thanjavur till 1030 AD when he passed away. It is not inconceivable that this would have been Sangrama's fate, too, if he had been captured. The manner of his imprisonment is not known.

Certain sources like Nilakanta Sastri mention that Sangrama Vijayatunggavarman was allowed to reign over his kingdom after paying a hefty tribute to the Cholas. Some sources also say that Srideva became the king of Srivijaya after Sangrama's capture. Lacking any real knowledge to take a stand in the matter, I have kept both possibilities alive, and also the hope of a sequel.

The princess's story, while largely lost to us, seems to be an interesting one. Dharmaprasadottunggadewi was the real wife of Airlangga, whose remarkable story is captured in brief here. Perhaps all the sources of her life, as with most of the characters in this novel, come from epigraphs. While one finds little consensus in the source material I referred to or on the Internet, the general understanding is that she was a Srivijaya princess or had some relation to the Srivijaya court and found herself in Airlangga's new kingdom. Some sources that I have referred to say that this happened before 1021 AD, which means they may have already been married before the invasion and she would have already been queen, while others feel that she may have only come into the court after the Chola invasion. For the sake of this story, I have assumed that she came after the invasion. The manner of her doing so and, in fact, her life in this novel, is fictionalized.

Airlangga began to establish himself around 1019 AD and founded the kingdom of Kahuripan nearly twelve years after *Mahapralaya* (fictionally depicted in this novel) which took place around 1006 AD. Alternate sources also mention that it could have happened in 1016 AD. But this dating, too, is debated.

On his part, Airlangga must have been inordinately fond of Dharmaprasadottunggadewi, since he appointed her *Parameswari*, or Queen Regent, and her daughter the heiress to the throne. He named his daughter Sanggramawijaya, and even built a Buddhist monastery dedicated to his wife called Srivijasrama. Either way, there was rapprochement with the Srivijaya. Truly, a wise man has no enemies.

There isn't too much information available about the Srivijaya empire out in public domain. And many of my assumptions are conjectures, but an excellent essay by Roy Jordaan called 'Who was Sri Sanggramawijaya' helped me fill in many gaps.

In fact, another interesting story goes that Rajendra Chola himself married a Srivijayan princess called Onang Kiu. This is mentioned in the *Sejarah Melayu*, the Malay annals that romanticize the founding of the great maritime empires of the region.

Coming back to Airlangga. Interestingly, his daughter, Sanggramawijaya, renounced the throne and became a *bhikkuni*, paving the path for her two younger half brothers to become kings. A desire for renunciation was not uncommon those days, and Airlangga, too, decided to abdicate his throne. Before doing so, he carved up his kingdom into two parts for either son. One was called Jangala, the other Kediri. Perhaps he was inspired by the Mahabharata, in which a similar carving of the kingdom took place. He was certainly enamoured with the work since he commissioned a *kakawin*, or epic poem, dedicated to Arjuna which has been mentioned here.

I was about to conclude with a chapter that alluded to a happy family reunion between daughter and father, and perhaps the seed of the idea planted in Airlangga's mind (after listening to Sangrama Vijayatunggavarman's adventures) of giving each brother a part of the kingdom to govern to prevent a war of succession.

But that would have been one lie too many.

This story could not have taken shape without the work and vision of the team at Hachette, who made this writer's job far easier than he had any right to expect. If you, the reader, have enjoyed this work, it is entirely due to the unrelenting efforts of Prerna Vohra, Arushi Pareek, Sucharita Dutta-Asane and Poulomi Chatterjee. A special thank-you to Prerna for suggesting that I try my hand at historical fiction and leave my myth-fiction comfort zone behind for a little while. Thanks are also due to Kunal Kundu and Haitenlo Semy for creating this wonderful cover, and to the amazing marketing team at Hachette, Avanija and Poorti.

Finally, as always, this book is dedicated to my mother and brother. It can't always be fun having a grumpy writer in the family, but you've always made me feel as if it is the most wonderful thing in the world.

GLOSSARY OF TERMS

Bali Dwipa: The ancient name of the island of Bali
Bhumi Java: The ancient name of the island of Java
Chakravarti: Emperor
Chola Nadu: Chola kingdom
Eelam: The ancient name of Sri Lanka
Gopuram: A large gatehouse tower at the entrance of a South Indian temple
Jambudwipa, Bharata, Bharatavarsha, Hind: The ancient and medieval names of India
Manakkavaram: The ancient name of the Nicobar Islands
Melaka: Malacca strait
Senapati: General
Shagun: Auspicious gift
Sunda: Sunda strait
Suvarnadwipa: The ancient name of the island of Sumatra (but historically also referred to the Indonesian archipelago islands)
Tamilakam: The land inhabited by the Tamil-speaking people
Vaidyasalai: Hospital
Yaal: Tamil harp

Palace of Assassins

ADITYA IYENGAR

Leper. Murderer. Hero.

The battle of Kurukshetra has come to its catastrophic end after eighteen long days. As Ashwatthama, the lone survivor of the Kaurava camp, slowly regains consciousness, he realizes, to his horror, that he has been condemned to a life of immortality and leprosy by Krishna, the mastermind behind his opponents' victory. Burning with hatred for the Pandavas for killing Duryodhana, his friend and saviour, and stricken with anger at his own fate, he vows to seek revenge.

An exhilarating tale of passion and redemption, *Palace of Assassins* masterfully recasts the events in the aftermath of the great war and presents Ashwatthama, one of the most misunderstood characters of the Mahabharata, in a whole new light.

For further details and information, please visit www.hachetteindia.com

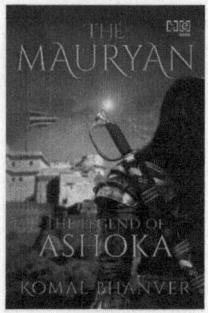

Emperor Chandragupta

ADITI KAY

**Building an empire is not easy, especially when there are
enemies everywhere and no one you can trust.**

India, 326 BCE. The world's greatest conqueror, Alexander, the
Greek emperor, is at its doorstep. In the east lies Magadha, ruled by
the Nandas, a dynasty driven by greed, lust and hunger for power.
From the embers of that lust and avarice a boy has been born,
raised by a tribe of peacock-tamers – a boy named Moriya forced
by the Nanda clan to be on the run.

Aided by Chanakya, a political strategist at odds with his former
rulers, who trains him in the ways of the world and christens him
Chandragupta, the young man ventures across the vast Magadhan
empire to form an army of his own and seek out the foreign invader.
This is the story of Chandragupta Maurya.